JUSTICE FOR MICKIE

BADGE OF HONOR: TEXAS HEROES, BOOK 2

SUSAN STOKER

CHAPTER 1

CRUZ LIVINGSTON TOOK a deep breath and willed himself to relax. He'd been undercover with the Red Brothers Motorcycle Club for a month—no, twenty-six days to be exact—and in his eyes, it was twenty-six days too long. Undercover assignments were never easy, but this had been like taking a fiery trip to hell the entire time.

He hadn't expected the job to be sunshine and roses, but he'd obviously gotten soft, because Cruz knew some of the shit he'd been forced to do to "prove" himself would haunt him for a long time. He hadn't killed or been pushed to rape anyone, thank God, but he'd threatened and beaten men up, and sold drugs. It was the selling of the drugs that had almost broken him.

It was ironic, the very reason he'd gone undercover —to *stop* the sale of drugs—was what he'd been forced to do from the very start of this assignment.

Cruz hadn't seen much of Ransom's supposed girl-friend, the person he was supposed to be getting close to in order to get information about the president. Her name was Angel, but from what Cruz could tell, she wasn't much of a girlfriend, more like a woman he was screwing. Cruz had seen Ransom fuck women in the middle of the clubhouse, not caring who was watching, so he obviously wasn't concerned about being exclusive with Angel.

Cruz's original plan had been to get in tight with the girlfriend and see what he could find out about the operation through her. But he had quickly found out that wasn't going to work. Ransom didn't give a shit about Angel, so it would look extremely odd for him to be cozying up to the woman.

MCs typically had two types of women hanging around—bikers' old ladies and club whores. The old ladies were somewhat respected by the other members of the club, and weren't ever disrespected by the whores or anyone outside the tight-knit group. The whores, on the other hand, were there to fuck and to use. Period. The whores knew their place, and never complained about it, ever hopeful that one day they might catch the eye of one of the members and become an old lady.

Cruz figured many of them continued to hang around for the drugs they were given in return for their services far more than they wanted to be an old lady. It was hard for him to fathom why any woman would allow herself to be mistreated as the whores in this club were, free drugs or not.

In the twenty-six days Cruz had been a prospect of the club, he'd seen some of the worst treatment of women he'd ever had the misfortune to observe in all his life, and that was saying something. His job as a member of the FBI included some pretty gnarly things, but watching as a drugged-out, half-conscious woman got gang-banged by ten members of the Hermanos Rojos motorcycle club, who didn't give a shit how rough they were, was one of the worst. The only reason Cruz hadn't had to participate was because of his prospect status. Until he was deemed "worthy" of the club, he wasn't allowed to participate in the orgies. Thank God.

Cruz knew he couldn't save everyone, but watching the women essentially get raped by the MC members brought to mind his ex-wife. She'd never been raped, but Cruz hadn't been able to save her from other seedy parts of life.

Cruz shook his head, trying to get back into the game. Standing in the middle of the Red Brothers' clubhouse wasn't the time to remember his fucked-up relationship with his ex-wife.

"Yo, Smoke, get your ass over here!" Ransom called from across the room.

Cruz had chosen the nickname Smoke when he'd joined the club. He hadn't bothered to explain it, letting the club members think what they wanted about the name. In actuality, it was his friend Dax who'd come up with the moniker. They'd joked that he was sneaky like smoke…getting into every crevice of the Hermanos Rojos's business and hopefully being the reason they were eventually taken down.

The only reason Cruz was able to infiltrate the MC was because an FBI agent who'd had a long-term undercover assignment at another club, near the border of Texas and Mexico, had vouched for Cruz when Ransom and his vice president had inquired. Simply being allowed in the clubhouse, and being privy to much of what went on there, was a huge step in being able to gather information on the club and hopefully stop one of the many entry points for drugs into the city.

He'd told Ransom and the others he was a part-time mall security cop. He had to have some sort of job, and doing anything directly related to law enforcement was definitely out, but he also needed a reason to look relatively clean-cut and not quite so "bikerish."

Cruz ambled over to where Kitty, Tick, and three other members of the club were standing.

"What's up?" Cruz asked with a chin lift to the guys.

"Got a job for ya," Ransom said with disdain, obviously annoyed at something. "I'm keeping some pussy on the side, but she's getting to be a pain in my ass. You know, demanding and shit, but I've got plans for her, so I can't piss her off. She called and demanded to come over to the clubhouse tonight. I don't particularly like her ass anywhere near here, but if I want to get in there and use her to get more high-class customers, I have to give in. I need you to go and pick her ass up."

Cruz's mind spun. He figured Ransom was talking about Angel, but he hadn't been privy to what customers Ransom thought he could get by using her. Cruz wondered just what other plans the president of the club had.

"Sure thing. What's the bitch look like?" Cruz's words were sneered with just the right amount of attitude.

"She's tall and skinny with big tits, which makes her nice to fuck. She's got long blonde hair and fancies herself in love with a real live MC president." The other guys laughed as if Ransom had said the funniest thing they'd ever heard.

"What's the draw, Pres?" Cruz knew he was pushing his luck, but he wanted to see if he could dig a bit deeper and see if getting in with Angel's friends was the only reason the man was hanging around her.

"The draw is that we're trying to expand business, and Angel is beautiful to look at but dumb as a rock. She's got access to a whole new set of customers… fancy-ass rich women, and we need to draw them in. She's so enamored of my role, and my cock, she'll do whatever I tell her to. I know she wants to continue to suck my MC president dick, so she'll do what I want, no questions asked."

Cruz didn't like what he was hearing, but kept his voice even. "So, I pick her ass up and bring her back here, then what?"

"Then we throw a lame-ass party with the old ladies, no whores around, she sees we're harmless, like a real-live, fucking romance novel or like that stupid-ass TV show, and she goes on her merry way. I get her hooked on me and the lifestyle she wants to believe in, as well as the drugs, and she'll be my ticket to selling to her rich friends."

Cruz's stomach turned. He wondered if this was how his ex had started out. He didn't know Angel, but there was no way he wanted to be a party to anything Ransom had in store for her, never mind her friends.

When he'd volunteered for the assignment, the goal was for him to gain some knowledge the FBI could use to remove just one of the avenues for drugs getting into the city, and if necessary, plant the seed for placing a more long-term agent inside the club. Since Cruz wasn't supposed to be there for months, he was to gather evidence about their drug-dealing so the agency could keep their eye on the club and, if things went as planned, bring down some of their contacts as well. No one knew how deep the Hermanos Rojos were with the big players.

Ransom wanting to use innocent women—although always a possibility; they'd known about Angel going in—was something that would never be all right with Cruz. If he could save Angel in the process of shutting down some of their supply lines before he got out, all the better.

"Sounds easy enough. Pick her up, bring her here. Got it. You got her address?"

"Better. I'm tracking her. Planted a bug in her purse. Bitch doesn't go anywhere without that huge-ass bag." Ransom flicked a small electronic device in Cruz's direction. "You'll see where she is. Bring her ass back here at eight. Not a second before. We'll do the party thing, I'll take her home, fuck her, and be back here by eleven. Then we can *really* party."

The other men around him laughed crudely.

Ransom focused on the other members of his club. "Make sure the whores are back by then. I'm in the mood for a gang bang tonight. Angel's tight pussy just won't be enough. There's nothing like fucking a whore when she's tied down and squirming for more."

Cruz laughed along with the other men at the president's words, while cringing inside.

"One more thing, Smoke," Ransom warned as Cruz started to leave.

Cruz turned back to the president and lifted his chin.

"Angel has a bitch of a sister who doesn't want her to have anything to do with the club. She's been riding Angel's ass, and I'm sick of it. Do whatever it takes to keep her skanky ass away, even if that means you put her out of commission for a while. That bitch had better not fuck with my plans, otherwise she'll find herself hurt in a way so she won't be *able* to mess with me."

CHAPTER 2

MICHELLE "MICKIE" Kaiser sat across from her sister in the small restaurant and tried to reason with her.

"Angel, those guys are bad news, seriously. I've told you this a million times."

"And I keep telling *you* to back the hell off. Ransom already doesn't like you. He knows how you harp on me and he's fed up with it. I was hoping you'd support me, and be friends with my boyfriend, but you haven't ever liked *any* of the men I've dated."

"You know that's not true. I just think you could do better. I honestly think Ransom is using you."

"How is he using me? Huh? Tell me that. He dotes on me, buys me stuff, and he *listens* to me when I talk, which is more than you do."

Mickie tried really hard not to lose her cool. "Think about this for a second, Angel. First of all, he's at least twenty years older than you. It's actually kind of gross. He's also never invited you to his house, wherever that might be. He comes to your apartment, fucks you, then leaves. He doesn't date you at all. No movies, no dinners, no nothing. Buying you skanky, whorish clothes to wear isn't love. He's creepy and scary as hell."

Angel flipped her hair so it fell in waves down her back. She leaned over the table and narrowed her blue eyes at her sister. "He loves me, Mickie. Why can't you be happy for me?"

Mickie threw her hands up and leaned back against the seat with a huff, not surprised Angel ignored everything she'd said. She tried to keep her voice low and reasonable. "I want you to find love as much as you do, but Ransom doesn't love you, Angel. He's using you. I don't know why, or how, but he is."

"He's *not* using me. He likes to hear about all my friends. He's *interested* in me and my life. And for your information, he invited me to his clubhouse tonight for a party. He wants to show me off to his friends. You'll see. He's fine."

"Oh my God!" Mickie was quickly losing patience with her younger sister. "This is *not* a romance novel. He's *not* a good guy, Angel. You aren't going to find hearts and flowers with him. Invited you to his clubhouse for a party? Do you know what goes on in those places? Again, this is not like one of those MC books you read. He does drugs, he probably runs guns—shit, he most likely has a stable full of women he pimps out."

"He does not! Jesus, you're always such a downer!"

"You don't know anything about him, Angel. I've done some research—"

9

"Oh hell no! I don't want to hear it."

"No, seriously, Angel. He's been arrested—"

Angel stood up from the table and put her hands on her hips and stared down at her sister. "No, I mean it. You've hated every guy I've ever dated. Just because you're embarrassed that you were boring in the sack and your husband left you for another woman, doesn't mean *every* guy is like *him*. Look at you! You'll never catch another man's eye. Your hair is too short—no one likes short hair! You're fat, have no sense of style, and you're a nagging bitch. It's not like you'll ever read one of my romance books and understand what the MC world is like. Under all his gruffness, he's a good guy. I've seen it. So leave me alone. Just because Ransom drinks and smokes and occasionally goes to a strip club, doesn't mean he's a bad guy."

Mickie ignored the hurt her sister's words caused and tried one more time. "All I'm saying is to watch your back. Please, Angel, I know you think MC guys are all marshmallows under their hard exteriors. That they do bad things for the good of the community, but these guys are *not* like that. They're doing bad things for the sake of doing bad things. They're breaking the law and they're scary, sis. Thugs. I don't want you hurt."

"Fuck you, Mickie. *You* aren't happy, so you don't want to see *me* be happy. I don't think I want to talk to you anymore. Good luck with your life. You're lonely and pathetic and you're going to be like that forever."

Angel stormed out of the restaurant, her blonde hair twitching behind her perfect body as she went.

Mickie pushed her plate away and dropped her head on her arms dejectedly. "That didn't go well," she mumbled under her breath.

Mickie had no idea why she continued to try to watch over Angel. It was absurdly obvious her sister wanted nothing to do with her. But it wasn't something she could just turn off. She loved her sister, no matter how badly Angel treated her. She held out hope that eventually Angel would grow up and they'd be able to have a sisterly relationship.

Mickie was ten years older than her; Angel had been an "oops" baby, and their wealthy parents hadn't really wanted to start over with another kid when she was born. They'd left a lot of her raising to Mickie, leaving her to do most of the babysitting. When Mickie was ready to head off to college, her parents convinced her to go to the local community college and live at home instead of going away. They hadn't wanted to lose their unpaid babysitter.

Mickie hated thinking badly about her own parents, but by the time she'd realized how they'd made her feel guilty over wanting to go away to school and how much Angel would miss her, she'd made her decision.

By the time Angel had reached middle school, she'd seen their parents manipulate Mickie so much, she'd learned to do it like a pro. Their parents gave her whatever she wanted just to shut her up and keep her out of their hair. Mickie had tried to teach Angel right from wrong but somewhere along the line, Angel had decided her sister was the enemy.

They couldn't look more different. No one ever guessed they were sisters. Where Angel was tall, slender, and light, Mickie was curvy and dark. She kept her black hair short and couldn't care less about makeup, fashion, or pleasing those around her. She said what she wanted to say, and to hell with what others thought. On the other hand, Angel wore full makeup in the sixth grade and had dated more boys than Mickie could even remember.

Angel's words had hurt, but Mickie was sadly used to them. She didn't want to take notice, but she couldn't help it. Anytime Angel didn't want to hear what Mickie was telling her, she'd strike back at her sister's looks or her disastrous marriage. There were days Mickie thought she looked good, but Angel's words could still sometimes hit her where she was most vulnerable, and she'd fall back into believing she wasn't as pretty as her sister.

Angel was also always telling her that she would never talk to her again, but Mickie knew the next time her sister needed something, she'd conveniently forget anything she'd said in the past and call her for help.

Ignoring the hurt in her belly, Mickie thought about this Ransom guy. He completely freaked her out. He was bad news, and she knew she'd never forgive herself if she didn't *try* to warn Angel. Even if they didn't get along, Mickie still loved her. She was her sister. Her younger sister. The girl who'd held her hand when she was small. Who Mickie had mostly raised. Mickie had known going into lunch that it was a long shot to try once more to talk Angel out of dating the president of the motorcycle club, but she'd had to try.

Mickie had to give Angel one thing, Ransom was a good-looking man. He was in his mid-forties and had dark brown hair. He had a beard, but it wasn't one of those beards that were long and straggly looking. Ransom kept it neatly groomed. It hung about an inch below his chin and actually looked soft. He was a few inches taller than Angel, probably a bit over six feet. He wasn't all muscle, he could probably stand to lose about fifteen pounds, but he wasn't obese. The few times Mickie had seen him, he'd been wearing his leather vest with nothing underneath. He didn't have a beer belly, but there was no six-pack present either.

All in all, he wasn't a troll, but it was the look in his eyes that freaked Mickie out the most. They were cold. Cold, hard, and empty, as if he didn't have any morals and didn't give a crap if what he did hurt someone else. And that was the thing. Mickie didn't want Angel to be the one he didn't care about hurting.

Mickie had done a bit of research about Ransom and his motorcycle club. It was really a gang. They called themselves the Red Brothers, or Hermanos Rojos, and one story had claimed it was because of the amount of blood they'd spilt around the city.

If that wasn't enough to scare the hell out of Mickie, she read that they'd been involved in drugs, owned a strip club that had been busted for prostitution more than once, and one member of the gang had been put in prison for murder the year before.

Every man in the gang had a tattoo that said "Loyalty to One," whatever that meant. Mickie had seen a picture of the tattoo on a newspaper exposé of the club. The men in the gang apparently were "honored" with the ink once they were voted in as full members. It was huge, and spanned their entire backs, from shoulder to shoulder and down to just above their butts. It was a takeoff of lady justice, but instead of being a woman, it was a man sitting on a motorcycle. He was holding a pistol in one hand in place of a sword, and rather than the scales of justice, he was holding up the severed head of a man who had been blindfolded. The letters RB were on one side of the vest the man on the motorcycle was wearing, and on the other side was the letter R. Above the image were the words "Loyalty to One" in beautiful scrolled letters.

The entire tattoo was creepy as hell, and Mickie couldn't believe that anyone would voluntarily get it put on their back permanently.

Even the women who hung around the men in the club were hard and scary looking. The same exposé about the gang included the tattoos the women got that read, "Property of...", and listed the man they belonged to. The words were put on the backs of their necks, as well as on their lower stomachs. One woman who was interviewed had proudly claimed they were inked in both places so no matter how their man was "doing them," they could see the brand on their skin.

Mickie shivered. She liked reading romance novels herself, and even liked the ones that portrayed submissive women to their dominant men, but she didn't think these MC relationships were like that.

Angel was twenty-four years old; more than old enough to make her own decisions, but Mickie knew this wasn't the *right* choice. But obviously trying to talk sense into her sister hadn't done any good.

Mickie sighed and kept her eyes closed as she rested her head on her hands and tried to figure out what she was going to do next.

CRUZ HELD his breath and tried to filter through what he'd just heard. He was sitting in the booth behind Angel and her sister. He'd arrived just after Angel, having followed her with the tracking device Ransom had planted in her purse.

Everything Mickie had tried to tell her sister had been dead-on correct. Ransom had been right in his assessment of Angel, she wasn't very smart, but she *was* beautiful. Cruz felt bad for the sister. He hadn't gotten a good look at her because he'd already been seated behind Angel when Mickie had come into the restaurant, and she'd come at the booth from the opposite direction of the one he was sitting in.

Angel hadn't sugar-coated her words, and Cruz had flinched when she'd laid into Mickie about her looks. No woman liked hearing she wasn't pretty.

While Cruz didn't have any brothers or sisters, he did have good friends he considered his family. If they wanted to warn him about a girlfriend, he might not necessarily agree with them, but out of respect, and due to his history with his ex and, yes, love, he'd listen to what they had to say.

The fact that Angel wouldn't even listen to Mickie was telling. She was used to getting her way and doing what she wanted. Spoiled was how Cruz would characterize her. Ransom wasn't the smartest person Cruz had ever met, but he wasn't stupid either. He couldn't be and have clawed his way to being the president of the MC. He'd chosen well in Angel. She was pretty, stubborn, spoiled, and clueless. She'd most likely do exactly what Ransom wanted her to do, including trying to sell her friends drugs if it came down to it. Damn.

He didn't like Ransom's threat against Angel's sister. It was obvious he had plans for Angel, and if her sister did somehow convince her that Ransom was bad news, the MC President wasn't going to be happy. He didn't even know the woman sitting in the booth behind him, but if her stubborn tone was anything to go by, she wasn't going to let the matter of her sister dating Ransom drop. The president was right to be worried about her.

Ransom's not-so-vague threat about hurting his pseudo-girlfriend's sister echoed in his mind. If Ransom had no issues asking Cruz to hurt her, he wouldn't have any problem ordering any of the other members of the club to do it as well. Cruz knew without a doubt that Ransom would do it too. He'd have her hurt to keep her away from Angel. And that was unacceptable. Cruz couldn't exactly warn her off without blowing his cover, but he could try to stick close to make sure Ransom didn't get near her. It wasn't a perfect plan, but if she got hurt and he didn't do anything to prevent it, he'd feel like shit. If push came to shove, he'd tell Ransom he was tailing the sister and keeping his eye on her. That should buy them both some time. If Ransom thought the sister was under control, maybe he wouldn't sic anyone else on her.

He thought about what his next steps were. He was supposed to meet Angel in a couple of hours and bring her into the lion's den, but he knew what he had to do before then. He'd ditched the idea of getting close to Angel because Ransom had been keeping her far away from the club up until now. He was gathering quite a bit of information without having to involve the woman, which was a relief.

Cruz got up and left the restaurant, going the long way around the table Angel had been sitting at so her sister didn't see him. Not that she'd notice him if he walked right by her. Her head was face down on the table.

He put his leather vest, which the members of the club called a cut, in the trunk of the small black piece-of-shit car the FBI had given him for the assignment. He'd wanted to have a Harley, but he'd been denied by the bean counters at the FBI. Damn the government and their budget cuts. They'd argued the expense was only worth it for long-term undercover assignments, not his short-term one. Cruz could've used his own bike, but didn't want to risk it getting wrecked, confiscated, or stolen while on assignment.

So Cruz had sucked it up and taken the shit from the Red Brothers about his lack of a bike. It wasn't normal for a prospect not to have a motorcycle, but somehow they'd bought it...with the groundwork story laid by the other agent in the southern club about how his previous bike had been stolen.

Cruz took out a pair of sneakers and exchanged his black boots with the zippers and rings on them for the more normal shoes. He also pulled a black T-shirt over his tank top, and even tucked it into his jeans to try to look more respectable. Cruz ran his hand briefly over his short crew cut. There was nothing he could do about the stubble on his face. It was too short to be called a beard, but too long to really be called a five o'clock shadow.

He took a deep breath and headed back into the restaurant toward the sister's table. Here went nothing.

MICKIE DIDN'T KNOW how long she'd been sitting at the table with her forehead resting on her arms when she heard someone talking to her. She lifted her head and saw an absolutely beautiful man standing next to her table.

She looked around, thinking he must have the

wrong table, but when she gazed back up at him, he was looking down at her and smiling.

"I'm sorry, did you ask me something?"

"Merely if you were all right. I saw your companion leave and you looked distraught, so I thought I'd check on you."

Holy freaking hell. Mickie looked around again, trying to see if someone was playing a joke on her. When she didn't see anyone, she looked back at the man standing next to her table.

He was tall. So tall Mickie had to tilt her head up to see him clearly. She'd always had a thing about tall men. There was nothing that made her feel safer than a man who towered over her. But then again, most men were taller than her five feet six inches.

He was wearing a tight, black T-shirt that didn't hide his extremely muscular arms. Even his forearms were tight and bulging with muscles. Mickie could just see the tip of a tattoo peeking out from the left sleeve of his shirt. It was done in shades of black, with no other color. Even though she couldn't make out what it was, she suddenly wished she could explore it in depth.

The man's jeans were well worn and tight in all the right places. His crotch was at her eye level and Mickie blushed and quickly brought her eyes back up to his face, trying to ignore the bulge that more than filled out his pants. His hair was black, like hers, but cut military-precision short. He had facial hair that looked rough, and Mickie briefly wondered what it might feel like against her skin. Would it be prickly, or soft?

She shook her head. She had to get herself together. "I'm okay. Thanks for asking."

"Are you sure? May I sit?"

The man gestured at the empty seat across from her. Mickie frowned. She wanted him to, she really did, but what was the point?

"Why?"

"Why what?"

"Why do you want to sit with me? You don't know me. I don't know you. You, looking like you do, can't possibly be interested in me, so why would you waste your time?"

The man shifted, leaned one hip against the table, and crossed his arms over his chest. He didn't look pissed at her words, but instead seemed amused. "I want to sit with you because I've been watching you since you walked in. I noticed you right off. You've got a cute little sway to your walk and I liked what I saw. You're correct in that we don't know each other, but I'm trying to remedy that. I don't know why you think I can't possibly be interested in you, but you're wrong. I'm probably overstepping some social boundaries by telling you so, but there it is. So as I see it, I'm not wasting my time at all. In fact, I can't think of anything I'd rather be doing right now than sitting here talking and getting to know you."

Mickie could only gape at the man. What. The. Hell?

"My name is Cruz. I'm very glad to meet you."

Mickie looked at the hand the man held out to her.

She glanced at the other hand resting on the table, no rings. His fingernails were short and well groomed. Mickie mentally shrugged and reached out to him with her own hand.

"Michelle, but I go by Mickie."

"It's great to meet you, Mickie. So, may I sit?"

Mickie found herself nodding. Holy shit. This wasn't like her, but there was no way she could turn this man down. If nothing else, she'd bring this memory back out later and bask in feeling good about herself for the first time in a long time. His attention soothed the hurt feelings from Angel's words.

Cruz eased into the seat across from Mickie. He was surprised by how attractive he found her. After hearing Angel's words, he'd assumed she'd look very different than she did. He was a bit ashamed of himself for thinking the worst. Mickie's hair was cut short, but still managed to frame her face in a way that was very pretty. She had large brown eyes and her lips were plump, especially since she kept nervously chewing on them with her teeth. Cruz couldn't see her body with the table in the way, but what he saw definitely wasn't a turn off. Her breasts were on the full side, way more than the A cup his ex's had been. And he had to be at least a foot taller than her.

She was the complete opposite of her sister...and his ex. Sophie had been slim, and even though Mickie was shorter than him, she was curvy. She probably thought she carried too much weight, but ever since discovering Sophie's slight frame had been the result of years of drug abuse, Cruz much preferred a woman who looked healthy. And Mickie certainly fit that bill.

He continued scrutinizing her. He watched as Mickie brought a hand up and smoothed her short hair back behind one ear nervously. She was wearing a light purple shirt that dipped low in front, showing off a hint of cleavage. Her eyes would meet his, then skitter away nervously. Her modesty and nervousness was endearing...and suddenly the entire undercover mission took a weird turn for Cruz.

He'd only meant to get to know her a bit today so he could accidentally run into her again later and talk to her, stick close to her to make sure Ransom didn't get some bright idea to do something drastic to keep her away from Angel. But suddenly Cruz wished he really was sitting here with no agenda and with no other motive than to get to know the woman sitting in front of him. Somehow he knew he could really come to like her.

If he wasn't undercover, and wasn't trying to keep her safe from a psychotic motorcycle club president, he might have seriously considered dating her.

"So, Mickie, you never did tell me if you're all right or not."

"I'm okay. Just a sister thing."

"Ah..."

"You have any brothers or sisters?"

Cruz decided right there to be as honest as he could with Mickie. If he was going to have to deceive her, he wanted to keep things as real as possible as long as he could. "No, I'm an only child. My parents wanted more, but it didn't ever happen. I do have some friends I consider my siblings, but I know it's not the same thing. You? Only one sister?"

"Yeah. She's way younger than me. My parents thought they were done having kids, then she came along."

"Wow, was that tough on you?"

"Yes and no. I was still young enough that I thought it was cool at first. She was my own living doll. Then my parents became less and less interested in raising another daughter, so the job mostly fell to me."

Cruz reached across the table and put his hand on Mickie's. "I'm sorry, that sounds tough." He pulled his hand back and leaned forward on his elbows. He'd wanted to keep his hand on hers, but knew it would be weird since they didn't really know each other. "I'm sure your sister appreciates everything you've done for her."

She gave a quick, short chortle. "I'm not so sure about that, but thanks for being optimistic. So, you from around here?"

Cruz nodded, letting Mickie change the subject. "Yeah, you?"

"Yeah, me and Angel have lived here our entire lives. You like San Antonio?"

"I do. There's culture, there's art, it's a city but if you drive twenty minutes in any direction, you're out of the city and can see longhorns and ranches."

Mickie laughed. "That's about right."

Cruz knew he was asking for trouble with his next question, but he couldn't stop wanting to get to know the woman in front of him. "Since we're learning about each other...what do you do?"

Mickie tilted her head and eyed Cruz critically. There was something about him that seemed...off, but she couldn't really put her finger on it. She mentally shrugged and gave him a vague explanation. She wasn't so stupid that she'd tell him everything about her. She didn't know him, after all. "Nothing too exciting, I assure you. I work at a car dealership in the service department. It's not very glamorous, but it pays the bills."

Cruz looked at Mickie in approval. "Good girl."

"What?"

"You didn't tell me which car dealership. Smart."

Mickie blushed. "I-I didn't—"

"It's fine. I was being honest. You shouldn't go blurting that stuff out to any ol' man who asks to sit with you and flirts shamelessly."

"Is that what you're doing?"

"If you have to ask, I'm obviously not doing it right. I guess I'm rusty."

"I'm just...guys don't usually flirt with me." She blushed again. Jesus, this guy was going to think she was pathetic if she didn't keep her mouth shut.

Cruz thought Mickie was adorable. He leaned farther on his arms and toward her a bit more. "Their loss is my gain."

Mickie shook her head in exasperation at Cruz.

24

Trying to change the subject, she asked, "So, what do *you* do?"

Cruz's stomach dropped, but he didn't show any outward emotion at her words. He'd hoped to distract Mickie enough that she'd forget to ask. Still, he'd learned over the years that keeping his answer truthful but vague was always the way to go. "I'm in security."

There was silence between them for a moment, then Mickie asked, "Security, huh?"

"Yup."

"Hummm. I guess I can see it. You're in shape, unlike a lot of security guards I've seen, so you get points for that."

Cruz swallowed back a laugh. "I'm not sure that's saying much, but I'll take it. Besides, it pays the bills," he intentionally repeated her words, happy when she smiled at him.

Deciding that the best way to make sure Mickie was safe was to stick to her like glue, at least when he wasn't at the club, he blurted, "I like you. Will you let me take you out sometime? Maybe for dinner?"

"Uh…I don't know."

Cruz knew he wasn't being very smooth, so tried to back off a bit. "I know, too soon, right? Okay, at least let me give you my number. You can text me or something. Maybe we can accidently meet for lunch again sometime?"

Mickie laughed. "You don't give up, do you?"

"Not when it's something I want."

She paused for a beat, scrutinizing him. Finally she

said. "Okay, give me your number. I'll have to think about it."

Cruz gave her the number to the phone he was using as Smoke. He couldn't keep her safe if she needed him by giving her his personal number, since he never carried that phone with him when he was at the club. When she contacted him, and hopefully she would, he'd add her to his contacts under a fake name so if the phone was compromised by one of the members at the club, *she* wouldn't be.

He looked Mickie in the eye. "I hope you use it. I really do want to get to know you." Cruz stood up reluctantly, knowing it was time to go if he didn't want to freak her out. "It was nice meeting you. I hope your sister comes to see what a treasure she has in you."

Mickie cursed the blush she knew was blooming on her cheeks…again. "It was nice to meet you too, Cruz."

"Bye, Mickie."

"Bye."

Cruz left the restaurant and Mickie noticed that his back view was just as nice as the front. She hadn't ever understood the phrase "you could bounce a quarter on that ass" until now.

She sighed. What the hell was she thinking? She looked down at the number she'd programmed into her phone. She really should just delete it. There was no way a man like Cruz would honestly be interested in her, but damn it felt good.

She clicked the button to turn the screen to her phone off and gathered up her stuff. Fuck it. Why wouldn't he be interested in her? Mickie knew she'd been taking Angel's words to heart more than she should.

She had a job, she was a good person, she might not be a size two, but it wasn't as if she was grotesque either, size twelve was more normal in today's day and age than a size two. So what if she had some fourteens in her closet too? Most women's weights went up and down...and besides, not every store had the same size chart. Whatever.

Mickie made up her mind. She'd text Cruz, see if he was serious. If he was, she'd go for it. She deserved it. Not only that, she wanted it.

The day seemed brighter as Mickie left, even though Angel and the damn MC were still on her mind. She had to do something, but she didn't know what. She'd have to wait and hope like hell Angel would come to her senses after the damn "party" tonight. Hopefully it would be out of control and would scare Angel shitless...and away from the club altogether.

CHAPTER 3

CRUZ LOOKED around the clubhouse in barely concealed disgust. The men had been on their best behavior from the moment he'd arrived with Angel. The music was loud, the booze was flowing freely, but it was extremely tame compared to some of the parties Cruz had been to in the last month.

After leaving the restaurant, Cruz had pulled over and donned his biker clothes, essentially putting back on his new identity, one he was beginning to hate. He continued to Angel's apartment and gathered her. He'd tried to be a dick to her as much as he could, while not risking Ransom's ire if she tattled about his actions to the president. Cruz wanted to show Angel that the bikers weren't nice guys. He didn't think his tactic worked, because the rest of the guys at the club were going out of their way to be solicitous and pleasant, at least for them.

Even the few old ladies who were there were taking

Angel under their wings. They'd taken her to a back room when she'd arrived, and an hour later when they'd come out, they'd all been acting as if they were best friends.

Cruz learned from Knife and Donkey, two of the more hard-core men in the gang, that the women were slowly going to bring Angel into the fold that night, including getting her high. It was all a part of their plan. They'd supply her with all the weed she wanted, and then eventually Ransom would pressure her into trying the harder stuff.

They were giggling and chummy when they came out of the backroom. The old ladies went to their men and Cruz watched as Angel weaved her way across the room to Ransom. When she got to him, he hauled her against his side with an arm around her neck. He didn't acknowledge her in any way, but merely kept on talking with Kitty and Tick.

Finally after a few minutes went by, Ransom looked down at Angel and asked, "Have fun tonight?"

"Oh yeah, everyone was so nice!"

"It's time to go."

"But, Ransom, I just got here," she whined.

"I *said* it's time to fucking go. Get your shit and I'll take you home."

"Okay."

Angel teetered her way back across the clubhouse floor on her four-inch heels, not knowing or probably not caring that all eyes were on her ass as she went. When she was out of hearing, Camel, a prospect who'd been voted into the club recently, said, "I gotta tap me some of that."

Cruz half expected Ransom to lose his shit, but it was more verification that the man didn't give a fuck about Angel when he merely laughed and said, "You'll have your chance. Patience, man. Everyone will get their shot at her when I'm done and when we're rolling in the dough her friends give us. I don't give a shit if you all pass her around...*after* I'm done with her and the club gets what it needs."

Everyone laughed and high-fived. Cruz joined in, sick to his stomach thinking about what Ransom had in store for Mickie's sister.

"Hurry up and get back, Pres. Bambi's coming over with a few of her friends after you leave. You know she likes it up the ass," Dirt informed his president with a smirk.

"Oh, hell yeah. I'll get Angel home, fuck her, and get back here. Half an hour, tops."

"You gonna let her orgasm tonight?" Tick asked. They all knew how Ransom used orgasms as a method of control.

"Fuck no. I don't have time for that shit and I don't give a fuck if she gets off or not as long as I do. I'll tell her she didn't pay enough attention to me tonight or some bullshit...how I like it when my woman does her drugs in front of me. She'll be begging for something to smoke the next time I see her."

Once again, everyone around them laughed crudely. "Well, hurry the fuck up. We need you to get the party started," Camel complained, knowing Ransom had one rule when it came to the club whores. He was the first to fuck each night. Once he'd had his fill of who he wanted, they were fair game for anyone and everyone else. No one was allowed to get any pussy until he decided he was done and permitted the other men to have their fun.

"Shut the fuck up, Camel. I'll get back when I get back. Don't piss me off."

"No disrespect intended, Pres."

They watched as Angel clipped her way back to them. Ransom smiled crookedly at her, shoved one hand down the back of her jeans, and grabbed hold of her hair with the other. He yanked her head back and kissed her long and deep. The hand at her ass moved up and squeezed her breast as he kissed her; he was obviously unconcerned with his audience.

As the other men catcalled, he lifted his lips off of Angel's. She had a dreamy look on her face. "Come on, let's go. I need inside that hot cunt."

Ransom led Angel out of the room with his hand at the back of her neck. It could've been a loving gesture; Cruz had seen his friend Dax put his hand on the back of his girlfriend Mackenzie's neck as they walked together sometimes, but he knew Ransom used it more as a controlling action than an affectionate gesture.

"Get on it, assholes. Get Bambi's ass over here. Ransom is gonna be ready to fuck when he gets back. Let's not disappoint him," Bubba ordered. The vice president's words were muted and harsh. He lifted his chin at Cruz. "Smoke, you're on lookout tonight. Make sure the pigs don't crash the party. The Snakes are bringing a shipment tonight. Don't fuck it up."

Cruz gave a short nod to the other man in response. Bubba was a large man—not muscular, but overweight. He looked like a heart attack waiting to happen, but Cruz had seen him take down one of the younger prospects the other day with absolutely no effort. He was big and mean, and took no shit from anyone in the club. He might be the VP, but he was also one of the best enforcers as well.

"No problem, Bubba. Are we expecting trouble?" Cruz wanted to know what he might be up against.

"We always expect problems, Prospect. That's why you're on fucking duty."

Cruz nodded in response instead of taking the other man to the ground for his asshole-ish tone and turned to head outside the big warehouse. It was located in the industrial part of San Antonio. All around them were other warehouses that held everything from vehicles to boxes and crates of merchandise. Inventory that was stored until it was either picked up and driven to the coast and put into shipping containers to be sent overseas, or trucked throughout the States. Eighteen-wheelers were entering and exiting the big complex day and night. It was actually a perfect hideout for the gang and their illegal activities. Of course, motorcycles didn't quite blend in, but it seemed the MC had done their work well, and everyone was either too scared to say anything, or they'd been bought off.

Thankful he didn't have to watch the orgy that was sure to go down that night, Cruz crossed his arms and leaned against the corner of a nearby warehouse. He knew there were other prospects standing around at other key points around the building as well. It wasn't likely anyone would just randomly show up, but it was another bullshit job the president got off on having the prospects do.

Cruz thought about the investigation; it was getting murkier and murkier every day. How the hell he was going to get Angel out of the shitstorm she'd found herself in, keep Mickie safe from Ransom's wrath, and find out who the mysterious new big dealer the club had somehow managed to procure, was all running through his brain.

On top of that, Cruz found his thoughts turning to Mickie. She hadn't been what he'd expected at all. She was spunky...and cute. She was a bit eclectic and obviously wasn't afraid to say what she felt.

On the other hand, Cruz couldn't remember the last time a woman had blushed so much. Every time he'd flustered her, she'd turned a light shade of pink. It was adorable and he was way too jaded for her, but that wasn't going to stop him from sticking close.

Feeling his phone vibrate, Cruz pulled it out, thinking it was one of the other prospects fucking with him. He was surprised to see a message from Mickie, figuring she'd make him wait longer before getting in touch with him.

Hey. Just wanted to say hi. It was nice meeting you today.

The text was short and to the point...a feeler of sorts. There was no commitment to it, so if he didn't answer, she wouldn't be embarrassed. But it also told Cruz a lot. She'd reached out in the hopes he'd answer. He immediately texted her back.

Hi. You too. I'm glad you got in touch. You want to accidently be at the same place at the same time tomorrow to feed ourselves?

Lol. Ok. Where?

Cruz smiled. God. He loved that Mickie didn't play hard to get.

Wherever you want.

The sub shop on Crystal Hill and Wurzbach Rd?

Cruz knew which one she was talking about. It probably wasn't a good idea for him to be seen in his "normal" clothes that close to the Red Brothers' hangout.

Actually, I was thinking Iron Cactus down on the River Walk.

Cruz sweated the ten minutes it took Mickie to respond.

I didn't peg you as a River Walk kind of guy.

Mickie was exactly right. Normally Cruz wouldn't be caught dead at the overpriced tourist trap that was the collection of shops downtown by the river. But he also figured none of the Red Brothers would be there either.

Figured for our first date, I'd treat you right.

A girl can't argue with that. See you there at one-ish?

Yes. Be safe until then.

Cruz stared at the words he'd typed on the screen. He'd told Sophie "be safe" every time they'd parted. Toward the end of their marriage, she'd merely rolled her eyes at him. Cruz didn't know why he'd said the words to Mickie, but there they were, in black and white. *Be safe.*

Thank you. I will. You too. Later.

Later.

Cruz tucked his phone back into his pocket and couldn't hold back the smile that crept across his face.

A bike pulling into the area brought him out of his musings of Mickie with a jolt. Cruz observed Ransom returning after having dropped Angel off, well within his thirty-minute estimate. Shortly thereafter, a car pulled up and three whores Cruz recognized stumbled out of the vehicle, obviously already stoned. The churning in Cruz's stomach wouldn't stop. Even though he wasn't inside, he could well imagine what was going to happen.

The prostitutes had Cruz thinking about his ex and finding her in their bedroom with three men.

The last time Cruz saw Sophie was when the SAPD had arrested her for prostitution and drugs. After their divorce, she hadn't stopped her illegal activities. He'd begged her to get help, but she'd refused, calling him a "fuddy-duddy," claiming she'd been using drugs for their entire marriage and that she'd never been satisfied by him in bed.

Cruz had met Sophie when he'd first joined the FBI. She'd been a senior at Georgetown and they'd met while at a bar one night. He'd fallen in love almost immediately. Sophie was tall and slender and her long blonde hair had blown him away. She'd been funny and gregarious and had made him feel as if he was the most important person in her life.

The reality more than lived up to his imagination. Sophie had been a wildcat in bed and Cruz thought he was the luckiest guy in the world. Eventually they'd made their way to San Antonio, where Cruz was still posted. He'd hoped being in a new city would strengthen their relationship, but instead it seemed to only exacerbate the issues they'd been having.

Sophie was known as the life of the party. She had a friendly disposition and she easily made friends wherever they went. However, it wasn't long before her party-girl attitude started to get old. At company get-togethers, she'd usually end up drinking too much and embarrassing the hell out of Cruz. Eventually it got to a point where he refused to bring her to any of the social functions he went to for work. He needed to maintain some sort of professional persona, and watching his wife flirt shamelessly and have to be carried home didn't cut it.

Sophie didn't seem to care. She'd simply shrugged and went out with her friends instead of accompanying

Cruz to work events. By the time they'd moved to San Antonio, Cruz was tired of making excuses and he knew they weren't working out as a couple.

His friends in the FBI were always complimenting him on how sexy his wife was and Cruz took their comments with a smile, but deep down, hindsight being twenty/twenty, he'd known he wanted more out of their relationship. He'd wanted a supportive partnership that was more than sex and parties.

The night Cruz found out about the real Sophie was one he knew he'd never forget as long as he lived. He'd gone to an annual charity event in San Antonio. He'd promised his friends he'd at least show up. He'd worked with various law enforcement offices throughout the city and had become close friends with five officers. They all joked that they were a living, breathing bar joke...a cop, Feeb, game warden, highway patrolman, doctor, and deputy walked into a bar...

But Cruz knew he'd never find closer friends than Dax, TJ, Quint, Calder, Hayden, and Conor. The other men, and woman, had all met during various cases they'd been on, and they'd bonded as a result.

Cruz had been at the charity event and felt like crap. He was coming down with the flu and had left early. He'd tried to text Sophie and let her know he was on his way home, but she hadn't answered. He'd entered their small suburban house and knew immediately something was off. He'd pulled his sidearm out and cautiously searched the house.

When he'd found his wife, he stood in the bedroom doorway, aghast, not able to believe the scene before him. Sophie had been on her knees in the middle of three men, alternating sucking one man and jacking off the other two. She'd been switching between the men, seemingly enjoying what she was doing. Cruz remembered the scene as if it was yesterday...

"What the hell?" He barked the words into the otherwise quiet room.

Sophie took her lips off one man's cock to peer around his leg, never stopping her hands from moving up and down the other two men's dicks. "Hey, Cruzch, I didn't eschpect you home scho early. Come join the fun."

Cruz could only stare at his wife as she went back to what she'd been doing before he'd interrupted, not caring her husband had caught her in the act. He looked over to the table sitting next to their bed and saw three lines of white powder, along with a plastic frequent-shopper card from the local grocery store. There were three used condoms on the floor by the bed and the covers were mussed, as if the group had just moved their sexual orgy to the middle of the room.

Cruz literally felt his heart break as memories careened through his mind and everything clicked into place with extreme clarity. All the nights Sophie came home from partying with her friends, immediately showering before joining him in bed. The weight she couldn't seem to put on. Her excessive frenetic energy and mood swings.

"Get the fuck out," Cruz clipped. When the men didn't move, he cocked his pistol and then warned in a deadly voice, "You have ten seconds to get your asses out of my house before I shoot first and call the cops second."

Even with Sophie trying to hold on to the men by their dicks, they managed to tear themselves away and brush past him on the way out the door. The last straw was when Sophie called, "Leave the money on the table on your way out."

Cruz thought back to Sophie's comment that he hadn't satisfied her in bed. He would've been hurt, except he'd dealt with enough addicts to know the only thing they could think of was their next hit. Besides that, he knew for a fact that they'd been more than sexually compatible...at least at the beginning of their marriage.

The officers at the San Antonio Police Department had known who Sophie was and had tried to go easy on her the first couple of times she'd been arrested, but it hadn't done any good. She'd simply not cared.

There was nothing left of the Sophie he'd once loved. She was lost to the drugs, her new life on the street and her pimp. Cruz had tried calling her parents to get her help, but they'd truly disowned her, as Sophie had told him early in their relationship. It seemed she'd entered a life of drugs while in high school. When her parents had been called to pick her up at a police station when she'd been taken into custody—after being caught in a hotel room with two men thirty years older than she was, naked and drugged out of her mind—they'd refused. One of her friends had been worried about her and had called her parents to try to get her some help. But instead, they'd washed their hands of her altogether. They figured that Sophie had made her bed and they'd had enough.

Cruz just wished they'd said something to him. Granted, he'd only met them once, but it would've been nice for them to have made an effort to reach out to him and let him know about their daughter. He mentally shrugged. The bottom line was that Sophie had put on a great show and he'd bought it hook, line, and sinker.

The backfiring of a car brought Cruz's attention back to the mostly deserted shipping yard. Even with the party going on inside the club, the area was quiet and the night passed slowly for Cruz. He hated knowing there wasn't anything he could do at the moment to help Bambi and the other two women who had been shown inside earlier, but his hands were tied.

The night was one for memories...both good and bad. He hadn't thought about Sophie in months, and after only a few hours of meeting a woman who was his ex's complete opposite, he'd rehashed their entire relationship. Cruz wasn't sure what to think about that. He'd already made the decision to get close to Mickie for her own protection, but he was beginning to think she'd be more than simply another job.

CHAPTER 4

MICKIE WIPED her hands on her jeans for the hundredth time as she made her way up the River Walk to the Iron Cactus. She'd waffled back and forth before actually texting Cruz the night before. Finally, talking herself into it, she'd sent him the noncommittal text, hoping he'd been serious about wanting to see her again. Never in a million years did she think he'd respond to her as soon as he had.

She hadn't lied when she'd told Cruz she didn't think he seemed like the type of man who would take a date to the River Walk. He seemed more…rugged or something. The iconic San Antonio River Walk was very touristy and didn't match the image of Cruz in her head. Mickie mentally shrugged. There were bound to be other things she'd learn about him that weren't what she expected.

Mickie couldn't help but think about her ex, and

how everything she'd known about him had been a lie. Troy was a piece of work. Mickie had thought she was the luckiest woman in the world. She'd married him when she was around Angel's age. They'd met at the dealership. Troy had brought his car in for service and they'd immediately clicked. He'd seemed so nice.

Troy had been thirty-one and quite wealthy. Mickie had money. Her parents gave her a monthly allowance to try to assuage their guilt over not helping much in raising Angel, but Troy had way more. He wasn't good-looking in the turn-heads-on-the-street kind of way. He was a bit of a nerd, but it was his perceived sincerity that had drawn Mickie.

He'd wined and dined her and had swept her off her feet. He'd even convinced her to wait until after they were married to consummate their relationship. Like a fool, Mickie had been convinced it was the most romantic gesture she'd ever heard of. She wasn't a virgin, but hadn't had a lot of experience either.

So they'd had a huge wedding, paid for mostly by Troy's family. She wore a wedding dress with a six-foot train along with six bridesmaids and six groomsmen, all friends of Troy's. The sex they'd had that night wasn't anything to write home about, but it wasn't awful either.

There hadn't been a honeymoon because Troy had claimed he was in the middle of a huge project at the accounting firm where he worked, but he promised they'd take a trip later. Later had never arrived. Troy had started working past five every day, and six o'clock became seven. Then eight. And slowly but surely, any intimacy between them turned tepid at best.

The lack of a sex life was what Mickie had stressed over more than anything else. She'd never been very adventurous, even before she'd met Troy, but they'd never had sex in anything but the missionary position. Mickie longed for more, but had never gotten it from Troy. They acted like roommates rather than man and wife, and slowly his lack of interest in her eroded any confidence she had in her own sexuality.

It wasn't until they'd been married for two and a half years that she found out the real reason Troy had married her. It had devastated her, and Mickie knew she'd never forget how gutted she'd felt listening to Troy talk on the phone with Brittany, one of the women who'd been a bridesmaid in their wedding, and who'd apparently been the real love of Troy's life all along.

"Yeah, Mickie has no clue. Brit, I promise, in another few months we'll get that divorce. You know I had to marry her in order to get my inheritance. Mum and Pop never liked you. It was a shitty thing to do, forcing me to marry or lose all that money, but now that I have control over it, I'll make sure Mickie loses interest in me and we can agree on an amicable divorce. I can guarantee the sex already sucks. When I have to fuck her, I don't bother even trying to make it good for her. Once she signs the papers that say she wants no alimony, I'm free for you, baby."

He'd been silent for a moment, obviously listening to Brittany on the other end of the line.

"Oh yeah. She never wants to rock the boat. She'll sign them, no contest. Swear. And yeah, I'll tell Mickie I'm working late again tonight and get to your place around three."

Another pause and Mickie felt the tears rolling down her cheeks, but didn't bother to wipe them away.

Troy's voice deepened as he responded to whatever Brittany had said. *"I can't wait to get you pregnant. Hopefully by this time next year, you'll be having my baby. I can't wait to start our family. As soon as you're pregnant, I'll tell her we've drifted apart and we'll be better off as friends. I have no doubt she'll sign the divorce papers. I love you, baby. See you later."*

Mickie had stood still in the doorway and stared at Troy with no emotion on her face as he'd turned around. All the blood had drained from his face and he'd had the nerve to stammer the clichéd phrase, "Mickie. It's not what you think."

She'd simply said, "You'll have divorce papers delivered within the week instead of waiting for her to get pregnant. I hope you have a good lawyer, because I'm sure as hell asking for alimony."

She'd received a fortune in the divorce, especially after Troy's long-term affair with Brittany was exposed. His parents despised Mickie for dragging their family name through the mud, almost as much as they hated Brittany, but Mickie didn't give a damn. As far as she was concerned, Troy and his parents had brought it on themselves. They hadn't allowed him to marry who he loved in the first place, and Troy didn't have the balls to stand up to them.

Her own parents were disappointed she and Troy couldn't get past "their little argument." Their attitude had saddened Mickie as much as the divorce itself.

Last she'd heard, Troy was now married to Brittany and they'd moved to Seattle. They'd had a little girl and Troy was employed by one of the best accounting firms in the state. "So much for karma," Mickie said out loud to no one in particular.

She sighed and stopped in front of the restaurant. She'd moved on. Older and wiser and all that crap. She was much more cautious now when it came to dating, and hadn't found anyone who had been able to break through her walls after Troy. More importantly, there wasn't anyone who she *wanted* to try with…until now.

Knowing she was running late—traffic had been horrendous because of an accident on the interstate— Mickie quickly opened the door to the restaurant and was hit with a wall of different sounds and smells. There was a large group of people in the bar area and the scent of spices and tequila hit her nose hard. Her stomach growled. Mexican was her favorite thing to eat and Mickie had forgotten just how good the food was here.

"Hello, Mickie. Thank you for not standing me up."

Mickie turned and saw Cruz next to her, as if he'd

materialized out of thin air. She shook her head. "I'm sorry I'm late. Traffic was a bitch. And seriously, I don't know who you've been asking out, but any woman would be insane to accept a date with you then not show up."

"Oh, you'd be surprised, honey. Come on, our table is ready."

Mickie melted a bit inside when his fingertips skimmed her lower back, guiding her in front of him, protecting her from the crush of people as they made their way behind the hostess, who led the way to a table.

They were shown to a booth in the back of the restaurant, away from the water. Mickie supposed it wasn't a prime seating arrangement, but sitting away from the people and in the dim light seemed just as intimate as if it'd been a candlelight dinner.

Cruz held her elbow as she sat, then surprisingly, opted to sit next to her instead of across the table.

"Do you mind?" Cruz asked, smiling and gesturing to the space next to her on the bench.

"Uh, no. I guess not," Mickie stammered. She'd never had a date want to sit next to her. Every time she and Troy had gone out, he'd sat across from her and buried his nose in his phone throughout the meal.

He sat and said nonchalantly, "I'd prefer to sit next to you. It feels more like a date that way." He shrugged. "I know…it's weird, right? Sorry, I'll just…" Cruz started to get up from the table to move to the other seat.

Mickie put her hand on his. "It's fine, Cruz. I have to be honest, you surprised me, but not in a bad way. Okay? I'm just not used to it. But I don't mind at all. Promise."

He laughed and settled back down next to her. "It's been a while since I've been out with a woman I wanted to impress. I think I've lost my touch."

"I think you're doing just fine."

"Really?"

"Really."

"Would you two like something to drink?"

The waitress's voice cut into their conversation and they both laughed. After ordering, and after the waitress had walked away, Cruz turned in his seat and looked at Mickie.

"So, come here often?"

Mickie giggled. "I've been here a few times, yes. You?"

"Once." At her lifted eyebrow, Cruz continued. "It was a celebratory dinner. I came with my friend and his woman, and the rest of our friends. She'd recently been through a horrific ordeal, and we were celebrating the fact she was alive, as well as our friendship."

"Wow, I'm glad she's okay. You sound like you're close with your friends."

"Yeah, I told you before they're like my brothers and sister. I don't think people like that are brought into our lives by accident, or very often."

At Mickie's silence, Cruz cursed again. "Shit. Sorry. That's a bit deep for a first date, isn't it? It's just—"

Mickie squeezed Cruz's hand that she still held in hers. "It's fine. Actually it's refreshing. It's real. I feel like most of us go through life being fake and lying so often it's hard to remember who we are deep down inside. I like that you aren't holding back. It's nice."

Cruz shifted uneasily. Suddenly he didn't like that he was getting close to her just to keep her safe from Ransom and the other club members. So far he liked her. She hadn't done anything crazy and he felt comfortable around her. Granted he'd only been in her presence for an hour, but an hour was long enough for some women he'd met in the past to go from interesting to bat-shit crazy. Hearing her compliment him made him feel worse about the reason why he was there, especially since he wasn't being completely honest with her.

Mickie looked at Cruz in confusion. It was as if her words, meant to be a compliment, had made him uncomfortable. "I didn't mean that in a bad way. Being nice is good. I like nice."

Cruz tried to relax and smile. He was doing a piss-poor job of making her want to hang out with him. At this rate, she'd excuse herself to go to the restroom and sneak out. "Sorry, and you should know...I like nice too. And I'll be on my best behavior from here on out, so you won't have to make up an excuse to ditch me."

Mickie smiled back at him. "Deal."

The waitress came back with their drinks and after quickly scanning the menu, they both made their choices.

"How's your sister? Have you had a chance to talk to her recently?" Cruz asked, hating to even bring it up, but wanting to know how much the party last night worked in Ransom's favor. When Cruz had seen him after the party was over early that morning, he'd been mellow and satisfied. Cruz hadn't asked about Angel, knowing it would seem weird for a prospect to be interested in his relationship, but he'd wondered.

Mickie sighed. "I called her this morning and she actually answered, which was surprising. But after listening to her, I knew she only talked to me so she could tell me that I'd been wrong about everything I'd told her yesterday."

"What was your fight over, if you don't mind talking about it?" Cruz asked.

"She's dating this guy who's not good for her, and she won't listen to me."

Cruz shrugged nonchalantly. "She's an adult, right? She's bound to make some dating mistakes as she learns what and who she wants."

"I'd normally agree with you, but not this guy. I'm assuming since you're from around here you've heard of the Red Brothers Motorcycle Club, yeah?" At his nod, she continued. "Well, she's dating the president of the club. She thinks he's misunderstood and a great guy, but he's not. I'm guessing you don't know this, but MC romance novels are very popular now. If you go online and do a search, there are a ton of them. Pages and pages of books with hot, built, tattooed men on the covers. They mostly tout these

SUSAN STOKER

big scary guys who are pussycats under all their bravado. They do slightly illegal things, but all in the name of keeping their communities safe. They don't deal drugs because that's wrong, and they might prostitute women, but only because they want to give them a 'safe place' to make money and to make sure no men take advantage of them. In the end they all end up together and happy as clams. It makes a good story. Hell, I read some of those books myself, and enjoy them. But my sister thinks *this* guy is straight out of one of those romance books. But he's not. I did some research. I'm scared to death for her. He's bad news."

Knowing he was treading on thin ice, Cruz waded in cautiously. He whistled low. "The Hermanos Rojos *are* bad news."

Mickie didn't even give him time to continue or to elaborate. She leaned one elbow on the table and put her head in her hand as she turned toward him. "I *know*, Cruz. Angel told me this morning that she went to their compound, or whatever it's called, while a party was going on. She said that it was all civilized and normal. She even said it was a bit lame. She told me she met some of the 'old ladies' and they were all very nice to her. They partied in the back, away from the men because that's their place, then Ransom brought her home. Something doesn't seem right about it, but I think she's even more in love with this guy than before. He's scum, and the more I try to talk her away from him, the tighter she holds on."

"I hope you aren't thinking about doing anything crazy."

Mickie sighed. "If I knew what crazy thing to do, I'd probably do it. Angel is spoiled and has said some pretty mean things to me in the past...but she's my sister and I love her. I know for a fact that anything I do to interfere will only make her more stubborn. She's a lot like me in that way." She smiled somewhat sadly.

Cruz hated seeing Mickie so dejected, but it wasn't as if he could break cover and tell her he'd keep his eye on her sister and do what he could to keep her out of danger. Deciding a change in subject was in order, he tried to flirt with her a bit, "So, tell me about yourself. I know you work at a car dealership, have a sister who drives you crazy and that you have hair that makes me want to run my fingers through it, but what else?" He smiled at the blush that bloomed over her cheeks.

"You can't ever ask a simple question, can you?" Mickie laughed and started playing with her napkin as she spoke. "I'm really not that interesting. I know I'm supposed to tell you all sorts of cool things, but I'm really just a nerd. I'm thirty-four years old and prefer to sit at home with a good book than go out and party. I've been married once, no kids, and have lived here all my life. I have my undergrad psychology degree from the University of Texas-San Antonio and I've only been to Mexico...not anywhere else out of the United States."

Cruz's hand lifted, as if it had a mind of its own, and pushed a lock of her hair behind her ear. He fingered the short strands hugging her nape, thrilled when she didn't pull away from his light touch. "I don't think you're a nerd, Mickie. Lots of people don't like the bar scene. I hate it, as a matter of fact. There are too many people, the noise is too loud, and drinking to get drunk never held that much appeal for me. What made you choose psychology?"

Mickie tried not to shiver each time Cruz's fingers brushed against the nape of her neck. Holy hell, if just the slight touch of his fingers made her horny, she was in big trouble. The chemistry between them was off the charts. It was crazy, but felt good at the same time. "I just really enjoyed learning about what made people do the things they do, and after a while I'd taken so many psych classes it just made sense."

"So, you like to know what makes people tick?"

"Yeah, but I couldn't find a job I liked. I know I'm way too picky, but I just couldn't see myself working as a social worker, or school counselor or something. Working at the car dealership isn't exactly my dream job, but it's entertaining sometimes and you'd be surprised how often I use what I learned in school." Mickie laughed, obviously recalling some of the antics of the customers she dealt with. "What about you? What made you go into the security field?"

Cruz took a sip of his drink and tried to figure out what to tell Mickie. He really wanted to tell her the story of how he'd decided to go into law enforcement, but he couldn't go into as much detail as he might've if she knew he worked for the FBI. He'd have to tread carefully.

"To understand why, you have to know a bit about me first. My mom passed away from heart disease when I was young. My dad remarried a couple of years later and I never really knew any mother other than Barb. We moved around a lot when they got married. We lived on the east coast for a few years, then my dad got transferred to Ohio. Then Barb took a job in southern California, so we moved again, but they quickly found out that the fast pace of life there didn't suit them, so we moved to Maine and that's where I finished high school.

"They're still there, retired and loving it. They live in a small, conservative town. Nothing much ever happens. My parents weren't rich, but they weren't poor either. I had everything I ever wanted as I grew up, so did most of my friends. The only real crime I had any experience with was petty theft every now and then." Cruz chuckled. "Well, that and underage drinking."

The waitress interrupted his story with their food. Once she left and they'd both dug into their lunch, Cruz continued between bites.

"My sophomore year in high school, we were in California, the only year we were there. One of my classmates' little sister disappeared. She literally was there one day and gone the next. There was a lot of speculation about what happened to her, but I think we all knew she wasn't going to come home. Avery seemed like a good kid. I didn't know her, but I heard her brother talking on the news one night, begging whoever took her to bring her back. She liked singing, dancing, dogs, and had a gazillion stuffed animals. I watched the news and read the papers about her disappearance. Before too long, the stories changed from interviews with her parents and brother and news about the search parties that had been organized, to other more recent sensational stories, like murders, climate change, and of course, politics.

"I never forgot Avery though. It was only about three weeks later when a couple hiking in the woods, nowhere near our town, found her body. A beautiful little girl, gone. To make a long story short, she'd been killed by a man who'd been kidnapping young women and kids all over the place. He'd been in our town a total of ten hours. Ten fucking hours. That's all it took for him to ruin at least four lives. Avery's parents divorced and her brother ended up joining the Navy."

"That's tough, Cruz. What did that have to do with you getting into security?"

Her question was a legitimate one, and Cruz tried to explain without giving anything about his career as an FBI agent away. "The police officers in our town weren't prepared for an in-depth investigation into Avery's disappearance. Her parents begged for help in finding their daughter, but after a token search, they said there wasn't much more they could do because there just wasn't any evidence. I guess stranger abductions are rare, and some of the toughest cases to solve. I saw firsthand how important it was for everyone to do *something*. Being involved in the search for Avery, and seeing how everyone came forward to help, really struck something in me. I know being in security isn't like being a police officer, but even if it's just helping little old ladies get their purses back after they're snatched away, it makes me feel good."

That last part was pretty lame, but Mickie seemed to buy it.

"That's amazing, Cruz."

He merely shrugged. "The best part of the story was that I saw on social media that Avery's brother recently found the asshole that killed his sister. He'd been hunting for him ever since he'd graduated high school. He'd apparently joined the Navy and become a SEAL and with some of his Navy SEAL buddies, they finally killed him. I never kept in touch with Sam, Avery's brother, but I bet if I'd stayed in California and finished high school there, we would've been good friends."

"That's an awesome story. Seriously. And you shouldn't feel bad about what you do. I mean...I don't know exactly *what* you do; I'm sure it's not like you're a Texas Ranger or anything, but I'm assuming you do your best to keep people safe now."

He let the Texas Ranger comment go, but made a mental note to tell Dax what Mickie had said...he'd get a huge kick out of it. It was obvious she hadn't meant it as it came out. "Stopping shoplifters or patrolling for trespassers is a long way from solving serial-murder cases."

"Yeah, but if there weren't people like you around, then it'd be chaos. Who knows what would be stolen or destroyed? It'd be anarchy." She smiled. "The teenagers would have a field day. Just the other day I saw a security guard make a group of little old ladies walk the correct way around the mall. Without people like you, the world would go crazy, I tell ya."

Cruz smiled. She was adorable, assuming he was a security guard and trying to make him feel good about it. There were some really good men he'd worked with over the years who *were* in the general security field, but he'd been honest when he'd told her it was a long way from solving serious cases.

"What's the craziest thing you've seen?" Mickie asked with her chin propped on her hand and leaning on the table. He loved the way she paid complete attention to him. She didn't seem to care about her cell phone, or what was going on around them. It was refreshing. He decided to feel her out a little bit. He knew she was worried about her sister, but he wanted to prod a bit deeper.

"I saw a drug deal go down one day."

"Oh my God! Really? What'd you do?"

"I called the cops. I followed the guy who sold the drugs, figuring he was probably more involved than the kid who bought them. Drugs. I can't stand drug use and what it does to families and to the user. Using is an insidious thing. At first it seems harmless, it makes people feel good, makes them feel invincible. The kid who bought the drugs didn't look like a hard-core druggie. He was probably getting it for a party or something. But drugs can easily take over a person's life. Each time, the fall gets longer and longer and they'll keep pushing their boundaries when it comes to what they'll do for that high."

Mickie put her now-empty plate to the side and asked earnestly. "It sounds personal for you."

"It is. My ex-wife got mixed up in it."

"I'm sorry, Cruz. That sucks."

"Yeah."

His response was whispered and Mickie could hear the sorrow in his voice. She put her hand on his forearm and squeezed gently.

Cruz sighed and put his hand over Mickie's. He could feel the body heat emanating from her palm through his sleeve and penetrating directly into his blood stream, or so it seemed. "She got hooked in high school, but I had no idea. She portrayed herself to me one way, and all the while she was prostituting herself to get money for more drugs."

"Wow. How long were you married?"

"Too long. I should've seen it."

"Cruz, you loved her. At least I'm assuming you did." Mickie waited until he nodded, then continued. "You gave her the benefit of the doubt. It's what you do when you love someone. You make excuses for them when they do things and you forgive them when they hurt you."

"Like you and your sister."

Mickie snorted. "Yeah, like me and Angel."

Cruz went back to the previous subject. "My ex is still here in San Antonio. Every now and then she gets arrested for prostitution. I feel like I'm the laughing-stock of all my friends. They all know about her."

"I'm positive your friends aren't laughing at you, Cruz. They probably feel bad for you, but that's way different than feeling sorry for you or laughing at you."

Cruz brought Mickie's hand up to his lips and kissed the back of it. "Thank you, Mickie. I'm sorry I'm such a downer. I didn't mean to dump all this on you on our first date."

Mickie laughed low in her throat. "This is one of the most interesting first dates I've ever had." At Cruz's skeptical look, she continued quickly. "Seriously. Most of the time the guy wants to talk about how great he is and how lucky I should feel to be with him."

"I don't know how lucky *you* are, but *I* feel lucky as all get out that you're sitting here with me."

"I'm not sure you know me well enough to feel lucky you're here. I have my own sob story when it comes to my ex."

"He was an idiot."

Mickie laughed at his immediate and honest-sounding response. "I'll agree with you on that one."

They smiled at each other. Cruz hadn't let go of her hand since he'd kissed it and he tightened his grip on her fingers. "Seriously, Mickie. I can't imagine what happened to make him decide not to be married to you anymore. From where I'm sitting, you're pretty amazing."

"Thanks, Cruz. That means a lot."

"Enough that you'll go out with me again?"

Mickie laughed. "Probably."

"Just probably?"

"Well, probably leaning heavily on the definitely side."

Cruz's voice got soft and rumbly and Mickie shivered at the promise she could hear in it. "Good. I have to say, I'm looking forward to getting to know more about you, Mickie."

"Me too."

"Can I call you?"

"Yes, I'd like that."

"And you'll keep in touch in the meantime?"

"Yeah."

"Good. Come on, I'll walk you out."

They stood from the table and Cruz helped Mickie up. He stepped back and led her out of the restaurant with his hand at the small of her back. Mickie didn't know what it was about the gesture that made her feel cherished, but it did. Maybe it was because Troy had never really touched her outside of the times they were in bed, but Cruz's hand against her felt wonderful.

They walked side by side down the sidewalk next to the water until they got to a staircase that led up to the street.

"This is me. I'm parked down the street up there," Mickie said.

"I'll walk you all the way to your car."

"Really, Cruz, it's fine, I can—"

"I'll walk you all the way to your car," Cruz repeated, his voice unrelenting.

Mickie looked up at his face and saw he was serious. "Fine, but it's really not necessary, it's the middle of the day."

"It's necessary to me."

Mickie smiled and simply nodded, giving in gracefully. They continued up the stairs and down a street until they got to a small public parking lot, where Mickie had left her car.

Stopping at the driver's side door, Cruz turned to Mickie. He took both her hands in his and brought each one up to his mouth. He kissed the back of her left and turned her right hand over and kissed the palm. "I've had a good time. Thank you for coming, Mickie."

"Me too. I'll text you and we can talk more this week. Okay?" Mickie didn't step away from Cruz, liking the feeling of her hands in his.

"That sounds great." Cruz leaned toward Mickie slowly, giving her time to move back. When she didn't, he briefly touched his lips to hers. He wanted to linger and savor their first kiss, but he didn't. He drew back and squeezed her hands once more before letting go. "Go on and get in. I'll talk to you soon."

"Bye, Cruz." Mickie opened her door and Cruz shut it behind her. She started the engine and turned to see Cruz was still standing near her car. She gave a small wave as she prepared to head out. He gave her a chin lift in return. Mickie pulled out of the space and headed toward the exit of the lot. She looked back once and saw Cruz headed down the street, back in the direction of the River Walk.

It'd been an interesting date. Intense at times, but she'd enjoyed being with Cruz and being the focus of his attention. She definitely hoped he'd call.

CHAPTER 5

"OH YEAH, take that ass. Give it to her."

Cruz threw back the last of the beer in the bottle he was holding and tried to ignore the actions going on behind him. It'd been five days since his date with Mickie and he'd never felt so unclean...maybe except for the time he'd gone to his doctor to be checked for any sexually transmitted diseases after learning the truth about Sophie.

This shit had to end. He had to figure out where and from whom Ransom was getting his drugs, see if he couldn't shut down the Red Brothers and get the hell out before he became a person he couldn't live with anymore.

Cruz was sitting around a table with Ransom, Tick, and two other prospects. Ransom was going over the prospects' new assignments. Every other day they were tasked with some sort of bullshit job, to prove their loyalty to Ransom and the MC.

It was ten in the morning, and behind them were three of the other members of the club and a girl who Cruz hadn't seen around before, but who couldn't have been more than twenty years old. Bubba had her bent over a table while Dirt and Camel cheered him on. They'd each had their shot already, and Cruz knew whoever walked into the room next would most likely take his turn as well.

Almost all of the men in the club were large, either tall and muscular, or overweight, and able to protect themselves and their president. The club whores were probably pretty at one point, but over time, through lack of proper diet, drug use and the abuse they took at the hands of the club members, they'd morphed into shells of the women they used to be. Most were average height, some were almost certainly underage, and because of the drug use, none carried much extra weight on their bodies. It made Cruz's stomach seize to watch as the MC members took their turns with them. Seeing the women helpless underneath the large, unrelenting bodies of the men fucking them was something Cruz knew he'd never forget.

This morning, Bubba and the others had tied the woman's ankles to the table legs, about three feet apart, and her wrists were bound with some sort of cord behind her back. They'd stuffed a ball gag in her mouth and Cruz had seen the drool pooling under her. She wasn't struggling at all, however, merely lying limp on the table as each of the men fucked her.

The woman's eyes were vacant. She was out of her

head with drugs and most likely didn't even realize what was going on, or if she did, she didn't care, only waiting until the men were done so she could get paid in more drugs. None of the men wore a condom, and Camel and Dirt had ejaculated all over the woman's back and hands when they'd orgasmed.

The entire scene was disgusting and obscene, and Cruz couldn't help but see in his mind first Sophie, and then Angel, lying across the table instead of the drugged-out woman.

"Got that, Smoke?"

Shit. "Sorry, what?"

Ransom laughed heartily. "You're a bit distracted this morning, Smoke. You're wishing you could join in, aren't you? Well, too fucking bad. You know prospects don't get to fuck. Club pussy is only for the Hermanos Rojos."

Cruz tried to look suitably chastised. "Sorry, Pres."

"Now, fucking pay attention. I don't like to repeat myself. Today you assholes are gonna take Angel out and sweet-talk her and her bitch friends. I gotta move this shit along. She's annoying as fuck and this needs to happen sooner rather than later. I promised my supplier this new market would be hot. It's taking too fucking long."

Thankfully, Tiny, another prospect, asked what was on Cruz's mind. "How will being nice to this bitch move things along?"

Ransom's fist came across the table and landed in Tiny's face almost before Cruz even saw him strike.

Tiny, ironically named because he weighed at least three hundred pounds, didn't really move with the force of Ransom's fist. His head went back, but that was about all that budged.

"What was that for?" he whined, holding his palm to his face.

"Because you don't ever fucking question me, prospect. 'Loyalty to One.' And *I'm* the fucking 'one.' If I tell you to take a shit in the middle of the River Walk, you'll do it without fucking asking why or whining about it. That's how this works. Once you prove you're loyal to me, and only fucking me—and part of that loyalty means you don't *question* me—then *maybe* I'll consider patching you in. Until then, you do what the hell I say, whenever the hell I say it. And today, the three of you are gonna pick up Angel, take her to Smoke's fucking mall to meet her rich-bitch friends, and you're going to show them how gentlemanly you can be. As a parting gift, you'll give Angel some joints and encourage her to share with her friends."

"Yes, sir. No problem," Roach answered meekly. Cruz and Tiny followed suit.

The outing seemed like a bullshit one to Cruz, but there was no way he'd say anything now. He'd have to watch it play out and see how it went. Ransom thought he worked security at the mall, and obviously decided it was the perfect place to take Angel and her friends in the name of introducing them to the MC.

Ignoring the group of men, now grown to six, who were gathered around the girl tied to the table, and who were cheering each other on even louder, Cruz and the other two prospects left the clubhouse to pick up Ransom's pseudo girlfriend.

"Fuck. I can't wait until I'm a full member. That there was prime pussy," Roach grumbled as they got into the panel van the club owned.

"I tend to like 'em a bit older," Cruz drawled.

"You're losing out, bro." It was Tiny who chimed in this time. "The younger they are, the tighter the pussy. I'm a big motherfucker and I need tight pussy to get off. Twelve and thirteen is ideal." He laughed at himself. "Don't get me wrong, I'll take pussy and ass no matter how I can get it, but I prefer the girls. They're just starting to get little titties."

Cruz swallowed the bile that rose up in his throat. Jesus fucking Christ, he had to get this job done sooner rather than later. He couldn't wait to bring these assholes down. He only hoped he didn't lose himself in the process.

MICKIE TRIED ONCE AGAIN to get through to her sister. "Angel, why don't you come over here? We'll go get manis and pedis together."

Angel sighed heavily into the phone. "No. Ransom is sending some of the guys over and they're taking me to the mall to meet up with Cissy, Kelly, and Bridgette."

"Why would MC guys want to go with you to the mall?" Mickie asked in what she thought was a reasonable tone. The entire thing made no sense to her. There was no way rough-and-tough motorcycle club men would want to hang out at the mall with some spoiled, rich twenty-somethings. They were up to no good and Mickie didn't like it.

"Maybe because they *like* me and want to get to know my friends?"

Mickie knew there was nothing she could say that would sway her sister. There were so many things she *wanted* to say, but nothing that Angel wouldn't take offense to at the moment.

She settled for asking her sister, "Be careful then, okay? Will you call me when you get back?"

"No. I'm not twelve anymore, Mickie. I don't have to call you when I get back and I don't have to ask permission to do anything either."

"I just worry about you."

"You don't need to. I know you don't approve of Ransom and his friends, so therefore, I don't want to hear anything else you have to say about them."

Mickie stared at the phone in her hand. Angel had hung up.

She sighed. The only bright spot in her life at the moment was Cruz and his texts. They were really funny. Mickie had tried to keep her communication with him to a minimum, they didn't really know each other after all, but he'd made that hard. Cruz was charming, even in his texts. He always told her how nice it was to hear from her and he made her feel special.

Mickie clicked on the app and read the last text from Cruz from the day before.

Green beans or corn on the cob?

Mickie had answered with corn. His next text had made her laugh out loud.

Guess I'm going back to the store this afternoon then. :)

Whatever you get is fine. I can eat green beans.

Nope, you want corn, you're getting corn.

They'd set up their next date. Cruz had invited her over to his apartment for dinner. Mickie supposed she should feel awkward and nervous about going to his place, but she didn't. She knew she'd just met him, but so far he'd seemed pretty sincere. And while their first date hadn't exactly been textbook, considering some of their topics of conversation, she still was interested in getting to know him better.

She enjoyed talking with him and it felt good to be the center of a man's attention again. Even though their relationship, if it could be called that at this point, was new, she really wanted to trust a man again. Troy had ripped her heart out and had really done a number on her, but to not trust anyone ever again was letting Troy win, and she refused to let that happen.

Mickie typed a quick text, letting Cruz know she was thinking about him...and wanting to run something by him. She hoped she wasn't being paranoid, but thought maybe a second opinion would reassure her that's all it was.

Hey. Just thought I'd say hi.

His response took a few minutes, but she smiled when she heard the ding of her phone.

Hey back. How are you?

Good. I think I had some visitors this morning. Mickie jumped right into what she wanted to ask him.

??

I saw 2 motorcycles leaving my apt complex this am. Never seen them b4. They could've been visiting someone, but it was early and the guys were wearing leather vests. Think they could've been Red Brothers?

Maybe. You have mace?

Yes.

Good, always carry it & have it out when you walk to your car. Call me if you get worried and I'll come and escort you.

U don't have to do that. They didn't do anything, but with Angel and all, it freaked me out a bit.

Your instincts are probably right on. Let me know if anything else weird happens. Ok?

I will. Sorry 2b a downer.

Never apologize for letting me know you're worried.

Talk 2u later?

I'll check back to make sure you're good.

Ok. Bye.

Bye.

Mickie put the phone down and sighed. Darn Angel. Somehow she'd known the bikes were connected to Angel and the MC. She'd have to be extra vigilant just in case.

Cruz's offer felt good. Even though they were still

getting to know each other it felt nice that she had someone to contact if something did happen.

CRUZ FELT his phone buzz in his pocket and pulled it out. Mickie. After their text conversation this morning he'd had to force himself not to beat the shit out of Ransom. He hated more than anything that the president was messing with her. He'd hoped he'd convinced Ransom she wasn't really trouble, that she and Angel didn't get along, but obviously the man was still keeping her on his radar.

He knew if Ransom was having the members watch her apartment he'd have to make sure if he was seen there, it could be construed as being a part of the role he was playing…keeping his eye on Angel's sister to keep her out of their club business.

Looking down at the phone, Cruz didn't dare let the grin that was dying to come out show on his face in case the assholes he was with wanted to know what he was smiling about.

Just when I think the world has gone crazy, u text me with something completely normal & innocuous. Thank u. And…I don't look anything like Julianne, but thanks. :) Thinking about u.

Earlier he'd sent a short message: *I just realized who you remind me of…Julianne whats-her-name from that dancing show. Hot.* He'd attached an older picture of the woman when she'd had her hair cut in what the

Internet called a "pixie cut." Her hair was blonde, but in Cruz's mind, she and Mickie could've been twins.

Cruz stuffed the phone back into his pocket and tried not to let her words get to him.

Shit, who was he trying to kid; the fact that Mickie was thinking about him had already burrowed deeply into his bloodstream and gotten stuck there.

"There she is. Fuck, she might not be twelve, but I'd still fucking tap that." Tiny's words cut through the warm fuzzies he'd gotten from reading Mickie's text like a knife slicing through butter.

Cruz looked up and saw Angel leaving her apartment as she turned and locked her door. She was wearing a tight pair of jeans that left nothing to the imagination, her thong was clearly visible over the back of her pants. She wore a cropped T-shirt, and as she made her way toward the van, they could all see it was tied in a knot under her breasts. Her belly-button ring was glinting in the sun as she ambled toward them.

"Fuck yeah. I think we'd *all* love to tap that," Roach agreed wholeheartedly.

"Shut the fuck up. We can't get anywhere near her or Pres would have our heads. Keep your dicks in your pants and remember we have to make sure her and her friends have a good time today," Cruz growled out grumpily.

"Yeah, yeah. Shit. Who pissed in your fuckin' Wheaties, Smoke?"

Cruz ignored Tiny's comment and got out of the van just as Angel approached.

"Hey. Ready to go?"

"Yeah. Thanks for coming to get me, Smoke."

Cruz grunted in reply and assisted Angel into the front seat. Roach was driving and Tiny was sitting in the seat behind him. Cruz climbed in and sat behind Angel.

"Hey, Roach, Tiny. How are you?" Angel asked politely, as she settled into the seat.

"Good. How're you?"

Angel giggled as if she was a teenager. "I'm good."

"Ransom sent a present for ya," Roach told Angel. He held out a joint.

"Cool. He's always thinking of me. Got a light?"

Tiny leaned forward from the back and flicked his lighter. The three men watched as Angel lit the marijuana cigarette and coughed as she inhaled.

"Thanks, Tiny."

"Who're we meeting today, Angel?" Roach asked.

The three continued to make small talk as they made their way to the mall. Every time Angel talked too much and let the joint burn, Tiny or Roach would encourage her to take another hit. By the time they got to the mall, Angel was high as a kite. Mission fucking accomplished.

The rest of the afternoon was more of the same. Cruz went through the motions of being nice to Angel's friends and observed Tiny and Roach slowly winning the four women over. They carried their bags and were quick to compliment them.

At one point, when Cissy asked Angel if she was all right—Angel had been giggling uncontrollably at any and everything—Roach threw his arm around the slender woman, leaned into her ear and whispered, "She's feeling awesome. Haven't you ever smoked a joint?" When Cissy had looked up at Roach in shock, he'd told her, "No? Well, shit. We'll have to educate you then."

Cruz had to admit, Roach and Tiny were good. Ransom had picked his prospects well. By the end of the shopping trip, the seven of them were sitting in the panel van in the parking lot. He'd taken them to the employees-only parking area; since he had an employee pass as part of his cover, Cruz figured maybe the cops would pay less attention to the obvious-as-shit van here than if he was parked amongst the Mercedes and more expensive cars that people typically drove to the mall. The women were giggling and laughing after sharing two joints.

"Oh my God, this is so awesome! You guys are the best friends I've ever had!" Bridgette enthused.

"I know. I love you guys!" Cissy joined in. "Angel, you never told us how great this stuff is!"

Trying to sound experienced, Angel huffed, "I wasn't sure you were cool enough to take the chance."

Kelly pouted. "That's not fair. You know we're just as cool as you."

Tiny winked at Roach and Cruz. He leaned over

and whispered in Cruz's ear, "And so it begins. Never fails. It's all a competition with these rich bitches."

"When can we do this again?" Cissy asked Angel.

Looking perplexed, Angel looked to Roach and stammered, "Ransom gave me these…"

Roach stepped into the conversation as if he were a puppeteer holding the strings of the marionettes that were Cissy, Bridgette, Kelly, and Angel.

"You know this stuff isn't cheap, Angel. He likes to spoil you, but it's not like it grows on trees."

Bridgette took the bait. "Oh, but we have money, don't we girls? We don't expect to get it for *free*."

"Yeah, I got access to my trust fund last year. I've got lots of money," Cissy said.

Cruz inwardly groaned. Jesus fucking Christ, these women needed a keeper.

"That's good, sweetheart," Roach crooned, leaning into Cissy. He bent down and licked her neck, right by her ear. "You got any right now? I've got some more stuff you could take with you if you wanted. No, wait! I got an idea. You wanna get some more of your friends together? I bet you've got some other cool friends who would be up for it, yeah?"

Bridgette chimed in next. "Oh yeah. Cissy, we could get a group together next weekend! Your parents are leaving the country, aren't they? We could use their house. They have that big room that would be perfect. It'd be like high school!"

All four women giggled hysterically.

"All right. That sounds awesome. But how about

instead of having it at one of your houses, you guys all come down to the clubhouse? It's private and secure and all your friends can meet the MC members. We'd love to have you join us for one of our parties."

When the girls nodded enthusiastically, Roach continued reeling them in. "I'll need a down payment. Give me some dough now, and I'll get you the address of the club. You bring some of your friends and the MC will be waiting and we'll have enough cigarettes for everyone," Roach said smoothly.

When the four women opened their purses and pulled out their wallets, Tiny took Kelly's wallet out of her hand and helped himself to two hundred dollars. He closed the wallet and handed it back, leaning into her and nibbling on the lobe of her ear. "That should do it, *ma chère*. I can't wait to hang with you and your friends."

Roach collected money from Cissy, and Cruz reluctantly pocketed five hundred dollars from Angel and Bridgette.

"Because you ladies have been so generous, we're gonna send you home with a few gifts from the Hermanos Rojos MC. Make sure you share with your girlfriends, and remember, only invite the friends you think can handle it and won't go blabbing to the cops or their daddies. If it works out, you can come and party with us all the time." Roach winked at the girls.

After the longest thirty minutes of Cruz's life, the three girls staggered out of the van and into the parking lot. They each had two joints tucked into their purses as they made their way toward their cars. Cruz knew it wasn't safe for them to drive, but there was absolutely nothing he could do about it right now, not while keeping his cover.

With Roach insisting he drive, Cruz climbed into the driver's seat and headed back toward Angel's apartment. She was sitting between Roach and Tiny in the backseat and every time he looked in the mirror, he saw the two men pushing their luck. Tiny had pulled her leg up and over his and his hand was on her thigh, rubbing up and down, getting closer and closer to her crotch with each pass. If she'd been wearing a skirt, Tiny's hand would've been way past neutral territory.

Roach had buried his face in Angel's neck and was licking her like she was an ice cream cone, sucking her earlobe into his mouth each time he reached it. Cruz even saw him push his tongue into her ear once as well. She was giggling but not stopping them, lost in the good feelings of the pot and the sexual tension in the air.

Cruz cleared his throat loudly and said in a threatening voice, "Ransom's."

Tiny's hand stopped its journey upward, but Roach only looked up and smiled evilly.

"Angel, we're here," Cruz announced loudly when they pulled up to her apartment complex.

Without giving her a chance to move, Roach put his hand on her chin and pulled her face toward his. He held her still while he thrust his tongue into her mouth and devoured her. Cruz could see the pressure of his fingers on her chin, even as she struggled lightly in his grasp.

When Roach finally pulled back, he forcefully turned her head toward Tiny, and kept hold of her while Tiny also took possession of her mouth. Cruz heard her whimper once while being ravaged by Tiny.

Finally, when the man leaned back, Roach said in her ear, "We know you're Ransom's. We don't disrespect our president. We don't take what's his without permission. But if you're gonna be his, you gotta know he likes to share."

Roach finally let go of her chin and Cruz watched as she turned slowly to look at Roach. He ran his hand down her cheek gently, as if he hadn't just been holding her chin hostage in his grip. Cruz could see the fading white spots on her skin as the blood made its way back into it.

Angel smiled shyly at Roach. "I'll see you guys next week at the party?"

"Yeah, Angel, you'll see us next week at the party. Make sure you only invite the cool girls that can handle it. Yeah?"

"Yeah, Roach. I'll make sure. I've had a good time today. Thank you for coming with me. Is Ransom gonna come see me? I really want him."

Cruz knew marijuana could make some people horny; Angel was obviously one of those people.

"I don't know, Angel. But I'll tell him how good you were today."

"Yeah, tell him that. I was a good girl for him."

For the second time that day, Cruz felt the bile creep up his throat. Time to get this show on the road.

"Come on, Angel. Let's get you inside."

Cruz came around the side and opened the van door and helped Angel out. She wobbled on her feet and leaned into him. "You gonna kiss me too, Smoke?" she asked with a smile.

"Nope. I think you've had enough. Time to go inside and take a nap."

Cruz lifted his chin at Roach and Tiny, telling them he had this, and he carried Angel's bags, and held her around the waist as he got her to her door. He had to unlock it for her and practically carry her inside.

He dropped the bags just inside the door and helped Angel sit on her couch. As soon as he let go, she toppled over sideways. Cruz shook his head. He could do anything to her and she'd have no idea. It was a good thing he'd walked her up, and not Roach or Tiny. Cruz knew they wouldn't have hesitated to take advantage of her, their prospect status be damned.

Cruz squatted next to the couch and shook Angel's shoulder. When she opened her eyes and looked blearily up at him, he told her sternly, "Call your sister, Angel. Let her know you're home and you're okay."

"She's a fuddy-duddy."

"She loves you. Call her."

"Oh, all right."

Angel closed her eyes and rested her head back down on the cushion. Cruz had no idea if she'd do as he asked, but he hoped so. He'd done what he could. It wasn't nearly enough.

He stepped out and closed Angel's apartment door behind him, making sure it was locked from the inside before shutting it. Cruz went back to the van and climbed into the driver's seat once more.

Tiny and Roach hadn't moved. They sat in their seats, smirking at Cruz.

"She all tucked in safe and sound?"

Cruz nodded curtly. "You were pushing your luck there, Roach."

"Pffft. That bitch was squirming in our hands. She wanted it."

"She's Ransom's."

"Yeah, for now. But he doesn't give a shit about her except when he wants some pussy and to get her friends hooked. Once he's done with her, she'll need some comforting."

"Ransom doesn't like to share, that was bullshit."

"Yeah, but what Ransom doesn't know won't hurt him. It's not like I'm gonna bring her to the club and fuck her. Ransom has the right idea, keeping her on the side. I'll do the same shit. Once he's tired of her, I'll move in. Rich fucking pussy whenever I want it. Can't pass that up. When I'm done with her, I'll move on to her rich-ass friends. They're all dying for MC dick. I'm happy to oblige. Having them start coming to our parties was the best idea Ransom ever had."

Cruz shook his head but didn't say anything. He knew he'd never change their minds, and protesting any more would be suspicious. They'd been getting away with whatever they wanted for a long time. He vowed to protect Angel as much as he could and do whatever was necessary to prevent any of her friends from getting hooked on drugs, like Sophie had.

Cruz knew he should break things off with Mickie. Today proved that all the more. But he couldn't. For one, she was the only bright spot in his life at the moment, and two, Cruz had a feeling Ransom was going to act on his threats against her, and he wanted to be sure she was safe from the club and all the crap that went down there. He knew it'd be a miracle if Mickie would forgive him for his role in what was happening to her sister. He knew he was treading a thin line, but Cruz wasn't going to stop courting her. He couldn't.

CHAPTER 6

CRUZ PULLED up in front of Mickie's apartment and took a deep breath. She'd texted him thirty minutes ago and asked if he'd be able to help her. When he'd learned why she needed his help, he'd been furious.

Apparently Ransom was sick of Mickie butting into Angel's business and had ordered Tick to make a statement. Thankfully Tick had only slashed her tires. It could've been a lot worse. Cruz had told Ransom he was keeping a close eye on Mickie, but after Angel told Ransom about how Mickie was still on her case, especially after her trip to the mall, Ransom had apparently lost whatever patience he'd been holding on to.

Cruz saw Mickie standing by her car, staring down at her phone. She looked sexy in a pair of jeans and a T-shirt. She glanced up and saw him striding toward her. She put her phone in her pocket and greeted him.

"Hey. Thanks for coming. I wasn't sure who else to call. I mean, I have other friends, but they're either working or busy. Not to say you weren't doing either, but I figured—"

"I'm glad you got ahold of me. How did this happen?" he asked, gesturing to her car. Cruz could see the muscle in her jaw flex as she ground her teeth together.

"Honestly? If I had to guess, I'd say it has something to with that damn motorcycle club."

Cruz was impressed with Mickie's intuition, but asked anyway. "Why?"

"Because I was pissed at my sister the other day and let her have it. I tried once again to get her to see that the man she's dating is a thug. I'm sure that conversation got passed along and this is the result."

"That's a pretty big leap."

Mickie looked up at Cruz and cocked her head as she observed him silently for a moment. Finally, she said in an even tone that somehow conveyed anger, frustration, and irritation all at the same time, "I work at a car dealership, Cruz. I'm a divorced thirty-four-year-old woman who minds her own business. I don't go clubbing. I don't hang out on any street corners. I go to the movies with my friends; I sit at home and read books. The biggest law I've broken is not returning my library books on time. I *might* have a VHS tape that I never returned to the video store down the block that went out of business ten years ago. The only people I know who might do anything like this are connected to my sister. I irritated my sister recently, so it only follows that someone might want to get back at me."

"You think your sister did this?"

Mickie rolled her eyes and put both hands on her hips. "My sister wouldn't know the first thing about how to slash a tire...but that guy she's dating? Yeah. I can imagine this would be his very mature way of dealing with his girlfriend being harassed by her sister."

Cruz couldn't help it, the grin formed on his face before he could beat it back.

"You think this is funny?"

Cruz got serious. "Your tires being slashed by someone in a motorcycle club? Absolutely, one-hundred-percent no. But you? Yeah. I've got to say, you've either had a lot of practice, or you're a natural. That sarcastic tone conveys just a hint of snark with a bit of sassy thrown in for good measure."

Mickie smiled for the first time. "How can I be laughing when I'm so pissed?"

"Because sometimes it's better to laugh than to cry."

"You've got that right."

"So," Cruz stated, getting down to business. "You got any extra tires hanging around?"

"Yeah, one. The spare."

"Don't think that's gonna cut it here."

"Didn't think so."

"You know you're gonna have to replace all of them, right?"

Mickie sighed. "Yeah."

"Can you cover it? I know you said you had some cash from your folks, but this could end up being expensive."

"Yeah. It's fine. Besides, it's not like I can decide it's not worth the cost."

"I'm afraid you're right."

"Can you drive me to the shop? I'll buy the tires and see if they'll get a tow truck out here to get my car."

"No problem. But I'll be happy to bring you back here and change the tires for you."

"I can't ask you to do that."

"You didn't. I offered."

Mickie studied Cruz for another moment. She honestly would never have contacted him if she hadn't been desperate. She had a million things to do that she'd been putting off, and it just figured that this weekend of all weekends would be the one when Angel's boyfriend would choose to make his point. "If you're sure you're not busy…"

"I'm sure."

"Then thank you. I'd be very grateful if you could help me. But this isn't a date."

"What?"

"This isn't a date," Mickie repeated. "There are rules for dates."

"Rules." It wasn't a question, but Mickie saw the smirk on Cruz's face.

"Yes. First rule, the woman gets all dressed up so she can impress her date." She gestured to her outfit. "I'm not dressed up and there's no way I'm impressing anyone dressed like this. Second rule, the woman always offers to pay, to be polite. But I'm not offering— I'm paying. Period. Third rule, there's absolutely no drama allowed on the date. I think this constitutes as drama. Hence…this isn't a date."

Cruz's smile lit up his face and made him look years younger. "Deal. I'm still fixing you dinner later this week. We'll call this a friend doing another friend a favor then…all right?"

Mickie beamed at him. "Deal."

"Come on, friend. You've got some tires to purchase."

The trip to the tire shop was relatively painless, except for the cost of the new tires, which was absolutely ridiculous, considering there was a good chance her sister's boyfriend would just ruin this set as well.

On the way back to her apartment, Mickie asked, "Do you think I should make a police report? I mean, I figure you probably know more about it than I do."

Cruz glanced at her before sighing. "If you don't have any proof it was your sister's boyfriend, or that he asked one of his friends to do it, I'm not sure what good it will do."

Mickie nodded. "Yeah, that's what I figured. I even called the main office to ask about security cameras, but they don't have any that were pointed toward my car since it was parked at the back of the lot."

When Cruz opened his mouth, Mickie hurried on. "I know, I know. I shouldn't park back there, it's not safe, but I wanted to get my steps in for the day." At the blank look on his face, she explained further. "Steps. You know, you're supposed to get ten thousand steps in every day to stay healthy. It's good exercise."

"It might be good exercise, but it's not safe," Cruz returned.

"Obviously," Mickie grumbled. "But now I'll park nearer to my building because the lady in the office said the cameras are pointing at the buildings, and the cars that are nearest to them are on the tapes."

He nodded, satisfied with her answer.

As they pulled back into the lot of the apartment complex, Mickie pointed out unnecessarily, "At least you have room to work out here. If I'd parked closer you would've had to work around the other vehicles in the lot."

Cruz didn't answer, merely shook his head in mock exasperation. He popped his trunk and hefted out one of the tires, leaning it against the car. He got the jack out of the back and went to work on the first tire.

Cruz worked quickly and efficiently. It was warm out, as it usually was in Texas, but he showed no discomfort. He removed the lug nuts and jacked up the car. Before she knew it, the first tire was on her car and Cruz had moved to the second one.

"Can you talk and work?"

Cruz looked up briefly at that, surprised. "Yeah, why wouldn't I be able to?"

Mickie shrugged. "I don't know. My ex could never do two things at once. He had to concentrate on one thing at a time." She saw Cruz's lips twitch, but her opinion of him grew when he declined to comment on what would've been a great opening for a sexual innuendo.

"I can talk while I do this, Mickie. No problem."

"I just figured, even though this isn't a date, that maybe we could still get to know each other better. How'd you learn to change a tire so quickly?"

"My dad taught me when I was around ten. We were driving across the country, moving to somewhere, I forget where now, but the tire on the car blew out on the highway. He stayed calm and pulled over on the side of the road. He got my stepmom out and safely out of the way, then he walked me through how to change the tire."

"Have you had much practice? It doesn't seem the kind of thing you'd do all the time, but you're obviously very good at it."

Cruz looked up at Mickie. She was sitting next to him, watching his hands as he worked on the tire. He'd never had a woman sit next to him when he changed their tire. Usually they were either inside a building or standing well away from him. She was refreshingly different from any other woman he'd met.

"Dad made sure I didn't forget. One day I went outside to go to school, and he'd taken one of my tires completely off my car. I remember I was so mad, but he simply shrugged and told me that tires didn't need changing only on the weekends when nothing else was going on. I needed to learn how to change it as fast as I could."

"Were you late for school?"

"Twenty minutes. Missed a quiz too."

Mickie smiled at him. "You've gotten faster at it."

They moved to the other side of the car so he could start on the third tire.

"Yeah. Anytime anyone in the neighborhood needed a tire changed, I got roped into it. It was annoying as all get-out at the time, but I'm grateful to him now."

"Me too."

"You want to learn?"

"Yes." Mickie's answer was quick and eager and Cruz couldn't help the chuckle that escaped.

"Cool. Watch me on this one and you can do the last one on your own."

"Can I ask something else?"

"Sure."

"How come you didn't become a cop when you graduated if you really wanted to help people?"

If Cruz had been eating or drinking anything he probably would've spit it out at her question, but other than a slight pause in what he was doing, he was proud of his non-reaction. "I didn't want to write tickets for people speeding and I didn't like all the politics that go on in police departments." It wasn't a lie. He'd thought about joining the force, but decided the FBI appealed much more to him in the long run.

Cruz knew he needed to turn the questioning around before she asked him something he'd have to outright lie about. "What's your favorite dessert?"

"What?"

"You asked a question, I get to as well...don't I?"

"Yeah. Of course. I just didn't expect that. My favorite dessert? I'd have to say cookie dough."

"Just the dough? Not the cookie itself?"

"Nope. I buy the bags of the ready-made cookies from the freezer section. You know, the little frozen blobs you're supposed to stick on a cookie sheet and cook? Yeah, I eat them raw. They're so yummy."

Mickie looked at Cruz. He'd stopped tightening the lug nuts on the tire and was looking at her in a way she couldn't decipher.

"What?"

"I was going to do my best to impress you by making sure I had whatever you told me was your favorite on hand later this week. But I'm not sure putting frozen cookie dough blobs on a plate is all that impressive."

Mickie couldn't help the giggles that exploded out of her mouth at the look on Cruz's face. And that only made her giggle harder. She held her stomach and giggled until tears rolled out of her eyes. Finally, when she had a bit more control, she choked out, "I'm so sorry, Cruz, but if you could only see your face... If it makes you feel better, I also like brownies."

One of Cruz's hands reached for her, but stopped short of actually touching her.

Cruz looked down at his filthy hands and resisted brushing away the wetness on her cheek. Watching as she'd laughed herself silly at his expense should've irritated him, but instead he found himself wanting to make her laugh again so he could see her unabashed zeal for life. He didn't often see that kind of pure joy in his line of work.

"I admit it wasn't what I was expecting, but I'll see what I can do to make sure I've got something you'll enjoy for dessert next week." He hadn't meant his words to be a sexual innuendo, but when Mickie started giggling again, he simply shook his head. God, she was funny.

"Come on, I'm done with this one, you ready to give it a try?" Cruz held a hand out to her and helped Mickie to her feet.

"I'm game if you are, but I can't promise to be as quick at it as you."

"Practice makes perfect."

"Let's hope I won't need to practice again anytime soon," Mickie mumbled as she stood and reached for the tire wrench. "Let's do this then."

Twenty minutes and lots of swear words later, Mickie's car had four bright and shiny new tires on it. Mickie was dirty and sweaty, but strangely enough, she'd actually had a good time. She felt good about finally learning how to change a tire, and Cruz had been very patient with her as she'd asked a million questions while changing the last tire.

"Thanks for coming over today. I appreciate it."

"Anytime. I mean that, Mickie. If you need anything, you can call me."

She nodded and then asked a bit uncertainly, "Are we still on for Friday?" She wanted to see him again, enjoyed being around him, but she felt like she'd forced him into helping her today and didn't want to presume he wanted to spend any more time with her.

"Absolutely. I'm looking forward to it."

"Me too."

"Are you good here now? I hate to say it, but I have to get going," Cruz told her.

"Yeah, I'm good. Again, I do appreciate your help."

"No problem. I'll talk to you later. Okay?"

Mickie nodded and watched as Cruz climbed into his car and waved once, then drove away. She was looking forward to dinner, even though she tried not to get her hopes up for anything. It was one thing to spend a few hours together hanging out like friends would, it was another thing altogether to get together with the expectation of seeing if a relationship was possible.

CRUZ ENTERED his apartment and went straight to his kitchen where he washed his hands, scrubbing off the dirt and grease from Mickie's tires. He then headed into his small living room and sat on the couch. He let out a breath, rested his head on the cushion behind him and thought about the afternoon.

He liked Mickie. Oh, he'd thought she was nice after their dinner the other day, but seeing her today made him look at her in a new way. She wasn't afraid to laugh at herself...or him. She'd dealt with the stress of having her tires slashed and having to pay for four new ones without any drama. She was genuinely interested in learning how to do something new. And perhaps more importantly, she was down to earth and seemed very easygoing.

He loved those traits in Mackenzie, his friend Dax's girlfriend, but never thought he'd be able to find a woman like her. But watching as Mickie giggled, and the fact that she didn't care that she was sitting on the ground in the middle of a parking lot, made his interest in her notch up a level.

His plan had been to make sure she was safe from Ransom and the rest of the motorcycle club, and while he'd still be keeping her from harm, now he was interested in her for another reason as well. Knowing if she ever found out why he'd originally spoken to her in the café, that all he wanted to do was keep her safe until his undercover mission was completed, he'd probably lose any opportunity to have anything long-term with her, he still made the decision right then and there to do whatever he could to get to know her better.

Hopefully she'd understand that while his initial motives weren't a hundred percent honest, what he was feeling for her had nothing, absolutely nothing, to do with her sister, Ransom, or the damn Red Brothers. It was all her.

CHAPTER 7

MICKIE KNOCKED on the door of apartment number sixteen. Cruz had given her directions when he'd called last night to confirm she was still coming over. The conversation had been short, and he'd apologized, saying he was in the middle of something.

She was nervous because Cruz had sounded weird. She didn't know what kind of weird, just that he hadn't sounded like the easygoing open guy she'd spent the afternoon with the other day.

She shook her head at herself in disgust. Mickie wasn't the type of woman to lust over anyone, but she thought she just might be in lust with Cruz. There was so much she didn't know about him, and Mickie knew it wasn't smart, but she couldn't help herself. She just plain liked him, not to mention the chemistry they had with each other was off the charts. She had no idea if he felt it too, but figured he must on some level. She wasn't ready to move in with him or marry him, but she wasn't ruling out jumping his bones.

The door opened in front of her, stopping her musings.

"Mickie, I'm so glad you're here. Please, come in."

Mickie stepped into the apartment and stared at Cruz. Jeez, he looked good. He was wearing a green polo shirt and a pair of khaki pants. Once again she could see part of his tattoo peeking out from the sleeve of his shirt. Mickie swore to herself she'd get a look at that tattoo sooner rather than later.

Cruz locked the door after she got in and turned to her. He put both hands on her upper arms and leaned down and kissed her on the cheek, then pulled back and held out his arm. "This way, milady. I've got some wine if you're interested."

Cruz tried to keep his voice level. Mickie was beautiful. He had no idea how anyone could've let her go. If she was his—

He broke off his thoughts. She wasn't his, most likely wouldn't be.

She was wearing a pair of black slacks and a pink short-sleeve shirt. It had a V-neck that plunged deeper than a regular T-shirt would. Cruz could see a slight bit of cleavage, but not enough to be indecent. The differences between her and her sister were striking.

Mickie's black hair was smoothed down and elegant while the other day it looked a bit chaotic. It fit her. One day she was casual and natural, and the next she was trendy and polished.

When Cruz had leaned over to kiss her cheek, her scent struck him hard and fast. She smelled...clean. He'd been buried in filth for way too long and her fresh scent had him hard before he'd even been able to try to control it.

Mickie looked around nervously as she made her way into his apartment. Cruz tried to see his place as she might. There was an entryway that held only a small table. It emptied into an open area. There was a couch separating the living area from the kitchen. He had a table up against one wall; he mostly used it when he was researching on his computer. The kitchen had granite countertops and there was a built-in bar with three stools in front of it. If he had company, they could sit at the counter and watch him cook.

Cruz helped Mickie sit on one of the barstools and poured a glass of red wine and placed it in front of her. She played with the stem of the glass and watched as he walked over to the table. He saw how uncomfortable she seemed and made a split-second decision to help her relax a bit. Even though they'd gotten to know each other a little the previous weekend, this was a date... and she was obviously nervous.

Cruz picked up his real cell phone and dialed. Without saying a word to Mickie, he began speaking.

"Hey, Mack. How are you? Yeah, it's really me. I know, I'll call again soon to touch base, but for now I need a favor. I've got a date over at my place and I want to reassure her that I'm not a serial killer."

Cruz held the phone away from his ear and smiled

at Mickie. They could both clearly hear the woman on the other end of the line screeching in delight.

He put the phone back to his ear and tried again. "Mack, chill! You're going to scare Mickie away. She knows I work in security, and I'd prefer you not give her a blow-by-blow of my employment history. If you think you can keep that on the down-low, can you please reassure her that I'm one of the good guys…for real? Okay, hang on."

Cruz held his phone to his stomach and took a deep breath. Mackenzie wasn't stupid. She knew he was undercover and with her reassurance, he knew she wouldn't say anything to give him away.

He looked at Mickie. "Mackenzie is my friend's girl-friend. Remember when I told you we all went out recently and celebrated her life? Yeah, this is her. I just want you to be comfortable around me. You went out on a limb meeting me here and I don't blame you for being nervous, but I swear to you that I'm not going to hurt you. I thought maybe talking to a woman who knows me would put you at ease a bit."

Mickie about melted in her seat. Not only had Cruz realized how nervous she was, but he'd found the perfect way to reassure her. She held out her hand without a word.

Cruz reached out and grabbed it. He brought her hand up to his lips and kissed the back before looking up at her without letting go. "Mack is going to be a bit over the top and probably a bit crazy. I'd appreciate it if you just went with it. She also has a tendency to ramble when she's excited or nervous...and she's definitely excited right now." He smiled, knowing excited was an understatement.

"It's fine, Cruz." Mickie pulled her hand out of his grasp and wiggled her fingers. She realized he was worried she'd somehow think less of his friend. It made him seem more...human. She didn't think anyone with nefarious intentions would not only try to make her feel more comfortable around him, but also be concerned about his friend as well. "Give me the phone."

He held it out and Mickie took it and put the phone up to her ear.

"Hello?"

"Hi! I'm Mack."

"I'm Michelle...Mickie."

"Mickie. I like that name. So you're there with Cruz? Isn't he a hunk? I mean, I have my own hunk, but if I didn't have Daxton, I'd totally go for Cruz. Okay, well maybe TJ... Oh hell. All the guys he hangs around with are to die for. Just wait until you meet them. I *hope* you'll get to meet them. I don't know how long you've been with Cruz, but seriously, they're all great people. And Cruz? You *so* don't have anything to worry about. Okay, maybe spontaneously combusting around him, but that's not necessarily a bad thing. Do you have any questions for me about him?"

"Only about a million."

Mackenzie laughed out loud. "Yeah, I know the feeling. I don't know what he really wants me to say, but I

97

SUSAN STOKER

swear on all the chocolate Easter bunnies in the world that Cruz is one of the good guys. I mean, he's a guy, so he's bound to fuck something up, they all do, but his heart is in the right place. You don't have to worry about him. I know his ex treated him like crap though. Oh shit, has he told you about his divorce? I didn't mean to bring it up if you haven't heard about it. Such a horrible situation all the way around, but seriously, Cruz is sexy as hell and I have firsthand knowledge of the fact that he's loyal to his friends. He'd do anything for them."

Mickie broke in before Mack could continue. "I appreciate the reassurance."

"No problem. When Daxton came over to my house for the first time, I made him give me not only his driver's license but his work ID as well. Then he insisted that I call his boss and make sure he wasn't carrying around fake IDs. Oh shit, I don't think Cruz wanted me to share that much with you, but I swear he's a good guy. Okay?"

"Okay. Thanks. I appreciate it. I *was* a bit nervous." Mickie looked at Cruz as she said the last words, knowing he was listening intently to their conversation.

"Good. I hope this works out with you guys. My best friend, Laine, and I try to have a girls' night out at least once a month, and we'd love to get some more girls to hang with us. I'll see if you're interested the next time we get together."

"That sounds good, but I don't know if—"

"Yeah, I know. But Cruz hasn't been out with anyone in ages. So if he's out with you, he has to be serious about it."

"Uh, I—"

"Yeah, sorry. I don't want to freak you out. You have a good night. Give him the benefit of the doubt. He might be guarded, but it's for a good reason. But that reason isn't to deceive you. All right?

"Yeah."

"Good, give me back to Cruz. Talk to you later!"

Mickie held out the phone to Cruz and said a bit dazedly, "She wants to talk to you again."

Cruz took the phone. "Thanks, Mack." He didn't take it away from his ear, but hooked his other hand around Mickie's neck and brought her into him. He kissed her forehead then let her go, taking a step away to give her some space. Mickie could hear Mack babbling in Cruz's ear as he moved to stand next to her. She took a sip of her wine as they finished saying their goodbyes.

"Yeah. Tell Dax I'll call him soon. Thanks again, sweetheart. I'll talk to you later. Bye."

Cruz clicked the phone off and placed it on the counter next to them. He met Mickie's eyes with his own and asked, "Do you feel better? I know we spent some time together, but you didn't look comfortable when you got here."

Mickie nodded.

"Sure?"

"Yeah, Cruz. Thank you."

Cruz's intense gaze didn't leave hers. "I'd like for you to meet my friends sometime."

"Okay."

"They're a bit crazy, but I trust them with my life. I'd do anything for them and I know they'd do anything for me too."

"I'm glad you have friends like that."

"You hungry?"

Relieved he was changing the subject—he was pretty intense normally, but seemed more so tonight—Mickie nodded and asked, "Are we having green beans or corn?"

"Corn, of course. It's what you said you liked."

"Just making sure."

Cruz smiled at her and stepped away. He snagged the phone off the counter and shoved it in a drawer in the kitchen as he walked by. It looked exactly like the phone he used at the club, but since it was his personal cell, he never carried it.

"I've got two steaks on the grill, as well as the corn on the cob and a salad. I thought I'd keep it simple tonight."

"I'm a vegetarian."

Cruz froze and looked over at Mickie. *Oh shit.* He'd screwed up right out of the gate. He'd asked her about what vegetable she wanted, but didn't think to ask her about the main course. Just as he got himself all worked up, he saw her smile.

"Gotcha!"

Cruz laughed and put a hand to his chest. "Don't do that to me, woman!"

"I have to keep you on your toes. Don't want you making any assumptions about me."

"I like that you can tease me."

"I like that I can tease you too."

They smiled at each other until Cruz turned to go out to the small deck off of the living room to get the steaks. The balcony wasn't huge, only big enough to hold the small grill and two chairs, but it was one reason he'd chosen this apartment over the others. Cruz loved to grill and wanted to make sure he had a space to do it.

After dinner, and after he'd brought out a tray with both brownies and cookie dough blobs on it,they relaxed on the couch. They'd talked about their favorite movies, foods, states, books, and even animals. The conversation stayed light and easy as they got to know each other.

They agreed that a night spent watching a movie on television was better than a night out on the town. Mickie admitted that since assuming responsibility for her sister, she hadn't made a lot of friends. When she was in college, she was too busy with school and Angel to bother making lasting relationships, and by the time she'd graduated, she'd lost the opportunity to make those close, lifelong bonds that most people made while in their early twenties.

Cruz told Mickie more about Dax and Mackenzie and even touched on some of his other friends, leaving out their professions in the various law enforcement agencies around the city.

It was approximately ten when Mickie looked down at her watch. "I can't believe how quickly time has gone by tonight."

"Do you need to go?"

"I should…" She let the words hang between them.

Cruz moved closer to Mickie on the couch and reached out to play with the hair around her ears. "Stay. For a bit longer."

Mickie hesitated, then nodded.

Cruz didn't say anything, but took his time really looking at Mickie. His eyes went from her eyes to her nose, to her lips, up to her forehead and then to her ears. They were constantly moving, and each time they landed back at her eyes, Mickie wanted to melt.

"You're beautiful, Mickie," Cruz said softly.

Mickie shook her head.

"You are. I don't know why you can't see it, but you are." His other hand came up and his thumb brushed over an eyebrow. It then moved down to caress the apple of her cheek. As it bloomed with heat, Mickie saw him smile. "So responsive to my touch. I wonder if you're this responsive everywhere."

His words weren't a question, more of a statement. He ran his index finger over her top lip, then her bottom one.

Mickie knew she was pushing it, but she opened her lips and sucked his finger into her mouth, smiling at the groan that escaped Cruz's lips.

"I want to kiss you," Cruz stated in a husky tone. He leaned into her, and Mickie could feel his hot breath against her lips. "May I?"

"Yes. God, yes."

Before the last syllable left her mouth, Cruz's mouth was on hers. The hand that had been at her ear moved to the back of her neck and held her to him. Mickie's hands came up to rest on Cruz's chest. They flexed as his tongue caressed her lips, teasing. Mickie opened wider and licked at him in return. Their tongues met and she felt Cruz shift her in his grasp.

The hand that had been resting at her nape, playing with her hair, was suddenly gripping it, and the hand at her waist was now pulling her into him. Mickie gave as good as she got. Not backing down, or shying away from the carnality of the kiss, she participated fully. One of her own hands crept up to his neck and she dug her nails in lightly. The other rested low on Cruz's belly and she could feel his muscles contracting as he moved her against him.

Cruz tasted like the coffee they'd been drinking and Mickie tilted her head to get deeper. She heard him groan and smiled against his lips. She, Mickie Kaiser, made Cruz groan. She felt powerful and, yes, beautiful.

She didn't realize Cruz was tilting her until she was under him on the couch. One of her feet still rested on the ground, and the other leg was against the back of the couch. Mickie shifted so Cruz could settle even deeper in the vee of her legs. He hadn't taken his mouth off of hers as they'd moved, and even now, as they got more comfortable, he refused to separate them.

Finally, Cruz lifted his head, pushing his hardness into her with his movement. "God, Mickie. You taste so fucking good."

Mickie could feel the blush consume her face as she looked up at Cruz. "Thanks."

"That didn't come out right—" he started to say, but Mickie brought her finger up to his face and put it over his lips.

"It came out exactly right. It was what I was thinking about you."

Cruz lowered his head and kissed Mickie hard. He didn't linger, but Mickie found herself totally consumed anyway. Finally, he pulled back again and sat up, bringing Mickie upright as he went. He kept one arm around her waist and pulled her into him. She put her head on his shoulder and closed her eyes.

Neither said anything for a moment. Finally, Cruz said, "It's late. You probably need to get going."

She did, but Mickie hated to leave. She sighed. "Yeah, I have to work in the morning."

"All right. We'll get together later this week?"

"Yeah, I'd like that."

Cruz smiled at her. "Good. Come on, up you go. If I don't let you go now, I might not ever." He stood, pulling Mickie up with him as he went.

Mickie gathered her purse and headed to the door with Cruz at her heels. "You don't have to walk me out."

"The hell I don't. I'm walking you to your car to make sure you get there safely. Then you'll call me when you get home to let me know you made it there without any issues."

"I will?"

"Yes."

Mickie smiled at Cruz. "Okay. Thank you."

"Thank you?"

"Yeah. For giving a shit if I get home all right or not."

"I give a shit."

"Yeah, so thank you."

Cruz smiled at Mickie. "Let's get you home before you turn into a pumpkin." Cruz took Mickie's hand and walked her out of his apartment to her little Honda Civic. He opened her door after she unlocked it. He crouched next to her as she got her seat belt on. "I'll talk to you in a bit. Okay?"

"Yeah, I'll text you when I get home. Thanks for a great night. Next time, my treat, okay?"

Cruz leaned in and kissed Mickie on the forehead before pulling back. "Okay, sweetness. Good night."

"Good night, Cruz."

Cruz stood and closed her door. He waved at her as she drove out of the parking lot. He sighed and ran his hand over the back of his neck as he looked down at his feet. Cruz hadn't lied to Mickie tonight. He knew he was riding a fine line with her, knew from the bottom of his soul it could go bad, but he couldn't stop. Being with Mickie was so refreshing after dealing with

SUSAN STOKER

the MC and the crap that went on there. The more time he spent with her the more he *wanted* to spend with her.

It wasn't about keeping her safe from Ransom anymore, although that was still a concern—it was about a man spending time with a woman who he was interested in.

CHAPTER 8

THE NEXT FEW weeks went by quickly for Cruz. Neither he nor Mickie had been able to get together after their date, but he was keeping a close eye on her.

Ransom had come into the club one night ranting about how he was going to kill Angel's "motherfucking sister" if she didn't butt out of his business. From what Cruz was able to understand, she'd had another conversation with her sister about all the parties she'd been going to and had actually threatened to call the cops on the club.

Knowing Mickie could really be in danger, Cruz had stepped up.

"I'll keep my eye on her, Ransom."

The president eyed Cruz for a moment before responding. "Fine. She's yours. If she so much as *thinks* about calling the fuzz, I'm holding you responsible."

Cruz knew what that meant. *He* was as good as

dead if Mickie followed through on her threat. "I'll be so far up her ass she won't have time to think about her sister *or* the cops," he reassured the president.

"I'll bet you'll be up her ass all right," Roach commented slyly.

Cruz had slugged him in the stomach hard, but hadn't said a word.

The club had upped its partying and were including Angel and her friends almost every night. They'd established somewhat of a routine, where the women would sit on one side of the room, smoking joints and drinking, while several members of the club entertained them. The other side of the room was more hardcore...and Ransom had slowly been allowing a few of the club whores and strippers to attend. He still wasn't allowing any full-out orgies, but Cruz had been there a few nights where it was obvious the couples weren't merely making out.

Angel was loving being the center of attention at the parties. Her friends were all very impressed she was dating the president of the club and were happy to shell out as much money as Ransom demanded in return for the unending joints.

The more parties they attended, the looser they got with the money—and their inhibitions. Cruz had hoped that the women would be smart and see what was going on, but so far no one had clued in. It even seemed a few of the women now thought they were "dating" some of the club members.

Bridgette and Cissy had even tried cocaine the other night at the party. Ransom was a first-class asshole, but he obviously knew what he was doing with the women. Cruz knew there was a party being planned where the women would be fully introduced to what it meant to be a "member" of the club.

They weren't old ladies, so that meant they were all being groomed to be club whores. Granted, the club had never had any whores who could actually afford to buy the drugs they were given, rather than earning it between their legs, but there was a first time for everything.

The nights Cruz got to speak to Mickie were the highlights of his existence at the moment. They might not have been able to get together, but the two-hour phone calls and the hilarious texts were almost worth the wait. Almost.

Cruz remembered the phone call that had really made him admit he was continuing his relationship with Mickie not to keep her safe...but because he honestly liked her. He'd called one night late after getting home from yet another party at the club. He'd never been a partier, and the constant loud music and half-naked whores, along with the stress of making sure he blended in with the uncouth club members, was exhausting.

He'd picked up his phone and dialed Mickie's number before he'd really even thought about it.

"Hello?"

Cruz could hear the sleepiness in her voice and cursed. "Hey, Mickie. It's Cruz. Sorry, I didn't realize how late it was."

"Everything okay?"

"Yeah. I just wanted to hear your voice." Cruz heard her stifle a yawn before she spoke again.

"I'm glad to hear from you too. How was your day?"

"Long. Yours?"

"Actually really good."

"Yeah?"

"Uh-huh. This woman came in, obviously stressed out. She had three kids with her and her car was acting up. She didn't have a sitter and had to bring them all with her. It was supposed to be a quick check-up, but the mechanic told her that it was most likely going to take all day. She looked like she was going to cry. I don't work the front, but I couldn't just sit there. I mean, haven't we all had days like that?"

"What'd you do?"

"I may or may not have kidnapped one of her kids."

Cruz almost spit out the water he'd just swallowed. "Uh, you do know that's illegal, right?"

Mickie giggled, and Cruz was reminded of when she'd lost it while he was changing her tire. He smiled remembering the look of pure and utter joy on her face then, and could almost envision it now.

"Okay, I might not have actually kidnapped her, but I asked the woman if she'd mind if I took her five-year-old and kept her busy for a while. I reassured her we weren't going to leave the building and that I'd be right around the corner. She was relieved, but still worried. She checked on us at least five times before she left us alone."

"Are you allowed to have kids working with you?"

"Well, no, but my boss was out today, so I just went with it. I got her some crayons from the waiting room and let her go to town. I made up scenes for her to color and we actually made an entire book."

"A book?"

"Yeah. I told her a story and she drew the pictures. I swear, Cruz, it was the cutest thing ever."

"I bet." Cruz could almost picture Mickie laughing and helping entertain a stressed-out mom's child.

"Luckily, the mechanics also had pity on the woman and they were able to get her car done before their estimated time. I was sad to see Rachel go, but her mom was super happy I'd entertained her for a few hours."

"Do you want kids?" The question came out before Cruz could think about it. They'd talked quite a bit, but it wasn't exactly the kind of question you really asked someone when you were first dating.

"Yeah. I didn't think I was really mom material. I mean, look how Angel turned out." Mickie sighed, but continued before Cruz could refute her words. "But I've been able to look back now and see that my own parents had a big hand in what happened. And now I know what *not* to do. I suppose I should be thankful to them for that at least."

"I think you'll be a great mother," Cruz told her honestly. "You saw how stressed that woman was today and didn't hesitate to jump in and help. And if you were able to keep that little girl entertained with only paper and crayons for several hours, you're going to be the most popular mom on the block."

"Thanks. I have no idea if it'll ever happen, but I'm not ruling anything out. What about you? Do you want kids?"

Cruz thought about it for a moment before answering. "I didn't think so until I saw Dax and Mack's relationship grow."

"What do you mean?"

"You know about my first marriage, it was a disaster, and I never wanted to bring a child into a situation where he or she wouldn't be the most important thing in my life. And I always thought having a kid would act as a dividing line between two people. That all the attention and love would be showered on the child, instead of the relationship. But seeing how Dax puts Mack first in his life, and in return she puts him first in hers, I got it. Having a child wouldn't tear that attention apart; it would only bring it together more."

"But your dad loves his wife, right?"

Cruz could hear the confusion in Mickie's voice, and he tried to explain. "He does. Barb is the best thing that could've happened to my dad after my mom died. But they don't...it's not an all-consuming love. They both loved me, but I also felt like an outsider around them as I got older. I never wanted any child I might have to feel like that. So I figured I'd be a better uncle to my friends' kids one day."

"I'd love to meet your friends someday, they sound like awesome people. And Mack was really funny on the phone."

I'd love to meet your friends someday. Her words settled into his psyche as if she herself burrowed into him. But they also scared the crap out of him. One part of him wanted her to meet Dax and all of his other buddies, but the other part of him knew that meeting his friends was just another step to this woman burrowing her way closer and closer to his heart. And the further in she got, the more it would hurt when she dumped him after finding out all his secrets.

Cruz had no idea when he'd be done with his undercover assignment, and there was no way he could let Mickie meet all the guys and Hayden before then. She'd know for sure he'd been lying to her. But he wanted it. He wanted to bring her around to the group barbecues. He wanted to put his arm around her and stand next to her and laugh with her at the things that came out of Mack's mouth. He wanted it all.

"I'd like that, Mickie." The words sounded inadequate to his ears, but they were completely heartfelt. He heard her yawn again. "I should let you go."

"Yeah." She agreed with him, but her tone was reluctant.

"I hate that our schedules aren't meshing. I want to see you."

"Me too."

"Okay, I'm going to do my best to see what I can do to make that happen, yeah?" Cruz asked.

"Yeah. I'm off this coming weekend."

Cruz sighed, thinking about the big party Ransom had planned for that Saturday. Now that Angel and her friends were regulars at the club, he was raising the stakes. He hadn't expounded on what "raising the stakes" meant, but Cruz had a bad feeling about it. Ransom was getting impatient with the paltry amount of money he'd been making off the women with the pot, and wanted to up the ante. It was likely he was going to officially push Angel and the others to start paying for the harder stuff.

"This weekend isn't good for me, dammit."

"You work too hard," Mickie told him sincerely.

If only she knew. "You should know that while I'm working, I'm usually thinking about you."

"Hummmm, interestingly enough, it's the same with me."

Cruz smiled. "I'll text you. We'll figure it out even if it's just for a quick lunch during your break."

"Cool. Be safe this weekend."

Cruz was startled by her choice of words. "Safe?"

"Yeah. With whatever security thing you've got going."

"Ah. I will. Sleep well, sweetness. I'll talk to you later."

"Later, Cruz."

Cruz had sat on the couch for a long while after hanging up with Mickie. She hadn't lambasted him for calling so late and waking her up. She was empathetic and did her best to help others around her. She wanted kids. The more he learned about her, the more Cruz was determined to keep her safe from the shit her sister had gotten involved with...and the more he wanted to keep her for himself.

CHAPTER 9

"LISTEN UP, assholes. We've got two things happening tonight. One, there's a big shipment coming in around eight. Bubba, Kitty, Knife, Dirt, Smoke, and Tiny, you'll head out to pick it up. Don't fuck this up. The other thing that's going on is Angel is coming over again tonight with her rich-bitch posse. Some of them have been getting nervous with all the whores that have been around. Tonight there will be *no* fucking on the floor in front of the rich-bitches. I'll allow that slut, Dixie, to be here tonight, but that's it. I don't give a shit if you take Dixie into the back and fuck her there, but absolutely not out here. Am I clear?"

There was a chorus of agreement from the members. Cruz was torn. He wanted to be at the club to watch out for Angel, he felt as if he owed it to Mickie, but he had no idea what he'd actually do if something went wrong. It wasn't as if he could risk his cover for her. And that was the horrible dilemma he faced, the moral conundrum he found himself in.

But ultimately, Cruz knew he needed to be at the drop-off. He needed to know who Ransom got his drugs from. That was one step to stopping the increase of all the shit into the city *and* ending his assignment. God knew the drugs would never stop, but if Cruz could cut off this one big supply, it'd make a huge difference, at least maybe for a while.

Ransom continued with his commands to his men. "I'm gonna push the bitch tonight. It's time to step it up a bit. I'll get her relaxed with the weed then bring out the blow. Nobody fucks with her tonight. Got it?"

"What about her friends?" Tick yelled out.

"I don't give a flying fuck about her friends. Just don't scare them away. We've got them almost where we want them. We've had too many lame parties with them to fuck it up now. Feel free to make them feel good, but no fucking on the floor. Feel them up, get them off, whatever, but don't screw this up for the club."

"Rich pussy. My fucking favorite," Donkey exclaimed, rubbing his hands together. Donkey had gotten his nickname because he liked taking women up the ass. He was a big man, all over, and Cruz felt extremely sorry for any woman who Donkey got his hands on. He wasn't gentle; he just took what he wanted.

Cruz glanced over at Roach; he could tell the man was jonesing for Ransom to be done with Angel so he could make his move. The way Roach had had his tongue in her ear when they were in the van was enough of a clue. So much for the 'loyalty to one' all the prospects were supposed to have.

If Ransom knew Roach had touched Angel, and what the man had said to her, he'd lose his shit, not because it was Angel but because for now, she was his property. Cruz knew better than to tattle. That was the quickest way to lose his standing in the club.

"All right, get the fuck out of here."

The members slowly made their way out of the room. Cruz strode over to where Bubba was standing with the others.

"Let's get the hell out of here, Smoke. We got shit to do."

FOUR HOURS LATER, Cruz walked back into the club-house with the other members who'd been tasked to pick up the drugs. The pickup was tremendously helpful for Cruz's mission, but he knew it wasn't over yet. They'd met with Axel, an extremely violent and dangerous gang member who Cruz knew worked hand in hand with some corrupt government officials in a small Mexican city just over the border.

The Mexican government had been working hard on battling corruption in their members and the police force, but so far the lure of the money drugs brought in was winning over doing the right thing.

Thankfully, Cruz hadn't had any interaction with Axel in the past, so his cover was safe for now. He just knew *of* him from Conor and TJ, both of whose agencies, Texas Parks & Wildlife Department and Texas Highway Patrol, had dealt with him extensively.

Bubba had met with Axel around Lackland Air Force Base, west of the city. They'd talked for a bit then they'd all gotten back into their vehicles and driven even farther west. Bubba had handed Axel a bag full of hundred dollar bills, and Axel tossed Bubba the keys to a truck and directions as to where the truck would be. They'd driven back into the city and found the truck sitting in the parking lot of a fast food restaurant.

Cruz was disgusted by how easy and simple the transaction seemed to be. Eighty feet away, inside the restaurant, kids were screaming and laughing and playing on the playground equipment. And here they were, driving away with almost two hundred thousand dollars in cocaine and weed. It was insane.

Bubba had driven the truck back to the MC hangout and now the guys were ready to party. Ransom had taken Bubba aside and they'd had a short conversation. Obviously satisfied with how the drop had gone down, Ransom clapped Bubba on the back and the two men had disappeared into a back room.

The party at the compound was in full swing. The music was loud, there were women everywhere, who the hell knew where they all came from, because they certainly weren't all strippers, whores, and old ladies, and the MC members were living it up. Cruz could tell they were holding themselves back because of Angel's friends, but they were still partying a hell of a lot more hard-core than most normal people would, and harder than when the women had been there in the past.

Cruz could spot Angel's friends easily. They were dressed as they always were when they came to the parties, as if they were at a fancy New Year's Eve party or something. Short skirts, high heels, glittery skimpy tops. They were sitting in a cluster around a table, laughing uncontrollably. It was obvious the first part of Ransom's plan was already in play. They were high from the joints they'd recently smoked and were having the time of their lives.

Donkey, Tick, Camel, and Roach were standing around the group of women, obviously waiting for their chance to make a move, while across the room, a crazy bastard named Vodka—because he'd once guzzled an entire bottle of the stuff and stayed standing throughout the night—and another guy who Cruz thought was named Steel, were sitting with Dixie. They were following Ransom's decree—barely.

Dixie was a club whore who'd do just about anything to score some coke. Vodka and Steel were sitting side by side on the disgusting, beat-up old couch, and Dixie was draped over Steel's lap, sucking Vodka's dick. Cruz could see Steel's hand moving rapidly under her skirt, fingering her as she serviced Vodka. His hand was on the back of Dixie's head, controlling the speed and the depth with which she took his dick down her throat.

Cruz turned away in revulsion. Jesus.

Just then, Ransom came into the room with Angel, who must've been waiting for him in one of the many backrooms. She made her way over to her friends, her hand a death grip on Ransom's arm. Cruz could tell he was tolerating it only because she was a part of his plan.

"Hey everyone! You remember my boyfriend, right? The *president* of the club." Angel winked ridiculously at her friends. They all tittered in response and greeted Ransom.

Angel continued, "He said he's got a surprise for us tonight."

Cruz winced, knowing what was coming.

"You ladies having a nice time?" Ransom asked. When all the girls nodded, he continued. "Good. Thank you for your generous donations to the party tonight, I'll personally make sure you're all rewarded. But let me know when you're ready for some *real* fun, and you've had enough of this pansy joint shit."

With that, Ransom peeled Angel's hand off his arm and stalked back through the crowded room, leaving Angel standing in front of her friends, embarrassed as hell. She looked around, confused about what had just happened, then slid over to stand uncomfortably next to a tall Asian woman named Li.

"What's he mean, Angel?" Li asked, brow crinkled in confusion. "We always have fun when we're here. We love partying with him and his friends."

As if they'd rehearsed it, Camel answered for Angel. "Coke, pretty lady."

The other women looked at him in surprise. Camel continued as if he hadn't just shocked the shit out of the country-club set. "And I'm not talking the fizzy-soda-pop kind. Those joints you've been smoking are fun, yeah, but they aren't anything compared to the high you get from snorting some coke. It makes you feel fucking invincible. You think the weed makes you feel good, shit, you have to try this. If you're scared to try it, no big deal, but I can personally guaran-damn-tee it makes orgasms stronger, longer, and for the ladies, makes you able to come all night long."

Cruz knew Camel didn't know what the hell he was talking about, but Angel's friends didn't know that. Cocaine did make the user feel euphoric and could make someone more energetic and talkative, but increasing their ability to orgasm? No. It *could* make the person using it have an increased reaction to touch, sight, and sound, which, Cruz figured, was where Camel was going with his orgasm comment.

Ransom didn't allow his MC members to use cocaine. He knew how addictive it was, and that having drugged-out members around the merchandise wasn't a good combination. Cruz had personally witnessed Bubba beating the shit out of a prospect when he'd first joined the club for stealing the cocaine he was supposed to be selling. That didn't mean the guys hadn't ever used before. Camel obviously knew what it felt like to be high on the drug.

There was silence around the table for a moment, then as Cruz could have predicted, Angel spoke up. "I'm in. Who else?"

When no one said anything, Angel sighed dramatically. "Fine. Y'all are pussies. I'll get Ransom to bring some over here and you can watch me. I'll show you I won't drop dead from it and then you can do whatever you want. It's not like using at parties is gonna make me into a drug addict." And with those words, she stormed away.

The mood in the room had changed a bit, though slowly but surely, the MC members moved in and worked their magic. Camel dropped his hand to Cissy's stomach and stroked her while talking into her ear. Donkey put his mouth to Kelly's neck and sucked hard, while at the same time holding onto her thigh and caressing her. Tick picked Li up off her chair and sat down in her place, holding her across his lap and against his erection as he ran his hands up and down her back, soothing, placating, and arousing.

While the other men were doing the same things to the other women, Roach was the most aggressive. He'd turned Bridgette's chair around so it was facing Vodka and Steel—and Dixie—on the couch. He stood behind her, whispering in her ear while running his hands over her chest, pausing every now and then to pinch her erect nipples. Bridgette's eyes were locked on the scene across the room as she squirmed in Roach's grip. It was obvious she was torn between embarrassment, and being turned on by what Roach was doing to her and what she was watching.

The men were using the women's altered states against them. The marijuana coursing through their systems was making them mellow and receptive to the guys' advances. They likely didn't feel any danger because they'd been coming to the club for nights on end. They knew the men, even if they didn't *know* them. Not to mention, Angel was encouraging the deviant behavior. It was a classic case of peer pressure. If Cruz didn't hate Ransom so much, he'd be impressed with the man. He was a master manipulator. Mickie would have a field day analyzing him with her psychology degree.

Cruz stopped his thoughts in their tracks. No way was he thinking about Mickie while he was standing in this pit of hell.

Angel came stomping back across the room with Ransom in tow. Ever the drama queen, she cleared the table nearest to her with one sweep of her arm. The glasses and bottles that had been sitting there crashed and broke as they landed on the floor. The women giggled nervously at her actions, but they must've been used to her over-the-top performances because they simply sat up straighter to get a better view of the drama that was about to happen.

Ransom smirked and set up the lines of cocaine on the tabletop. He tamped them down and held his hand out to Angel.

"Give me a hundred."

Angel reached into her purse and brought out a hundred dollar bill with no argument. They all watched as Ransom tightly rolled it up. He then handed it back to Angel and gestured toward the table. "Go for it. Show 'em how it's fucking done."

Cruz could see Angel was apprehensive, but Ransom didn't give her a chance to back down. He moved behind her and put his hands on her waist. He leaned in. Cruz only heard him because he was standing nearby.

"Go on. Fucking do it already. Any bitch of mine wouldn't be scared of this shit. You've done it before with the old ladies, what's the difference now? You a part of my MC or what?"

Angel squared her shoulders and put the rolled-up bill to her nose and bent over. She stood up and coughed and ran her hand under her nose, wiping away any white powder that might be clinging there.

"That's my good girl," Ransom told her. "Again." He put his hand on her back and pushed. Angel almost fell on the table, but caught herself at the last second. Ransom pulled her hips back and pushed his dick against her ass. His hands went to the bottom of her dress and he slowly ran them up her sides, pushing her dress up as he went.

As Angel leaned down to snort the second line Ransom had set out for her, he brought her dress all the way up and over her ass. Angel was wearing a black thong, her ass now visible to everyone in the room.

Ransom ran his hands over her tan cheeks and then leaned into her.

When she was done, he pulled her up against him and gave her another joint to smoke. Ten minutes later, when Ransom knew the drug would most likely have taken effect, he addressed the women sitting around the table, who were now watching Angel and Ransom with fascination.

"Listen closely, ladies. Watch and fucking learn." He turned his head and spoke in a normal voice to Angel. "How do you feel, Angel? Can you feel it coursing through your veins?"

"Uh-huh." Angel vigorously nodded.

Ransom ran his hands down her sides and held Angel closer. One of his arms went around her chest, holding her against the front of him. His other hand went down and cupped her pussy. Her skirt was still rucked up around her waist. He was hiding her from her friends, but it was obvious what he was doing.

"And this? What does this feel like? Does it feel different?"

"God, Ransom!"

"Answer my fucking question. Now."

"Yeah, it feels different."

"How?"

Angel's head rested back on Ransom's shoulder and she rolled it back and forth. She grabbed his arm around her chest and the other hand went down to where he was now rubbing against her clit.

"Hands off, Angel. Don't even think about fucking stopping me."

Angel immediately retreated, putting her hand back on his arm.

"You want me to make you come? Right here in front of your friends?"

Angel simply moaned.

"I won't say it again. Give me a fucking answer."

"Oh God, Ransom, Please."

"Please what, bitch?"

Angel's hips were now thrusting against Ransom's hand. Cruz couldn't help but stare in morbid fascination as Ransom manipulated not only Angel, but her friends as well. Each rub over Angel's clit was meant to show her friends how wonderful the cocaine high was...even though the two really had nothing to do with each other.

Every one of the other women sitting around the table was silent and still, watching intently. The other MC members were *not* still. They were in various stages of caressing Angel's friends. Some nonchalantly and others more blatantly, but none as overtly sexually as Ransom.

"Please, let me come."

Ransom abruptly removed his hand from Angel's crotch and brought it up to her mouth. "Suck it."

Angel opened and Ransom shoved the three fingers he'd been fucking her with into her mouth roughly. Angel kept her eyes closed as she licked and sucked her juices off his fingers with no complaint as he worked them in and out.

"Now, finish the last line and then you'll tell me how it fucking feels when I ask, without hesitating, and I'll think about letting you come."

Angel obediently leaned over the table and quickly snorted the last line of white powder. Ransom snagged the rolled-up bill from her hand and shoved it into his back pocket, not missing a beat and never missing a chance to pocket easy money.

"Please, Ransom. You promised, please."

"You don't call the shots here, whore. You know that."

"I'm sorry. Please..."

Ransom brought her back against his chest again. "Put your hands up around my neck."

Angel did as he asked, once again resting her head on Ransom's shoulder.

Ransom inched one hand back down to her pussy and grabbed her throat with the other. He forced her head back farther as he squeezed her neck tightly. Angel coughed and gagged, but didn't otherwise try to remove his hands; she just kept undulating against him and trying to get herself off.

"Now, tell me what I want to know, bitch. Describe how this feels. Tell all your friends how it's different. How it's better."

Angel started slowly, but picked up speed as she described what she was feeling. Her voice was raspy and low, because her air was being restricted, but her friends could still hear her. "I'm wet. Really wet. I can feel every slide of your fingers inside me. Your fingernails scraping against my walls. It's heightened, as if I can feel every molecule of your fingers. They feel big. Huge, almost like it's your cock."

Ransom smirked. "You see, ladies? There's no better aphrodisiac than a bit of blow. It's completely harmless. As your friend here will demonstrate, it can make you multi-orgasmic. You think she cares you're all watching her? No. All she cares about is getting off. And I can guarantee it'll be the best orgasm she's ever had. Right, whore?"

His hand went to work between Angel's thighs. He smacked her pussy three times, making Angel twitch in his grasp. She started to move her hands from behind his head and Ransom tightened his grip on her neck and growled, "Leave them there, cunt."

Angel moaned and obeyed, squirming in Ransom's grasp.

Ransom reached up and lowered Angel's dress so that one breast was exposed to the group, who now stared as if hypnotized by the show before them.

He pinched her nipple between his thumb and forefinger until Angel was standing on her tiptoes groaning.

Ransom was smirking as he continued his demonstration. "The increased blood flow to her extremities is making everything I do to her feel twice as good as it would without the coke. There's no other feeling in the world like this."

Ransom's hand went back down to her crotch, holding Angel tightly against him as he delved under her thong once more. It didn't take long, only ten or so seconds, and Angel was howling and everyone watched as she orgasmed in Ransom's arms. Without letting her recover, he continued his assault on her clit.

"Now, she just came, but watch—I can make her come again and again, something she can't do without the blow. I know, I've fucking tried."

Angel screamed again and lost the battle to stand fully upright. Only Ransom's arm around her neck kept her standing.

"One more, bitch. Give me one more."

"I can't, Ransom, please, stop, it hurts!"

"Shut the fuck up. I'm in control here. You *will*. Put your fucking foot up."

When Angel didn't move, Ransom nodded at Camel, who was standing next to them. Camel leaned over and grabbed Angel's leg roughly and forcefully hooked the heel of her shoe on the bottom spindle of the nearest stool. The action opened her up to Ransom even more. He increased the speed of his thrusts inside her pussy and rolled her clit roughly with his thumb, her thong no barrier to his fingers.

He shifted and finally took his hand off her neck, only to snake it down to pinch her exposed nipple. They could all see the tip begin to slowly turn red from the pressure. He then pulled it away from her chest. Angel whimpered in his arms, but didn't otherwise fight his rough handling of her body.

"See girls? She's loving this. She doesn't care where she is or what I do to her. This could be you. All it takes is a bit of blow." He took Angel's earlobe between his teeth. "Come again, bitch. Come now." He let go of her nipple and as the blood rushed back into the nub, he grabbed her entire breast in his hand and squeezed hard enough that Angel would have bruises in the morning.

That was all it took. Angel came again with a screech, yelping Ransom's name.

Cruz observed the display with disgust. It was obvious Ransom didn't give a shit about Angel, he was just using her. Well, it was obvious to *him*. Hell, Cruz could tell the president wasn't even hard. He wasn't getting off on what he was doing. It was all a show, a ploy, and Angel and her friends were playing right into his hands.

When Angel had calmed somewhat, Ransom pulled her dress down and her bra up to re-cover her breast and removed his fingers from between her legs. He wiped his hand on her dress with what Cruz could see was barely concealed disgust.

"Now, who's in?"

The women around the table didn't immediately agree, but eventually the alcohol and weed they'd ingested made them lose enough of their inhibitions that they all decided to try it.

Ransom twisted with a smirk and slapped Angel on the ass. As he turned away, he said, "Thanks, bitch."

Angel hadn't recovered her equilibrium from the

orgasms and didn't respond. Her hands were on the table in front of her and she leaned over it, trying to catch her breath. Bubba pulled out several small baggies of coke from his pocket and started making the rounds to Angel's friends, pocketing money, giving instructions, and handing them his business card so they could get in touch with him when they wanted more.

Cruz turned away. He didn't want to hang around and watch all the club members get these naïve women off. They had no clue they'd been played by a master.

As Cruz walked to the other end of the warehouse to get away from the depravity, he thought about how he could stop Ransom and his club from getting the rest of the drugs onto the streets, and how he was going to explain to Mickie that he'd stood around and watched as her little sister had been so crudely put on display for Ransom and all his club buddies. It was one thing to know she was having sex with the man, but if Mickie had seen what had just happened, she'd be as horrified as he was. He knew it.

CHAPTER 10

GOOD MORNING.

Good morning, Cruz.

All ok there? No more incidents? Cruz had started texting Mickie each morning to make sure none of the other club members had taken it upon themselves to send her another message. If that happened, he'd have to make a stand, but so far they'd all stayed away from her.

Nope. All was good this morning. How'd the job go last night?

Cruz had told her he had to work a private party at the Alamo the night before. He hated lying to her, but telling her he was hanging out at a party thrown by the same motorcycle club she was trying to convince her sister to ditch, obviously wasn't going to work.

Good. No problems.

See any ghosts?

He laughed out loud at that. He recalled another

conversation they'd had about how fascinated she was with the history of the Alamo and the downtown area, particularly regarding the spirits that had to still be around.

Not this time, only real people.

Darn.

Have a good day at work. I'll talk to you later?

Sounds good. Later Cruz.

Bye

An hour or so later, his personal phone rang.

"Cruz."

"Hey, it's Dax. How're you holding up?" Daxton Chambers asked, sounding concerned even over the phone line.

"I've been better."

"It's been almost two months. You doing okay?"

Cruz ran his hand over the top of his head. "I'm getting there. I've been reporting what I've seen and heard back to the field office. They say another couple of weeks and I'm out."

"A couple of weeks? Come on, man, you know they don't need you in there while they're doing the paperwork to shut them down."

"I can't leave right now." When Dax didn't say anything, Cruz reluctantly repeated, "It's personal. I can't leave now."

"I don't like it, man, but I understand. You know I'm here if you need me. Just say the word and I'm there."

"I know, and I appreciate it."

Changing the subject, Dax said, "So, Mack tells me

she was your wingman when it came to a certain woman…" He let the sentence hang.

Cruz laughed. "Yeah, she was great. Thank her again for me."

"That's it? That's all you're giving me?"

Cruz chuckled at the disappointment he heard in his friend's voice. "She's amazing, Dax, but it's not going to go anywhere."

"Why do you say that?"

"Because. I'm fucking undercover. There's no way."

"Don't say that. I didn't expect to find Mack, yet, here we are."

"That's different."

"How?"

"For one, you weren't pretending to be someone you aren't with her."

"When you're with this woman, are you pretending?"

"Not really, but there's no way she's gonna forgive me when she finds out what I'm doing and that I'm not *just* in security."

Dax chuckled at that, but sobered quickly and said, "If there's something between you, you never know."

Cruz sighed and sat on a chair at his kitchen table. He'd spoken with Mickie several times since their last date, and every time he talked to her, he swore she just got better and better.

"I'm not sure I can forgive *myself* for what I've had to do this time, Dax."

"Take the afternoon off and come and visit with me and Mack."

"Thanks, but I can't."

"You know the offer is always open."

"I know, and I appreciate it."

"All right. You take care. I'll make sure Mack's around the next time I call, I know she'll want to talk to you."

"Sounds good, talk to you later. Bye."

"Bye, Cruz."

Cruz clicked off his phone and put it on the table. He thought back to the last week. After Ransom had gotten Angel off in front of her friends, and they'd bought a shitload of coke, the party had disintegrated into a disgusting display of the club members getting the ladies completely shitfaced with the drugs. The guys had then taken the women to different parts of the warehouse and gotten them off, much as Ransom had done to Angel.

Cruz had finally left, to the jeers of the club members because he didn't have any pussy to play with. It'd been three days since he'd spoken to Mickie because he'd felt guilty as hell about what had happened to her sister. If he was honest with himself, it was also because he felt dirty.

He put his head in his hands and let out a deep breath. He was being an idiot. This was a job. That's all.

But he knew he was lying to himself. Mickie had become very important to him in a short amount of time and he hated the double life he was living.

He hated being in the club, but he was happy that being there gave him a reason to talk to Mickie, and to see her more often than he probably would've been able to swing if he wasn't supposed to be keeping his eye on her. He hated when Ransom asked for updates on the "sister situation," as he called it, but enjoyed being able to be around her.

Later that morning, the phone on the counter rang and Cruz stood up to answer it. It was "Smoke's" phone that was ringing. Without bothering to check who it was, he turned on his MC persona as he answered.

"Yo."

"Hi, Cruz?"

Fuck. "Hey, Mickie." He immediately gentled his voice.

"Hey. Whatcha doing?"

"Sitting around thinking about making something to eat. You?"

"Feeling sorry for myself. Want to go grab something together?"

"Everything all right?"

"No."

"Mickie? Talk to me."

Cruz heard a big sigh on the other end of the line.

"It's nothing new, Cruz. It's Angel. We had another big fight today. I'm losing her and it's freaking me out."

Instead of asking more questions, Cruz suggested, "Want to meet at the pancake place on Timberhill and Grissom?"

"Yeah, I'd like that. Thirty minutes?"

"Perfect. Drive safe. I'll see you soon."

"See you. And thanks, Cruz. Bye."

Cruz hung up and immediately turned toward his bedroom.

It was obvious Mickie was feeling down and had called him to try to cheer herself up. He couldn't deny that it made him feel good inside that *he* was the one she wanted to talk to when she was sad. She was so open and trusting. Just being around her made Cruz feel calm.

But the thing that made him recognize he'd completely fallen for her was the realization that the second it dawned on him that she was feeling down, he'd done whatever he could to cheer her up.

He'd never felt that way about Sophie. He didn't like it when she wasn't happy, but he didn't feel this all-consuming need to see to her. Cruz knew he should go into the club and see what Ransom had planned for later, but Mickie came first. It wasn't until after he had hung up that he realized he'd already put Mickie before everything else in his life. His job, his friends…and he'd continue to, if it came to that.

Cruz pulled up to the restaurant in his little car and entered. He saw Mickie sitting at a booth in the back of the small room and made his way to her. The second she saw him, her face lit up in greeting.

Mickie had been nursing her cup of coffee for a few minutes when she saw Cruz come through the door. She waved him over and smiled as he arrived at the table.

"Hey, Cruz. Thanks for coming."

"The pleasure's all mine, believe me." Cruz scooted into her side of the booth and leaned over and kissed Mickie on the side of the head. "Are you okay?"

"As okay as I can be, knowing my sister is making the biggest mistake of her life."

"What's she done now?"

Before Mickie could answer, the waitress came over to their table. Cruz didn't have to look at the menu to know what he wanted to eat. He told her what he wanted and Mickie also ordered. Mickie picked up their conversation as if they hadn't been interrupted.

"I called Angel this morning and she sounded completely out of it when she answered. I asked how her job was going and she told me she'd quit. *Quit*, Cruz. It's not like she was working her dream job or anything, but what the hell does she think she's going to live on?"

"I was under the impression she had some money."

"She does. We do, but it's not enough for her to live on forever. I mean, I know I took Troy for half of everything he had, but I actually like working. Angel has to do *something*. She can't just sit around and eat bon-bons for the rest of her life. The thing of it is, she didn't sound like herself. She was totally unconcerned she was sleeping at ten in the morning. In the past, she always got up by eight so she could go to the gym and work out when all the hotties were there. Her words, not mine."

Cruz put his hand over Mickie's on the table. "Is she still seeing that guy?"

"I think so. I mean, she didn't say specifically, but when I asked about him, she told me to butt out and hung up on me. I swear if I didn't know better, I'd say she was high or something. Angel's done some pot before, when she was in high school, but this was different I think." Mickie sipped her coffee.

"What's going on behind those pretty eyes?"

Mickie looked at him. "She's my sister. I have to help her, whether she wants it or not."

"Mickie—"

"Don't take that tone with me, Cruz. I'm an adult."

"So is Angel."

"Yeah, but—"

"No buts about it, Mickie."

"Is that how you felt about your wife?"

Mickie wished she could take back the words as soon as they were out of her mouth. It was a shitty thing to say.

She put her hand on Cruz's arm and immediately apologized, "I'm sorry, Cruz. That was uncalled for. I just…I thought about following her one night to see where she went with that asshole Ransom. If I can take some pictures of him doing something illegal, get her to see that he's not a good guy—"

Cruz took Mickie by the arms and turned her toward him. "Abso-fucking-lutely not. Terrible idea, Mickie. No way."

"What am I supposed to do then?"

He spoke without thinking. "Let me ask some of the guys I work with. Some work as private investigators on the side. I'll see what they know about the MC."

"You'd do that for her?"

"No, I'd do it for *you*." Cruz stared into Mickie's eyes as they teared up.

Mickie leaned forward and put her arms around Cruz. "Thank you. Having you ask your coworkers if they know anything makes me feel like I'm not so alone in trying to look out for Angel. You have no idea how much this means to me. She's my only sister. I don't know what I'd do if something happened to her."

"Don't get your hopes up; I'm not sure what I'll find out. It'll probably be nothing, and even if they do know about the club, I don't know what good it'll do you." Cruz felt like he had to warn her. He had no idea what information he could give to Mickie that would satisfy her, but there was no way he wanted Mickie *anywhere* near Ransom and his fucking compound.

"I appreciate you even seeing what you can find out. I'm not sure it'll do any good, because I think Angel already knows Ransom isn't exactly on the up and up, but she doesn't seem to care. But maybe if he's doing something *really* bad, I can call the cops and turn him in. That would get him out of her life."

The waitress arrived with their food and Mickie sat back. They ate their meal with no more mention of Angel. Mickie seemed contemplative, but Cruz thought it was only natural with all she had going on in her life.

When they were done, Cruz paid the bill and they left the restaurant.

"What are you doing for the rest of the day, Mickie?" Cruz knew he would have to show up in the evening because of a job Ransom had for him and some of the other members, but he didn't want to let Mickie go. He loved spending time with her; she made him feel like a better person, even if it wasn't true.

Cruz had no idea what Ransom had in store for Angel or her friends that night, but he hoped now that Ransom had introduced them to cocaine, he'd lay off having parties almost every night and concentrate on supplying them with drugs individually.

The club members were headed out to pick up another shipment of drugs later that evening though, and Cruz knew he couldn't miss it. Bubba was in charge again, and he'd already tasked Cruz and some of the other members to go with him to do the pickup. Cruz was hoping to finally get enough information on the suppliers of the drugs to pass along to his boss so he could get the hell out of the op.

"I was gonna go home and wallow in my uneasiness about Angel...got something that could compete with that?" Mickie joked, holding onto Cruz's arm as they walked to their cars.

"How about spending it with me?"

Mickie stopped, causing Cruz to stop as well.

"I'd love to."

Cruz smiled, loving that Mickie didn't play games with him. If she wanted something, she said it. If she was hungry, she ate. If she was in a bad mood, she didn't pretend she wasn't.

"Great. Is it okay if we just go back to my place and hang?" he asked as they continued walking.

"You don't want to go to the mall?" Mickie teased.

Jesus, the last place he wanted to go to with her was the fucking mall. "No way."

She laughed. "I was joking. Got any good movies?"

"Yeah, I have a whole collection you can look through."

"I get to choose?"

"Sure."

"Not scared of what I'll pick?"

Cruz guided Mickie to her car and waited as she unlocked the doors. Once she clicked the locks, Cruz backed her against the car and caged her in with his arms. "Mickie, it's my place. It's not like I have a secret stash of romantic comedies for you to choose from."

Mickie giggled.

Cruz leaned in and smirked as her giggling stopped. "I hope you like action flicks. I'm not sure I've got anything else." He put his head to Mickie's neck and nuzzled her ear.

"I-I like them."

Cruz felt Mickie's hands go to his waist and hold on to his shirt. He purposely breathed in her ear before saying softly, "Good."

"On one condition…"

Cruz pulled back and looked at her. She was smirking at him. "One condition, huh? Okay, shoot."

"I want to see your tattoo." Mickie ran her fingertips over the edge of his T-shirt, right above the tattoo that snaked up his upper left arm.

"You like tattoos?"

"Never really thought about it before, but on you? Yeah, I think so."

"Deal. You can pick the movie and I'll let you see my tattoo."

"Cool," Mickie breathed as she looked up at him.

He drew back, knowing he was a second away from kissing the hell out of her. He put his hands on Mickie's face, tilting her head so she was looking up at him. "You want to follow me?"

"Uh-huh."

Cruz smiled; she was so fucking cute when she was flustered. "Okay then, let's get you ready to go." He kissed her on the lips briefly, wishing more than he could say that he could linger, and drew back. He turned her and put one hand on her back and waited for her to open her door.

She sat and Cruz held on to the car door. When she was belted in, he leaned his forearm on the roof and said, "Drive safe, I'll see you in a bit."

"Okay. You too." Mickie breathed out a sigh of relief once Cruz headed toward his car. Jeez, he was absolutely lethal. Over the last few weeks she'd gotten to know him pretty well—at least she thought she had. Every time she saw him, he took her breath away. He was just so freaking good-looking, and he was interested in *her*. It was crazy.

She wasn't one to believe in insta-love, but she'd taken her time with Troy, been very cautious, and look how that turned out. It wasn't as if she'd jumped into bed with Cruz on that first date, but she was definitely moving faster with him than any other relationship she'd had.

But the difference this time was that they were talking more. On the phone, via texts...without face-to-face contact, they'd had to rely on getting to know each other by *talking*. She liked it. She knew more about Cruz than she ultimately knew about Troy. But that really wasn't saying anything since apparently she knew nothing *real* about Troy.

Mickie would've been over the moon, if only it hadn't been for her sister. She knew she'd have to confront Angel, sooner rather than later. Something major was up with her and Mickie knew in her gut it wasn't anything good. She needed to get to the bottom of it, if only she knew how.

But first, Mickie had an afternoon to spend with Cruz. She shivered in delight. Maybe she'd be able to convince him to take their physical relationship a bit further than they'd taken it in the past. Mickie was ready—more than ready.

CHAPTER 11

CRUZ'S GAZE swept from the road in front of him to his rearview mirror. Mickie was a good driver, and kept his car in her sights. Seeing her trusting him, following him wherever he wanted her to go, made him come to a decision. He was simply going to go with it with Mickie. As Dax had said, he had no idea how this would all play out in the end, but Cruz knew he'd never forgive himself if he gave up on whatever was starting between them without at least giving it a chance.

He wanted Mickie. She was cute, funny, and down-to-earth. She cared about her sister even when Angel was being hurtful, and was about as normal as any woman he'd ever dated...and that appealed to him more than he thought it would. He wanted someone who would love him as much as he loved her back. He wasn't sure if Mickie was that woman yet, but he'd be an idiot to let her go. She was the first woman since

Sophie who he could even *imagine* himself in a long-term relationship with.

Soon they were pulling up in front of Cruz's apartment complex. He got out of his car and headed over to Mickie's Honda. He met her at the front of the car and took her hand in his as they headed to his door.

It seemed natural to hold on to her. Cruz had no idea why this woman made him feel this way, but it was what it was, and reiterating his thoughts on the way to his place, he wasn't going to fight it anymore.

Their quirky courtship, which thus far had mostly existed via phone, was completely different from anything he'd ever had before. As much as he'd thought he loved Sophie, he'd never felt anticipation when his phone vibrated. He'd never woken up wanting nothing more than to talk to her, and he never went to sleep hoping her voice would be the first thing he heard in the morning.

The more Cruz got to know Mickie, the more he realized what he had with Sophie hadn't been true love. He thought about Dax and Mack. Their love was what he wanted. After what Dax had been through, watching Mack literally die in front of his eyes at the hands of a serial killer, and how it'd affected him, Cruz knew *that* was what he wanted. Not the dying part, but the love part. He hadn't understood it...until now. Until Mickie. He wasn't sure he loved her yet, but he certainly cared a whole lot about her.

Cruz unlocked his apartment door and held it open

for Mickie. She walked in and put her purse on the table by the door.

"Go on and choose what you want to watch. Movies are in the cabinet by the television."

Mickie headed over to his entertainment center and squatted down next to the cabinet with the DVDs. He went into the kitchen and got two cans of soda. Cruz went back into the living room and settled on the sofa.

Mickie held up *Beverly Hills Cop*. "Too cliché?"

Cruz laughed and stood up to put the movie into the DVD player. "Hell no. I love this movie." He scrunched up his face and raised his voice, mimicking Eddie Murphy, "Disturbing the peace? I got thrown out a window!"

Mickie immediately finished the quote. "What's the charge for getting pushed out of a car? Jaywalking?"

Cruz gawked at Mickie, not believing she could actually quote *Beverly Hills Cop*.

Mickie laughed. "I love it too. Eddie Murphy's the bomb."

"Will you marry me?"

Mickie laughed again, even as her heart beat wildly in her chest at his words. "Shut up."

Cruz sat on the couch next to Mickie and took her hand as the music started. They sat watching the movie for a while, Cruz smiling at Mickie mouthing various lines as Eddie Murphy said them. "At the risk of interrupting you, I just wanna say, thanks for coming over today."

Mickie looked over at Cruz. "I think that's my line. I

was stressed about Angel and you offered to help me pull my head out of my ass."

Cruz lifted the hand not holding hers and brushed it over the side of her head. "I'm sorry about your sister. Seriously."

"I know."

"You'll figure it out."

"I hope so."

"Are you hungry?"

Mickie looked surprised at his change of subject. "No. We just ate."

"Thirsty?"

Motioning to her drink on the table next to the couch, Mickie shook her head.

"Comfortable? Need anything?"

"Cruz? I'm fine. What's up with you?"

"I just want to make sure you're comfortable and all's good."

"I'm fine."

"How into this movie are you?"

"Uh, it's good, but if you need to do something else, it's okay, I can go."

"I don't want you to go. I can't hold back anymore. The more I learn about you, the more I have to have you. You're loyal to your sister. You work hard, you're not selfish or spoiled. You're sexy as hell and I can't get you out of my head. I'm done waiting. I want to taste you. I want to feel your curvy body under mine. I need it. If you don't want that, please, tell me. Otherwise, this is happening. Right now."

Mickie swallowed hard. Cruz was dead serious. He wasn't smiling, he wasn't teasing her. She could feel her nipples harden under her cotton bra. Dear Lord. This handsome man wanted her. She didn't have to think about it. She'd decided earlier that she hoped Cruz wanted to move their physical relationship forward. "I want it."

"Thank fuck. Come here." Cruz hooked his arm around her back and tugged her into him as he fell sideways onto the couch.

Mickie tried to prop herself up so she didn't squish him as she looked down into his eyes.

"Relax, Mickie. I need to feel you against me."

"I'll squash you."

"Hardly. Mickie, you weigh nothing compared to me. Put your legs on either side of my hips. Straddle me. I like feeling you against me. That's it…" Cruz put his hands on her hips and held her to him. She was astride his stomach, which was probably good; he didn't want to scare her with how hard he was.

He ran his hands up from her hips to her sides, then back down. Then he did it again, going higher this time, until they were just under her breasts. Cruz kept his hands on her, soothing her, gentling her. "Relax into me. You won't hurt me."

Cruz felt when Mickie put her full weight on him. Her legs relaxed and he could feel the warmth of her core against his stomach. Her hands were braced on his chest and she was looking down at him as if she was starving and he was her last meal. It was a good look on her.

Wanting to move their lovemaking along, Cruz said, "You want to see my tattoo now?"

"God, yes. Please."

Cruz took his hands off her and put them up by his head. "Take off my shirt."

Mickie looked down at the exquisite man underneath her. She'd been nervous about sitting on him, but as he'd run his hands over her body, she relaxed more and more. Now she lifted her hips and reached under her to grasp his T-shirt and ease it up his chest. She teased them both by removing it slowly.

As she revealed his abs, Mickie gasped. "Wow, Cruz. You're built." She scooted backwards until she rested on top of his erection. She leaned down and kissed his stomach as she continued to ease his shirt upward. She kissed his belly button and then each of the defined muscles she revealed as she raised his shirt. Mickie felt him inhale at the first brush of her lips against his stomach. She usually wasn't this forward or fast with men, but there was something about Cruz that made her lose her inhibitions.

"That's not where my tattoo is," Cruz teased, breathing deeply to try to control himself. The feel of Mickie rubbing against his erection and her lips so close to his waistband was playing hell with his good intentions.

Mickie raised her head and watched as Cruz lifted

his arms straight up so she could push his shirt completely off. Her eyes were glued to his left biceps and shoulder as he brought his arms back down, hauling her hips back up so she was straddling his stomach again.

She pouted at him. "I was comfortable where I was."

"Yeah, but if you want this to last for more than two minutes, I need you here right now."

Mickie smirked. "Two minutes?"

Cruz chuckled at himself. "Yeah, you've got me so hard if you'd ground yourself against me any longer, that's how long I would've lasted."

Mickie blushed and covered her cheeks with her hands when he laughed at her. "I don't think anyone's wanted me like that before."

"Well, rest assured, I do. You wanna take a look at this now or later?" Cruz asked seriously, gesturing to his shoulder with his head.

Mickie brought her hands down from her face and leaned into Cruz. "Now. Definitely now." She smoothed her right hand up his arm and over his tattoo to his shoulder. His tattoo was of a large bird with its wings spread. She wasn't sure what kind, maybe an eagle, maybe a hawk, but whatever it was, it was big, spanning the width of his muscular biceps. It was done in shades of black, which made the intricate artwork all the more beautiful. The initials AR were under the tattoo in curly feminine writing, a direct contrast to the hard, masculine lines of the tattoo. Mickie ran her fingertip over the letters, guessing their meaning. "Avery's initials?"

Cruz looked up into Mickie's eyes as she examined his ink. "Yeah." She leaned down and kissed his biceps, right in the middle of the tattoo. He'd been nervous to show her, as the eagle on his arm was the exact same eagle that was depicted on his FBI badge. He wasn't sure she'd understand why he'd felt the need to put Avery's initials on his arm, but he shouldn't have been surprised.

"She'd be honored."

"That's not why I got her inked on me."

"Why then?" Mickie sat up and braced one forearm on Cruz's chest, looking him in the eyes as she did, running her fingertips over his arm. She obviously approved and that made his stomach clench in relief. Not everyone understood tattoos, and while he wasn't covered in them, this one meant everything. It was who he was, what he stood for. She might not understand that right now, but it still touched him that she seemed to understand the tattoo had a deep significance for him.

Cruz realized she'd asked a question. He smoothed her hair behind her ear as he answered.

"To remind myself that behind every victim, there's a family. There are people who love and miss their loved ones. I saw what Avery's family went through. Her brother Sam spent years trying to find whoever killed her. There wasn't anything the police could do for Avery, but they owed it to her family to investigate and find the person who'd killed her, not make her brother spend a lot of his life doing it.

That's why I have her initials there. To remember. I might only be in security, but I try to remember that what I do can make a difference in people's lives." Cruz tacked the last part on...feeling it was lame, but trying to link it to what Mickie thought he did for a living.

"I have something to say, but it's inappropriate as hell."

Cruz blinked at Mickie's seemingly abrupt change in topic. "Okay. Go for it."

"Even knowing why it's there and what it represents...I gotta say, all it makes me want to do is rip the rest of your clothes off and fuck you right here, right now."

Cruz felt himself grow even harder, if that was possible, at Mickie's words. "Yeah?"

"Uh huh. I typically don't like tattoos. But yours? Combined with your body? Oh yeah. It works for you, Cruz. It most definitely works."

Cruz smiled and tightened his hold on her hips. "I've showed you mine. Gonna show me yours?"

Misinterpreting him on purpose, Mickie said, "I don't have any tattoos."

"You've got other things I wanna see. Better things."

Thinking about what he would see when her shirt and pants came off, Mickie bit her lip nervously.

"Don't even, Mickie." It was as if Cruz could read her mind. He brought one hand up and tugged her lip out of her teeth. Then he ran his fingers down her chest, not lingering at the hard nipple he could feel as he went, until he reached her hip again. He ground her against his stomach and sat up, bringing her with him.

Mickie slipped down so she was straddling his lap again. Cruz held her hard against him, making sure she felt how much he needed her.

"Hang on, I'm moving this to my bed."

Mickie squealed as Cruz stood and she grabbed his shoulders, tightening her legs around his waist so she wouldn't fall.

Cruz stalked down the hall, groaning as he felt Mickie's heat against his erection. She squirmed against him as he walked. He kicked open his bedroom door and made a beeline for his bed. He dropped Mickie on her back and immediately caged her in as he came down over her.

"Scoot up."

Mickie did as he asked and he continued, "Don't be nervous, Mickie. You have no idea how much I've wanted this, wanted *you*. Ever since I sat across from you in that restaurant that first day, I've dreamed of seeing you naked and getting my hands on you. I admit, I've thought about your nipples...I can already see they're extremely sensitive."

Mickie glanced down and clearly saw the outline of her nipples against her shirt, even through her bra. She'd always cursed her big nipples and how they were continuously embarrassing her, but now, seeing Cruz look down at her as if he couldn't wait to lick her all over, she wasn't embarrassed at all. She arched her back, urging Cruz on.

Cruz swallowed hard and ran the tip of his finger lightly over her nipple, feeling it bead even more at his touch. "Your curves are sexy as hell. I can't wait to dig my fingers into your hips as you take me. I'm hard everywhere. I want a woman who's soft and can take what I have to give. Can you take it, Mickie? Can you take me as I am?"

"I can take you, Cruz. God, can I take you."

"Thank God. I've jerked off to the thought of you more than I did when I was a teenager. Don't make me wait. Please. Show me what you've got under there, Mickie."

CHAPTER 12

MICKIE HAD no idea what had come over her, but she wanted nothing more than to rip off her clothes and be naked for Cruz. The thought of him masturbating when he imagined what she looked like was overwhelming. She reached down to her pants and undid the button of her jeans.

Cruz caught her hands in his, stopping her.

"I thought—"

"Oh, I want you naked, have no doubt, but I want to do it my way."

"Then hurry up, Cruz!"

"Slow. My way is slow."

"I hate slow," Mickie complained with a pout.

Cruz chuckled, somehow knowing she'd say something like that. "You'll love it by the time I get done with you."

Mickie groaned and put both hands above her head

and sighed dramatically. "Let me know when you're done down there."

Cruz laughed again, not remembering the last time he'd had this much fun while making love to a woman. "Much obliged, ma'am. Just close your eyes and forget I'm here then." Not looking up to see if she'd done what he asked, Cruz leaned in and put his nose against her belly, nudging her shirt up until he was nuzzling against her skin. He inhaled deeply.

"What are you doing?" Mickie asked nervously, shifting under him.

Cruz held her hips tightly with his hands, silently asking her to be still. "You smell amazing. You're so wet for me. I can smell your arousal. That, along with whatever soap or lotion you've used, is a fucking aphrodisiac."

"Cruz—"

Whatever Mickie was going to say was cut off when Cruz moved quickly and unzipped her jeans. He shifted his head down until his nose was right over her mound. His hand pressed against her panties once, then his nose was there again.

"Cruz!" Mickie exclaimed, trying to push his head away.

"Easy, Mickie," Cruz murmured. "It's okay. I'm going to spend quite a bit of time here, you might as well get used to it."

Mickie giggled nervously and lay back again. "I still say fast is better."

Cruz did pick up his head at that. "You'll change your tune, sweetness, just give me some time."

Mickie just shook her head at him.

Cruz lowered himself and inhaled her unique scent once more. He hadn't been lying to her earlier. He'd jacked off to the thought of her body, of having her under him, of her scent, more often than even Cruz was comfortable admitting. It wasn't just lust, although there was a healthy dose of that; it was more. He admired her, and he knew, just *knew* she wouldn't want to be anywhere near him once she learned everything about his assignment. She was too loyal to her family, to Angel, to be able to forgive him. He might only get one shot at this, at having her, and he wasn't unselfish enough to do the right thing, to let her go.

He'd debated over and over whether he should pursue anything with her, even after his pep-talk to himself in the car. But sitting next to her on the couch, listening to her giggle and quote *Beverly Hills Cop*, had tipped the scales for good. He couldn't stay away from her. Cruz needed her.

He moved his hands until they were under her and lifted her pelvis into the air. "Push your pants down, Mickie. My hands are busy."

Obviously thinking he was getting on with it, Mickie hurried to do as he asked. She pushed her jeans down as far as she could reach. After she toed off her sneakers, Cruz lowered her hips back to the bed and finished taking her jeans off. She lay under him now in her panties, still covered from the waist up.

Cruz looked down at her. She was wearing a pair of gray cotton undies.

Seeing Cruz eyeing her underwear, Mickie apologized. "I'm sorry they aren't sexy, I didn't—"

"Not sexy?" Cruz interrupted, looking up at Mickie incredulously. "Are you kidding me? I've never seen anything sexier."

"Cruz, I'm a sure thing here. You don't have to lie."

"I'm not fucking lying, Mickie. Jesus, you have no idea." Cruz shifted and ran the index finger of his right hand down from her belly button to her anus, over her panties, and then back up. With the other hand, he pulled the cotton tight until it outlined her crease.

Mickie could feel herself grow even wetter at his actions. She clenched her inner muscles, wanting and needing more.

"No, you aren't wearing silk, and it's not a thong, but what I've got in front of me is a hell of a lot sexier than anything I've *ever* seen before." Cruz leaned down as if inspecting her, and he inhaled deeply. "Your panties are light gray. That means as they get wet, they turn dark gray." He ran his fingertip over her folds once more. "And right here, right now, they are so dark gray, they're almost black. You're soaked, Mickie. And getting wetter right in front of my eyes. There is nothing, and I mean nothing, sexier than that. Knowing you want me? That you're enjoying my touch and my words? Nothing. Fucking. Sexier."

Mickie whimpered. "Oh my God, Cruz. Seriously. Please, I need you."

"And you'll get me, Mickie. You think I'm not taking you after seeing how wet you are for me? Smelling how excited you are? No fucking way. But you'll get me on my time, not yours."

"I had no idea you were this sadistic."

"Oh, this isn't sadistic, Mickie. This is worship."

"I wish you'd worship faster then."

Cruz couldn't help it, he laughed. "After this, you'll get fast. Guarantee it. But I want to savor you. I want to unwrap you slowly, learn exactly what you like and how you like it. There'll never be another first time for us. I want to savor it. Now, lay back and enjoy."

Mickie lay back with a huff and Cruz smiled up at her. "You won't regret this, Mickie. Whatever happens in the future, I hope to Christ you don't regret this."

"I won't."

"Promise?"

"Promise."

With that, Cruz bent his head and got to work. He nipped and licked and stroked until Mickie was begging mindlessly. Finally Cruz moved her soaked panties to the side and ran his finger up her folds, with nothing between them.

"Oh my God."

"You have no idea how good you feel." Cruz didn't know if Mickie was really hearing him. She had a light sheen of sweat covering her from his teasing and her panties were literally soaked with her excitement.

"Let's get your shirt off, yeah?"

Mickie sat up so fast and had her shirt off before

Cruz could even help. He laughed as she reached behind her to undo her bra clasp.

Mickie looked into Cruz's laughing eyes and smiled sheepishly. No longer embarrassed about what she might look like because she was so turned on, she told him, "I figured if I didn't get this off before you took over, you'd take another year to get to it."

Cruz didn't bother to respond, his eyes were locked on her chest. "Jesus, Mickie. Your tits are more beautiful than I could have imagined."

Mickie blushed at his crude words, loving them all the same. Having had enough of his slow pace, she brought her hands up to her breasts and lifted them, as if offering them to Cruz. "Large areolas, hard nipples."

Cruz ran his index finger around her right areola, and when she began to drop her hands, he ordered, "Keep them there. I like you offering yourself to me." Cruz looked up at her face when she moved her hands back under her breasts. "And I like that blush too."

Mickie knew she was breathing fast, but she'd never had a sexual encounter like this. With Troy, he'd just climbed on, did his thing, and rolled over. He'd never taken the time to really look at her before. None of the other men she'd been with had ever been this...intense, either. Mickie wasn't sure she liked it, but she certainly didn't hate it.

"Cruz..."

"And I like that pleading tone of your voice too. Hold them there." Not giving her time to say anything else, Cruz leaned over and put one hand under hers on her breast and lifted it higher. He put his mouth over it and sucked. When he heard Mickie's swift intake of breath, he took her nipple between his teeth and nipped. Loving how it got even harder under his teeth, he worked it with his tongue as he sucked harder. It wasn't until Mickie squirmed that he gave in and released her.

He brought his hand up and rubbed her breast soothingly. "You are amazing. I've never seen such big nipples before. It's as if they're begging for me to lick and suck them."

"Please, Cruz."

"Take off your panties," Cruz ordered in a guttural voice. "I thought I could make this last longer, but I have to have you."

Mickie scrambled to do as Cruz asked. He was just as busy getting rid of his own pants. He stood next to the bed, gazing at her. Mickie licked her lips as she stared at his body. His erection was long and hard. He was big—bigger than anyone she'd ever taken before.

She refused to get nervous. She could take him; women's bodies were meant to stretch around a man's. She reached out for Cruz.

Cruz forced himself to stay still as Mickie's hand gripped his cock. A bead of semen appeared on the head of his cock and almost fell to the floor. Mickie's hand caught it and rubbed it into his skin as she caressed him. Withstanding her touch for a beat, Cruz took a deep breath. Then, knowing he couldn't handle it much longer, he took her wrist in his hand and put a knee to the bed. He grabbed the other wrist and brought it above her head and pinned her hands there.

"As much as I crave your touch, this would cease to be slow and move quickly to Mach-10 if I let you continue to touch me."

"But—"

"No, not this time. Later, yes. I'll let you explore. I'll even beg you to touch me, to lick and suck me, but not now. Not this first time. Keep them there." When she nodded, he released her and ran his palms down her forearms to her biceps, over her shoulders, over her breasts, tweaking both nipples as he passed them, over her soft stomach and down to her hips. Cruz could see Mickie was breathing hard, and her eyes were firmly on his body as he moved.

Cruz shifted until his weeping dick brushed against her thigh.

"You're wet for me too." Mickie's voice was soft and incredulous.

"Yeah, there's nowhere I want to be more than buried deep inside your body, feeling you snug against me as I take you."

"Then do it already, Cruz. Jesus."

"Soon, Mickie. I'm enjoying myself here."

"Can't you enjoy yourself faster?" Mickie whined, squirming against him as he moved his fingers closer to her core.

"Nope. Not until I taste you."

Cruz reached up suddenly to his pillows and

grabbed one, shoving it under Mickie's hips. "That's better. I can see you easier."

"Cruz…"

He ignored the pleading sound of Mickie's voice and scooted down the bed. He took her bottom into his hands again and tilted her up farther, until his head was directly over her weeping center. He blew against her folds and watched in fascination as she clenched in his grip. "Fucking beautiful, Mickie. I swear I can see you throbbing. Here's the deal—I'm going to make you come for me at least a couple of times before I make my way inside you. I want you nice and wet. If I'm going to take you without hurting you, you have to be soaked and ready for me."

"I'm ready now, Cruz."

"No, you're not. You're wet, but not wet enough. I want to see you dripping for me before I take you. Literally. I want to see your juices coming out of you before I push inside your hot body. Now hush and let me concentrate." Ignoring her cute groan, Cruz didn't mess around, he concentrated on her clit, licking it with a steady pace, then increasing his speed as she shifted under him. Cruz held her close, not letting her squirm out of his grasp and away from his rapidly flicking tongue.

It was only about three minutes later when he felt Mickie come for the first time. He quickly pushed one finger inside her, feeling her inner muscles clench around him. She threw her head back, lifted her hips, and moaned out his name. Cruz didn't let up, but instead kept at her. He lapped at her clit remorselessly, sliding a second finger inside her and curling them upwards so he stroked against her G-spot as he continued his assault on her clit.

"Too sensitive, please, Cruz. Oh my God…"

Cruz ignored her and kept going. Finally after her third or fourth orgasm—it was hard to tell as they were practically nonstop—he eased away from her body. He turned his head and kissed her inner thigh, enjoying her breathy pants and her still-shaking muscles. "*Now* you're wet. You're so wet you're leaking down your ass. You're soaking my pillow. I don't think I'm ever washing it. I want to sleep with my nose buried in it, remembering this vision right now."

"Please, for the love of God, Cruz. Shut the hell up and fuck me already."

Cruz kissed her rosy clit once more, enjoying the jolt of her body as he made contact with the sensitive bundle of nerves, before sliding up Mickie's body. He reached over to the table next to the bed and snagged a condom from the drawer. He hadn't brought a woman to his place in a very long time, but even though he'd never been a boy scout, he was always prepared.

He quickly rolled the latex down his erection and placed the tip against the shiny lips of her sex. "Slow and steady, Mickie," Cruz told her, not looking away from where he was about to take her. "If I hurt you, let me know. But I'm not stopping. No fucking way. I'll slow down and let you get used to me, but I'm coming inside." He looked up finally.

Mickie looked completely wrung out. The short hair on her forehead was sticking to her with the sweat that had accumulated there. Her face was red and she had a rosy blush on her upper chest. Her nipples were hard and reaching toward his ceiling. And her hands. Jesus, her hands. They were still where he'd placed them. She hadn't moved. Even during the orgasms he'd forced her through, she'd had the presence of mind to keep them right where he'd put them.

Cruz suddenly wanted her hands on him. Wanted to feel her clutching him to her.

"You can touch me, Mickie. Please put your hands on me."

Her hands immediately came down from over her head and rested on his biceps. She dug her fingernails in lightly, holding on, and nodded at him. "Fuck me, Cruz."

At her words, Cruz pushed in. The angle the pillow put her hips at allowed him to drag himself along the top wall of her sex. He pushed in an inch, then withdrew. Then he pushed in two inches, and pulled back out until she only had the tip of him.

Mickie raised her hips on her own and took the two inches back. Cruz pulled away again and followed her down as her hips lowered. He gained another inch and waited. When she pushed up impatiently, he pulled back, teasing her.

"Cruz, for God's sake—"

Before she could finish her words, Cruz pushed in until he couldn't any more. Then he pulled her hips up, and gained another half an inch. Cruz could feel his balls flush against her backside. They both groaned.

"Okay?" he managed to ground out, not knowing what he'd do if she said no.

"Oh yeah, more than okay." Mickie's fingernails were digging into his upper arms harder now. "I've never been this full before."

Cruz couldn't help but flex against her at her words. God, she was sexy. Cruz had never regretted wearing a condom before in his life. It was automatic to glove up before having sex, but this, this was something different. He wanted to fill her up with his juices. He wanted to watch it slowly leak out of her after they were done. He wanted to soak his pillow, which was still under her ass, and his sheets with their juices.

He shook his head. Jesus, this wasn't permanent. He had to keep reminding himself of that.

He pulled out then slammed back in, loving hearing her moan under him. "Hang on to me, Mickie. You wanted fast? You're about to get fast."

"Oh yeah. Finally. Thank God."

Realizing he hadn't kissed her since he'd brought her into his bedroom, Cruz leaned over, letting go of her hips so he could brace himself over her. He shoved in as far as he could go then brought his mouth down to hers.

He delved into Mickie's mouth, learning what she liked and what she didn't. Cruz sucked her tongue into his mouth and scraped it with his teeth. Then he took her lip and sucked on that. Finally, he thrust his tongue into her mouth and rocked his hips into hers. Kissing Mickie while she took all of him into her was insanely intimate. He'd kissed and he'd fucked, but something about this moment, right now, was more than just kissing and fucking.

Cruz broke contact with her lips and sat up, continuing his assault on Mickie. She smiled up at him. Cruz looked down and saw her breasts undulating with each of his thrusts. His Mickie was all natural and he loved it. He palmed one of her breasts and squeezed as he took her. Knowing she'd need more stimulation if she was going to come again, Cruz ordered, "Touch yourself."

"Wh-what?" she asked in confusion.

"Your clit. Make yourself come one more time. I want to feel you suck my cock in. Do it, Mickie. I'm hanging on by a thread here. I want you to come one more time before I lose it."

Mickie immediately took her right hand away from his arm and snaked it between them until she was touching herself. She rubbed her clit then moved her fingers down until they were caressing his shaft as he thrust in and out of her.

"Oh my God, Cruz. That is so hot."

"Stop fucking around, Mickie. I'll let you watch some other time, but for now, please, do it. Make yourself come."

Mickie didn't break eye contact as she moved her finger up and harshly stroked herself. Cruz could feel her orgasm getting closer and closer. He took her nipple between his fingers again and squeezed it…hard. Harder than he would've if she hadn't already come several times and if she wasn't about to come again. "Now, sweetness. Oh yeah, I can feel it. Squeeze me, yeah. Oh yeah. Fuck!"

Cruz felt Mickie lose it right before he did. He thrust once more and ground himself inside her as far as he could. He saw spots in front of his eyes as he emptied himself into the latex surrounding his cock.

When he finally came back to his senses, he realized he was lying on top of Mickie and she was stroking his back calmly. He immediately rolled over, taking Mickie with him, holding her hips against his own, making sure she didn't lose him in the process of them moving. She ended up sitting astride him. She pushed up and looked down, blushing.

"Wow."

"Yeah, Wow. That was amazing, Mickie. *You* were amazing."

"I think you did all the work."

"No way, it was all you."

Mickie giggled and Cruz groaned.

"When you laugh, I can feel you clench around me."

Mickie stopped laughing and blushed again. "Uh, don't you have to get up and…you know, get rid of the condom or something?"

"Yeah, but I'm comfortable where I am."

"Yeah, but—"

"And you might not realize this, sweetheart, but I can feel how wet you are because it's dripping down my cock and covering my balls and the sheet under-neath us."

"That's gross, Cruz."

Cruz reached up and brought Mickie down onto him. He linked his hands at the small of her back and she cuddled into his chest and he thought about what she'd said. Had hanging around the MC made him cruder and more demanding in bed? Cruz didn't think so. It was Mickie. She brought out all sorts of things in him, the biggest being the ability to be his true self in bed.

"It's not gross, hon. It's us. Sex is raw and dirty and nasty...and completely wonderful. We can wash ourselves and the sheets. We can clean up and be back to normal in a heartbeat. But sharing this with you, sharing our bodies' natural reactions to each other and what we did together? That's fucking beautiful, not gross."

Cruz felt Mickie snuggle deeper, as if she were trying to burrow into him, and it made his heart clench. He tried to memorize the feeling of her in his arms, knowing as soon as she found out what he'd done—or not done, in the case of her sister—she'd look at him with disgust instead of the soft, sated eyes she was wearing now.

Cruz felt her sigh against his chest. "Tired?"

"Mmmm."

"Take a nap then. I don't have to be anywhere for a while."

Mickie began to move, and Cruz held her tightly to him. "Right there, Mickie. I like the feel of you on me."

"I like the feel of you *in* me."

Cruz chuckled when he felt her stiffen. "Didn't mean to say that, did you?"

"No," Mickie said, disgruntled.

"I like the feel of me in you too. Sleep."

"Has anyone told you that you're awfully bossy?"

"No."

"Well, you are."

Cruz merely smiled. He was content. For someone who had spent the last two months in the underbelly of the worst MC the city of San Antonio had ever seen, he was pretty damn happy at the moment.

He hadn't lied. He could feel his come leaking out of the condom and onto his skin and the sheet under him, but he wasn't about to move. He'd get up later. For now he wanted to cherish the feel of Mickie in his arms, sated and warm.

He couldn't remember ever feeling like this after being with a woman. He was usually antsy to get up and out of bed. Not with Mickie. He laughed lightly, hearing Mickie's soft snores. She was adorable, even when asleep.

Cruz tightened his arms and leaned up and buried his nose into her hair. He tried to memorize her smell, knowing he'd be back in the pit of hell soon enough.

CHAPTER 13

BUBBA SHOOK hands with Axel as he delivered another shipment of drugs. Cruz, Kitty, Camel, Vodka, and Roach stood next to them as they discussed their future business.

"We down for another delivery next week?" Bubba asked.

"So soon? Fuck, man. Not sure I can make that happen," Axel told him, running his hand over his head.

"Fucking make it happen. Ransom wants that shipment."

"He better watch himself, you know Chico Malo won't like Ransom overstepping."

"Fuck that. If Chico Malo isn't enough of a bad fucking boy to deal with a little competition, then he doesn't deserve to be in the business."

Axel shook his head. "Dios mío, Bubba. You have no idea what he can do."

"Doesn't matter, man. If Ransom wants his shipments, he's getting his shipments. We can do business with *you* or find someone else."

Axel put up his hands. "Calm the fuck down, man. I'll see what I can do. I'll talk with Chico Malo. You know he only supplies who he wants, when he wants, and if he thinks you're trying to take over this area, it's not going to go well."

"You talk to him then. Ransom will be waiting, but tell him not to take too long." Bubba turned his back on Axel, a serious diss, and headed for the van.

"Fucker," Axel murmured under his breath.

Without a word, Vodka took a gun out of his back waistband and pistol whipped Axel. The man was on the ground, bleeding and disoriented, before anyone could move.

Bubba turned around, nodded at Vodka's action, spit on the ground and continued to the van. Camel and Kitty followed him, unconcerned about Axel. Cruz and Roach approached Axel, who was now sitting up— Cruz because it was expected, and Roach because he wanted to get his licks in as well.

Roach coldcocked Axel with his fist and Cruz could tell he'd broken the man's nose. Blood poured out and dripped down Axel's face. Everyone knew if Axel wasn't half conscious he'd be using the pistol they could see in the waistband of his pants, but he currently made for an easy target.

Roach laughed as Vodka leaned down to Axel. "There is no 'see what you can do' when it comes to what Ransom wants, motherfucker. If Ransom says he wants more drugs, you'll fucking get him more drugs. Got it? You don't want to be on Ransom's bad side."

Roach kicked the man, aiming for his kidneys. Knowing it'd look weird for him just to stand there and watch, Cruz aimed a kick at the man as well, trying to avoid anything vulnerable. Vodka watched as Cruz and Roach beat the man on the ground until he wasn't even flinching from their blows.

"That's enough. Let's get the fuck out of here." Vodka spit on Axel's bloody body as he passed, and Roach and Cruz did the same thing.

As the group traveled back to the clubhouse, Cruz thought about what he'd just found out. Chico Malo was the man in charge of a large criminal empire in Mexico. He was on the FBI's most wanted list for the amount of drugs he was importing into the States, as well as for the alarming number of bodies that were found in his part of Mexico.

The Mexican drug lords sometimes gave themselves innocuous nicknames, knowing the dichotomy between the cutesy names and what they did would freak people the hell out. In Chico Malo's case, it definitely worked. He might be called the "Bad Boy," but everyone knew he was no boy. He was one bad motherfucker, and no one had the guts to go against him. Ransom was insane for drawing a line in the sand and getting the attention of the notorious, dangerous, drug dealer.

But this could be the proof the FBI needed to nail Chico Malo. He'd had no idea Axel was dealing directly with the notorious Mexican drug lord. Oh, he and the FBI had had Chico Malo in their sights for years, but if they could catch him in the act and get proof, it'd go a long way toward trying to get the "legitimate" Mexican officials to do something.

If Axel was scared of the man, that was saying something. Axel was a dangerous drug dealer in his own right. If Ransom thought he could take over Chico Malo's empire and become a big fish in the drug world, Cruz knew he was sadly mistaken. Ransom was a big fish in his own small pond here in San Antonio. He wouldn't last a day in the Bad Boy's sandbox.

Cruz needed to get the intel to his boss as soon as possible. He had no idea when a confrontation was going to happen between Chico Malo and Ransom, but he knew it was coming. There was no way the Mexican drug lord would take the threat from Ransom lightly. Iron control, it was how all drug lords kept on top... that, and killing off their competition.

Cruz felt his phone vibrate in his pocket at the same time the ring tone sounded. He was loath to take it out in front of the others, but he had to. It could be Ransom or any of the other MC guys. It'd be suspicious if he didn't answer.

He pulled the phone out of his pocket and felt his stomach drop when he saw it was Mickie calling. She hardly ever called him. She usually texted.

He began to put the phone back into his pocket so he could call her back later when Roach said, "Why don't you answer it, Smoke?"

Not having a ready excuse and knowing it'd look weird if he didn't answer, Cruz merely shrugged. "Didn't want to bother you all with a conversation with my latest pussy, that's all."

Realizing he was making a mistake and there was no way this call could go well, but feeling pressured to answer, Cruz clicked to pick up the call.

"Yo."

"Hey, Cruz. I was wondering if you wanted to get together tomorrow? I have to work, but we could meet for lunch."

"Can't."

"Oh, okay. Tomorrow night maybe?"

Cruz could hear the confusion in Mickie's voice. She'd gone from happy and bubbly to uncertain, and all it took was one word from him. Cruz wished he could fucking kill all four men who were now openly listening to his conversation.

"Nope. Can't then either." Cruz tried to keep his part of the conversation short, in the hopes Mickie would end the call before he said something she couldn't forgive him for.

Before Mickie could say anything else, Camel called out, loud enough for Mickie to hear, "You need some dick, baby? I've got some, say the word, *beg* for it, and I'll be right over!"

The other men laughed, loudly.

"Uh…I guess I called at a bad time."

"Yeah, I guess you did."

"He's fucking busy, bitch! Leave him the fuck alone.

If he wants your pussy again, he'll come to you. Now hang the fuck up already." That was Vodka. He was a hard bastard and never pulled any punches.

Cruz heard Mickie's inhalation. Her voice was wobbly as she said softly, "I just wanted to let you know how much I enjoyed today. That's all. Sorry to have bothered you."

Cruz clicked off the phone at hearing the dial tone. Fuck. Double fuck. He knew Mickie was probably remembering how she'd begged him to fuck her and most likely thought he'd blabbed about it to his "friends."

He didn't have to fake the scowl on his face as he turned to Vodka. "Thanks a lot, asshole. Now I'll have to work double-time to get back in there."

"Fuck it, man. No pussy's worth that."

"It is when I'm not allowed to have club pussy." Cruz knew he was treading on a thin line with that statement, but he couldn't let Vodka think he could push him around.

"I could talk to Ransom about that."

"Whatever, man. Ransom isn't going to let prospects fuck club pussy, and you and I both know it. Just shut the fuck up about it already."

Bubba laughed. "I'm sure you can make it up to the bitch later. After we get back and let Ransom know what went down tonight you can go to her, make her suck your cock and she'll be begging for you to give it to her again."

Cruz hated that he grew hard at Bubba's words. It

wasn't his words, *making* someone take him in her mouth didn't do anything for him...at all, but remembering how Mickie *had* begged him to fuck her that got to him; that and the thought of her on her knees sucking him off. And that made him remember her smell, the feel of her clenched around him, and how she'd blushed when they'd finally gotten out of bed that afternoon and she'd looked at the huge wet spot they'd left on the sheets.

Seeing his erection and misinterpreting the cause, Bubba sneered, "Liked that, huh? There's hope for you yet, Smoke."

Cruz just lifted his chin in response and kept quiet. He tried to think about anything but Mickie in his bed, at least until he could get the hell out of the MC clubhouse that night. Then all bets were off.

They pulled into the warehouse district and climbed out of the van after Kitty stopped at the back loading dock. They all headed inside to report back to Ransom about Chico Malo and Axel.

The only thing Ransom said when Bubba told him what Axel had warned was, "He's not the only supplier around here. If he wants to get into a war on my turf, he'll get a fucking war."

Cruz mentally shook his head. What a conceited asshole. There was no way Ransom would win a war against Chico Malo and his thugs.

"Oh, and Smoke here wants a piece of club pussy," Roach teased.

"No fucking way," Ransom growled. "Club pussy is

just that, *club* pussy. When you've proven you're a part of this MC, you can have club pussy. Until then, keep your dick in your pants."

Everyone laughed and Cruz scowled at Roach.

"He's just pissed because the bitch he's screwing called and got upset," Bubba explained after they'd stopped laughing.

Cruz's gut clenched at Bubba's words. He didn't like to hear Mickie referred to as "the bitch," even if Bubba didn't know who he was talking about.

"I got it, Smoke," Ransom said seriously. "Angel's bitch-face sister is still on her case. Why don't you fuck *her* to get her off her sister's back? We need that money to expand business. I'm not going to lose it at this stage in the game to some cunt who has mommy issues."

If Cruz thought he was tense before, it was nothing to how he felt now. Every muscle in his body clenched and it took everything he had not to jump the man and beat the shit out of him. Luckily, before he could do something stupid, Roach chimed in.

"Yeah, although you'll have to close your eyes. Heard she's short and fat. But I guess pussy is pussy, right? You could always do her doggy style, then you wouldn't have to look at her."

"I'm not fucking the sister because you want to get her out of the way," Cruz said shortly, forgetting for a second the role he was playing.

Ransom was out of the chair he'd been sitting in and had punched Cruz in the face before he could defend himself.

Cruz immediately picked himself off the floor, ignoring the throbbing coming from his face. Ransom threw a mean punch.

Knowing hitting the president of the club back was tantamount to suicide, Cruz controlled himself... barely. He clenched his teeth and bit back the angry response on the tip of his tongue.

Ransom sat back down as if he hadn't just punched Cruz. He calmly said, "If I tell you to fuck someone, you'll do it. Loyalty to One, or have you forgotten already? Don't think for a second, Smoke, I don't have my eyes on you. You're new here. I don't care if one of Snake's boys vouched for you. I don't trust anyone, and that goes double for prospects. I was only half kidding anyway. I don't think that bitch of a sister of Angel's even *likes* cock. She's probably a muffer."

Cruz forced himself to stay calm and not lose his shit. It was better Ransom thought Mickie was a lesbian. Maybe that way he wouldn't order any of the other members to get it on with her to keep her out of Angel's business. Cruz knew, as well as everyone standing around, that if Ransom ordered someone to fuck Mickie, they would, no questions asked, whether she was willing or not.

"I'm loyal, Ransom, but I'll find my own pussy, thank you very much."

"Just remember what I said, Smoke. You're loyal to *me*, or you'll be loyal to no one ever again."

Cruz nodded once and turned and left. As a threat, it was pretty impressive. Cruz knew that however this went down, he'd have to make damn sure Ransom and the rest of the club had no idea he was undercover. They'd spend the rest of their lives trying to take him down, along with anyone he cared about.

He couldn't handle being around anyone in the club anymore. Each day it was getting harder and harder, and now that he had the information he needed, Cruz hoped like hell his stint with the MC would be coming to an end.

After he spoke with his boss, he had to figure out how to make it up to Mickie. They'd had an incredible afternoon, and he prayed it hadn't been ruined with one short phone call.

CHAPTER 14

MICKIE BLEW her nose and tried to think objectively about what had happened yesterday. She'd called in sick today, knowing there was no way she'd be able to deal with disgruntled customers complaining about how much it cost to fix their cars.

When she'd heard his friends during their call yesterday, it was obvious he'd told them all about what they'd done. Intellectually she knew men talked with each other about stuff...especially sex. But she hadn't expected Cruz to be as crude as he'd been.

The short conversation didn't make any sense with what she knew about him. He was in security. He had the initials of a long-ago murdered little girl on his arm. He told her he wanted to do what was right for the families of crime victims. It all was a confusing mash of memories in her brain. The man she'd spent the afternoon with didn't mesh with the one she'd talked to on the phone. Who would hang out with the

183

kind of men who'd use such harsh language and brag about…fucking…loud enough for someone they didn't know on the other end of a phone line to hear? Were those the coworkers he was going to talk to about the MC?

But ultimately, it was Cruz's behavior that hurt her more than any words the other men had said. She'd thought they'd made an honest connection. She'd never been so uninhibited and passionate—and he'd gone and bragged about it.

He'd sounded so different, ugly. Mickie had never heard him talk to her in that tone of voice before. It made her feel…small.

Well, fuck him. She wasn't going to sit home and sniffle over him anymore. She wasn't taking any crap from a man ever again. She was worth more than that.

Mickie sighed. She knew it would take more than an internal pep-talk for her to get over Cruz. She'd really been falling for him. It was everything about him. He was funny, and interesting, and she'd never known a man so…amazing in bed. That wasn't really the word she was looking for, but it'd do. He'd been concerned about her, and only her. At least until the end and his own orgasm. But to have him make her explode that many times in one go? Incredible, and something she thought only happened in romance novels.

To be honest, she wasn't sure she'd liked Cruz's intensity at first. One orgasm was fine, great actually, but when he wouldn't let up, even when she'd told him she was too sensitive...it had been pleasurable, but in a somewhat painful way. She'd seen a video online once where a woman had been strapped down and her boyfriend, or whoever he was, had forced her to orgasm over and over with a vibrator. It had looked painful...and exhilarating. Mickie understood for the first time how that woman must've felt. Luckily, Cruz had stopped after four for her, but she had no illusions. He could've gone on all day.

No. She had to stop.

Mickie got up and took a deep breath. Then another. Fine. She could do this. She'd take a shower then go see Angel. She hadn't talked to her in a few days, so she'd stop in, find out what she was up to, and see if she'd found another job.

An hour later, Mickie was ready to go. She grabbed her purse and opened her door—and stopped dead in her tracks.

Seeing the box on her doorstep took her aback. She nudged it with her toe and felt that it wasn't heavy.

Mickie looked up and down the hallway to the apartment. No one was there. She sighed. It could be another way for the MC to try to scare her, she imagined a dead rat or something being inside, but since it had a large pink bow on it she figured it was most likely from Cruz. Mickie had no idea who else would leave her a present. She picked it up and brought it back inside her apartment. She debated about opening it before going to see Angel. Knowing she'd never been good at waiting, Mickie reached for the bow and pulled and tugged on the top of the box.

It came off easily and she looked inside. Sitting at the bottom was a metal police car. It wasn't anything special, and Mickie was more confused than ever. She picked up the note that was in the box and cautiously opened it.

I AIN'T FALLIN' for no banana in my tailpipe!
 I'm sorry. If you're willing to listen, I'd like to explain.
 Cruz

MICKIE LOOKED BACK DOWN at the police car. She picked it up and turned it around and laughed out loud. Cruz had stuck a rolled-up piece of yellow paper into the little tailpipe on the toy car. *Beverly Hills Cop.* The man was quoting "their" movie. Mickie held the car to her chest and squeezed her eyes shut. She would not cry. She would not cry. Taking a deep breath, Mickie opened her eyes and placed the car carefully back into the box. She read the note one more time and sighed.

She wanted more than anything to hear what explanation Cruz had for what had happened and what she'd heard, but first, she needed to check on Angel. After that, maybe she'd see what Cruz had to say.

Who was she kidding? Of course she'd hear what Cruz had to say about how he'd treated her and about the men he was hanging around with. She wanted, and deserved, an explanation. She might be an idiot for wanting to give him a second chance, but she'd never felt about anyone, even Troy, the way she felt about Cruz.

Mickie pulled up to her sister's apartment, got out of her car and walked up the outdoor stairs to her door, knocked once, and didn't get a response. Concerned, Mickie went to the end of the walkway and looked down into the parking lot. Angel's car was there, so she should be home. It was possible she'd been picked up by one of her friends to go shopping or something, but this early in the morning, it was unlikely.

She went back and knocked on the door again. Finally, after getting no response, she dug into her purse and pulled out an extra key to Angel's apartment. She'd almost forgotten she had it. She and Angel had exchanged keys a year or so ago, just in case.

Mickie pushed the door open and almost gagged at the stench of the apartment. She waved her hand in front of her face. Pot. Mickie would recognize the smell anywhere. She'd learned really quickly when Angel had been in high school what it smelled like.

Even more concerned now, Mickie walked quickly through the apartment, calling out for her sister. Mickie pushed open Angel's bedroom door and gasped at what she found.

Angel was on her bed, dressed in a black skirt so short it barely covered her womanly bits. She wasn't wearing a shirt, but instead had on a bra that covered almost nothing. She had bruises on her sides and around her breasts.

Mickie went to her sister's side and shook her shoulder, relieved beyond belief when she moaned and turned away from her touch.

"Angel, wake up. Are you okay?"

"Mickie? What the hell are you doing here?"

"I was worried about you. Come on, sit up."

"Leave me alone."

"No, now come on, let's get you up and at least dressed."

"I am dressed."

"Uh, no you aren't. You're missing your shirt."

"This *is* my shirt."

Mickie was horrified. "What?"

"This is what I wore last night at the club."

"Oh my God, Angel. What club let you in half dressed?"

"Ransom's."

"Okay, that's it. No fucking way. Come on, we're having this conversation now whether you want to or not. Get up, get a shower and we'll talk afterwards."

Instead of getting pissed, as Mickie completely thought would happen, Angel simply snorted. "You're so pathetic, Mickie. You're such a prude. Swear to fucking God. Okay, fine. I'll get up, take a shower, then we'll talk. Now leave me the fuck alone. I'll see you in the kitchen."

Mickie took a step back. Ouch. Okay, she knew

Angel didn't have a lot of love for her, and she'd heard worse, but still. There was a part inside Mickie that hoped one day they could have a sisterly relationship, but as the years went by that was looking more and more unlikely.

"Okay, Angel. I'll wait in the other room."

"Whatever. Get the fuck out."

Mickie went.

Half an hour later, Angel came into the kitchen looking somewhat better than when Mickie had found her. She was wearing a tight pair of jeans and a white tank top. Her bra was black and Mickie could see it easily through the thin material of her tank. It was skanky and a bit slutty, but knowing she had to pick her battles carefully, Mickie ignored it for now.

Angel crossed the room and went straight to the pot of coffee Mickie had brewed and poured herself a cup. She sat in the chair across the table from Mickie and huffed belligerently while crossing her legs.

"So, you wanted to talk? Talk."

"I'm worried about you, Angel."

"Yeah? What's new? You never think I can do anything, you think I'm an idiot, and you don't trust me."

"That's not true."

"Yes. It is. But I'll tell you something, Mickie. I don't give a fuck anymore."

"Angel—"

"No. You came over here today to talk me out of seeing Ransom again. I know you did. I *like* Ransom.

He makes me feel good. He's a good person. He does a lot of things for the community. He donates to charities for little kids and he even dresses up as Santa for the hospital. He's a lot of fun and he likes my friends. Not only that, but he fucks me hard and I *love* it."

"Angel!"

"What? You're a prude, Mickie. You're in your mid-thirties and you're way past your sexual prime. You have no idea what someone my age likes or wants."

"And you want to dress like a whore and hang out in strip clubs? Is that it? And smoking marijuana, Angel? That's what you want? You want to be a drug addict for the rest of your life? For the last time, Ransom is *not* into you. Let me guess, he's supplying you with weed, right? He keeps you high so you'll do stuff to him sexually? Oh, and let me go even further and guess that he's brought your friends into it too, right?"

Seeing the look on her sister's face, Mickie knew she was on the right track.

"That's it, isn't it? He used you to get to your friends. They're probably shelling out a ton of money to get weed, aren't they?" Mickie laughed with no humor. "I wonder when he's going to get enough of you...huh? Once he has all your friends hooked, he'll probably dump you. He won't need you anymore."

Angel suddenly stood up, knocking her chair backwards in the process. "Shut the fuck up! You don't know anything!"

Mickie sipped her coffee, trying to look unfazed on

the outside, but internally she was freaking out. "I don't? How often have you seen him since your friends have been buying weed from him?"

Mickie wasn't happy with the look that crossed her sister's face. It was one thing to be right, and another to hurt your only sister in the process.

"For your information, I saw him last night, at his club. And tomorrow night he's invited me to his club-house for a big party."

"Uh-huh." Mickie's voice dripped with antagonism.

"And because you asked, smartass, he might have sold us weed and coke but that's not why he's still with me."

"What the *hell*, Angel?"

As if she didn't hear Mickie, Angel continued, "He's with me because I can suck his dick so good it makes his eyes roll back in his head. He taught me to deep throat him and he told me no one has ever been able to take him so deep before."

In a horrified voice, ignoring her last statement, Mickie whispered, "Coke, as in cocaine?"

"Yeah, as in cocaine. It's fucking awesome. It makes everything so much...more. If you didn't have such a stick up your ass I'd let you try it, but I know it'd be a waste of good blow."

"Are you even listening to yourself? My God, Angel. We weren't raised this way. You're using drugs, for God's sake!"

"Yeah, and I *like* it. You have no idea how it feels to have a man look at you like you're the best thing that's ever happened to him. To know that *you* were the one who satisfied him."

"I do know how it feels, Angel, and it didn't take drugs to make it happen."

"Bullshit. There's no way you felt with Troy anything like what me and Ransom have."

Mickie didn't even argue or try to explain that it wasn't Troy she'd felt it with, she had more important things to worry about. "Angel, please, you know taking drugs isn't good. Let me help you."

"Help me? Jesus, Mickie. Get over yourself. I don't want your help, or *anyone's* help. I *like* the drugs. I *like* how I feel on them. Nothing you can say will change my mind."

"How about the effects of cocaine on your body then? Hallucinations, depression, psychosis, heart attacks, destruction of the lining of your nose, your teeth falling out, infertility or brain damage. That's just to name the things I can think of off the top of my head."

"Whatever. You've been watching too many public service announcements or something. I'm *fine*, sister of mine. I can stop whenever I want."

"That's what everyone says," Mickie said sadly.

"Well, I mean it. Now, get the fuck out. Oh, but give me your key first. I don't need any more surprise visits like this one. I feel like shit and I want to go back to sleep. There's that party tomorrow night that I want to make sure I'm in top shape for."

"Party?"

"Yeah, I told you. At the clubhouse. Shit, see? You don't listen to anything I say."

"Angel, you can't go."

Angel laughed in an incredibly mean way. "Watch me. Now give me my fucking key and get out. I don't want to see you again."

Mickie knew Angel well enough to know there was no use talking to her when she was like this. She sadly put the key to Angel's apartment on the table in front of her and stood up. "I love you, Angel. You're my only sister and I practically raised you. I only want what's best for you. I worry about you and I'd give my life for yours, no questions asked. But I can't stand watching you throw your life away. You're smarter than this. I know deep down you know what you're doing is not only wrong, but dangerous as well. Ransom is *not* a good guy. I'm sorry you can't see that, and I hope like hell you will before it's too late. But if not, even if it takes you years, I'm here for you. That's what family does."

"Oh for God's sake, seriously, get the fuck *out*. Don't pull that family bullshit with me. You've always thought you were better than me, and I'm sick of it."

Mickie shook her head sadly and turned to leave. She paused at the front door, hoping Angel would somehow come to her senses.

"Why aren't you gone yet?" Angel walked over to Mickie and pushed her...hard.

Mickie stumbled out the door and almost fell on her ass. When she regained her balance, she looked up at the pissed-off face of her sister. Mickie didn't even recognize the little girl she used to play Barbies with anymore. That girl was gone, and in her place was an out-of-control woman on the path to destruction.

Mickie winced at the loud bang of the door as it slammed shut. She heard the deadbolt click into place and the chain being put on.

Not willing to give up on Angel altogether, no matter that she'd just shoved her hard enough that if she'd fallen it would've really hurt, Mickie thought about what she could do to help her sister as she walked toward her car.

She stopped suddenly in the middle of the parking lot.

If she could get proof of how much of an asshole Ransom was, Angel would have to at least *listen* to her. She wouldn't like it, but maybe, just maybe it would work. It was a long shot, but Mickie didn't know of anything else she could do to get through to Angel.

She walked quickly to her car, trying to think through what she could do. It was dangerous; it wasn't like she was a secret agent. She knew she was acting a bit stupid, but it was either risk it or lose her sister altogether.

Mickie knew Angel was at a crossroads. She'd been serious when she'd told her sister that she'd die for her. She loved Angel. No matter how many harsh words she threw at her, Mickie knew deep down Angel loved her too.

She was betting on it.

CHAPTER 15

M<small>ICKIE READ</small> the text on her phone and sighed. It was the second time Cruz had texted her and she wasn't sure she was in the right frame of mind to listen to his excuses. Angel's words were still rattling around in her head. Her sister could always find just the right, or wrong, thing to say to hurt her the most. Mickie looked down at her phone.

I know you're still mad. Plze let me explain.

She quickly typed in a response to Cruz and threw the phone on the coffee table in front of her.

Today sucked. Can it wait until tomorrow?

Mickie closed her eyes and thought through her plan for tomorrow night. It was risky, but then again, so was what Angel was doing. She sighed as her cell vibrated with another text, most likely from Cruz.

Mickie leaned forward and snagged the phone, looking at the text. It was long, Mickie knew it would've taken Cruz forever to type it all out with the way he hunted and pecked on the keyboard screen.

Yeah. It can wait. But know this, I didn't talk about what we did with anyone. There's no way I could even come up with the words to even try to tell someone else what we did, how I felt with you in my arms. I know it's fast, and we still have a lot to learn about each other, but please don't doubt that yesterday was the most intense, beautiful experience of my entire life. I'll call you tomorrow. Sweet dreams.

"Oh my God." Mickie simply stared down at the screen of her phone in disbelief. Still whispering, she declared to the room, "He did not just say that."

Just when Mickie was ready to completely break things off with Cruz, he went and said something that had her wishing he was there with her right now. Was she being as blind as Angel? Was Cruz playing her as she thought Ransom was playing her sister? She honestly didn't think so, but she supposed it was possible. She hadn't met any of his friends, had only talked to the one woman on the phone during their first date at his place. And how did she even know Mack was really Mack? Maybe it was some skank he'd put up to it. Maybe everything he'd told her was made up…

Mickie sighed and put her phone down next to her hip and rested her head on the back of the couch. It was too much to think about right now. She hated doubting herself. She hated doubting Cruz. She so badly wanted him to be a good guy, but she was confused, and yes, still hurt by what she'd overheard. She'd let his words sink in and call him tomorrow.

As much as she was disappointed in what had happened last night, she wanted to hear what Cruz had to say. She sure hoped he had a good explanation. Even with all her confusion and doubt, she didn't want to give him up.

* * *

AFTER A RESTLESS NIGHT'S SLEEP, which was full of erotic dreams about Cruz, and nightmares about Angel, Mickie got up and showered. She had to go to work, which sucked, but she'd taken the day before off and knew her boss would be pissed if she called off too many days in a row.

She went into the parking lot, relieved to see her car still had four functional tires, and drove to work, thinking all the way about what her next step was with Angel. Mickie headed for her desk, calling out greetings to the mechanics and other administrative employees as she went.

Generally, Mickie liked her job and her boss, but she had a ton of stuff she needed to do, and working wasn't one of them. Sometimes it sucked to be a responsible adult.

Mickie wished Cruz was at the top of her list, but he wasn't. She had to figure out how to show Angel that Ransom was an asshole. Then she had to figure out how to convince Angel that she needed to get off of the drugs she was using and get her into rehab, if she needed it. Once she had that worked out, she could concentrate on Cruz and their relationship.

And that was the thing…Mickie had thought they *had* a relationship, but now she wasn't so sure. Was she a one-night stand to Cruz? Did he really care about seeing her again, or did he merely want to explain why he'd been so cold on the phone the other night and move on? Mickie sighed. She had no idea.

She settled into her chair at her desk while her mind was going a million miles an hour. Mickie started jotting her ideas down on a sticky note from her desk on what she was going to do that night. Angel was going to the Red Brothers' clubhouse for a party? Then so was she. It was a free country. If Angel could party with the MC, so could Mickie.

The phone rang. Mickie took a deep breath to get back into the proper head space for work, and answered.

* * *

OKAY, Mickie knew she was officially crazy. She was standing in her apartment, looking at herself in the mirror. After work, she'd gone straight to the mall and to one of the stores she normally wouldn't ever think about shopping in. It had leather and spikes and all sorts of other clothing that teenagers might wear. Mickie knew if she was going to crash a party at a motorcycle club, she'd better at least try to look like she fit in.

She decided on a pair of jeans that were too tight, but she'd managed to squeeze herself into a size ten. The denim hugged her ass and her thighs and actually didn't look too bad, if Mickie did say so herself. The jeans were cut so that the extra weight she carried around her waist didn't spill over the top. They were so low, Mickie kept looking back to make sure her ass crack wasn't showing. It wasn't. Barely.

The top was harder to decide on. Mickie figured black was the safest color to wear, and so she'd bought a push-up bra that literally squeezed her boobs together higher than they'd ever been squeezed before, and a short-sleeved shirt that had mesh on the upper part and was solid below.

Mickie tilted her head and eyed herself critically. This was the most provocative thing she'd ever worn, and to think she was going to wear it to a party where there were drugs, bikers and, most likely, prostitutes, was completely unbelievable.

She wiped her sweaty hands down her thighs. The deep vee of the shirt's plunging neckline showcased her breasts in the tight bra. The mesh was actually really sexy and allowed her to show off her boobs, while the regular material hid her less-than-flat belly.

Mickie snorted. As if anyone would be able to look at anything other than her boobs. They were hard to ignore in the outfit. Her C-cup breasts were looking more like double D's.

Mickie took a deep breath and immediately regretted it. She actually watched in the mirror as her nipple popped over the top of the bra and got stuck in the mesh that was covering it. She giggled nervously, and adjusted herself so she was adequately covered again. She made a mental note. *No deep breathing.*

Mickie had spiked her short hair up and even added a streak of pink along the side with temporary dye. She had no desire to walk around looking like a punk rocker after the night was over. She felt like enough of an abnormality as it was, but if she came to work with that bright-pink streak, her boss would have a heart attack.

She had applied makeup to her eyes with a heavy hand. Her mascara and eyeliner were caked on and she had eye shadow up to her eyebrows. Hating lipstick, but knowing it'd complete the look, Mickie had chosen a dark-red shade that even she had to admit made her look mysterious, and yes, sexy even. Mickie thought she looked about as ready as she was going to.

The last thing she needed was her phone. Mickie didn't have any kind of special recording devices that women always seemed to have access to in the movies and television shows. It'd be handy to have a pin or something she could wear that would record everything she saw, but since she was flying by the seat of her pants here, and not dating James Bond, she'd have to rely on her cell phone, which was kind of a crapshoot.

She set it to the camera mode and clicked it to video. She'd practiced the best place to stash it and finally settled on her back pocket. The jeans were so tight it would keep the phone still, and Mickie could put it halfway in her pocket and it would stick up enough so the lens cleared the material. Then all she had to do was turn around and face away from whatever she wanted to film and voila!

Mickie's phone vibrated in her hand, scaring the shit out of her. She laughed nervously and saw it was another text from Cruz. He'd been texting her all day, and Mickie had mostly ignored him. She could tell he was getting impatient with her though.

You gonna call?

Mickie's fingers flew over the screen in response.

Tomorrow

Why not now?

I've got something I have to do

What?

Something

Mickie, I hate this

Mickie closed her eyes. She hated it too. But she had to get through tonight. At first she thought showing up at one of the motorcycle club parties and getting evidence for Angel that Ransom wasn't a good person, would convince Angel to break up with him once and for all. But almost as soon as she had the thought, she dismissed it. Angel knew he was doing things he shouldn't be, and unfortunately Mickie knew in her heart Angel was doing some of those bad things right along with him.

So her plan to "save her sister" morphed into something different. If she could get evidence of Ransom doing drugs, or selling it, or hell, even soliciting a prostitute, maybe she could get him arrested. If he was in jail, he couldn't be around her sister. He'd get out eventually, but maybe it would be a while and in the meantime she could get Angel away from the club and the lifestyle. Mickie was afraid she was losing her sister too.

I'll call you tomorrow

Ok. I have a thing I have to do tonight, but I'll call you in the morning and we'll talk. I'll tell you everything.

A thing?

Yeah. A security job. I'll call you early. Maybe we can get some lunch or something.

Ok

There was so much more Mickie wanted to ask, but she didn't have the time and didn't want to do it over text anyway.

Her phone vibrated once more, but it wasn't a text from Cruz this time. It was Li. Mickie had called her and gotten Angel's friend to agree to take her to the party that night. She had to pretend to be interested in the MC lifestyle and the drugs she'd be able to get in order for Li to finally agree to take her, but Mickie was apparently a better actress than she'd thought, because after only a short while, Li had agreed. Even though Mickie had never hung out with Li before, she'd seen her several times and Li had been pleasant to her.

Whatever Angel's faults were, she obviously wasn't constantly talking about her annoying older sister to her friends. Which worked well in Mickie's favor at the moment.

Here

Be right down

Remembering not to take a deep breath, Mickie once more turned to her reflection in the mirror. She almost didn't recognize herself. Angel would be pissed when she saw her there tonight, but it was for her sister's own good.

Mickie ran her index finger over the metal police car she'd put on her kitchen counter and smiled at the fake banana in the tailpipe. Cruz had a good sense of humor and she hoped they'd get to further explore what they had together.

She gripped her phone in her hand, stuffed her license and some bills into her back left pocket and headed out. She locked her door and then looked up and down the hall. Seeing no one, she awkwardly knelt in her tight jeans and put her key under her mat. Not the safest thing to do, but it'd work for tonight. Better than trying to keep track of a purse or putting the key in her pocket and risking losing it.

Mickie stood up and headed to Li's car. This would work. It *had* to work.

* * *

CRUZ RAN his hand over his head and cursed. Mickie was still pissed at him and he hadn't been able to talk to her yet. He'd wanted to talk to her before the party tonight, but she'd been at work for most of the day, and then she'd flatly refused to let him explain after. Cruz knew something was up, but he had too much other shit going down to be able to devote his complete attention to Mickie. As much as he hated that, it was true.

After the meeting with Axel the other night, and learning Chico Malo was the supplier behind Axel and the Red Brothers, Cruz had contacted his boss at the FBI. Knowing there was another large party at the clubhouse, which would be a great distraction, the takedown was planned for that night.

After the party got started, the FBI, with assistance from the Texas Rangers and SAPD, would surround the warehouse and take down Ransom and the rest of the members of the club. It was a huge operation, especially because of the amount of MC members that would be at the party and the danger involved.

Cruz didn't like it. He knew Angel would be there tonight, along with her friends, not to mention the old ladies and club whores. There were so many things that could go wrong; it was almost a suicide mission to try to take down the club as quickly as the FBI was moving, but it was out of Cruz's hands. He was somewhat surprised at the speed of the operation, but also secretly thrilled. The FBI had been after Chico Malo for a long time, and the connection between the Red Brothers and the Mexican drug lord was an added bonus to the op.

Cruz didn't care why they were mobilizing so quickly, just that they were. The sooner he could end this mission, the faster he could come clean with Mickie and see if she'd be able to forgive him. He hoped they could continue their relationship after everything was out in the open, but he'd even be willing to start from scratch if that's what she needed

The plan was for the agency to take Cruz into custody along with the rest of the club, to try to alleviate suspicion that he was undercover. Once the dust had settled and everyone had been hauled off for interrogation and incarceration, Cruz would be able to sneak out and disappear.

This was the biggest party Ransom had thrown with Angel and her friends since he'd started playing her. Bubba had been busy supplying all of her friends with both weed and cocaine. The women had begun to contact Bubba themselves, instead of going through Angel. Ransom's plan had worked like a charm, and he no longer needed to keep stringing Angel along. He had her friends right where he wanted them, and she wasn't necessary anymore.

Cruz knew Ransom was planning on getting rid of Angel at some point during the party that night. He'd had enough of her "hanging on him" and was cutting her loose. He planned to make it very clear if she retaliated by taking her friends with her when she left, she'd regret it.

He was glad, on one hand, that Ransom was going to finally make the break with Angel, but didn't like to think about what Roach or any of the other members would do afterwards. Cruz was sure they were all dying to get their hands on her. If she was high on cocaine when Ransom scraped her off, there was no telling what she'd do to try to get back at him.

Cruz sighed. His "simple" undercover operation was anything but. It was fucked up ten ways to Sunday and all he wanted to do was hide in his apartment, in his bed, with Mickie.

"What's up your ass, Smoke?" Camel demanded, walking into the large room. "Still pissed you can't tap any of that?" He gestured to the other side of the room where Ransom was currently taking one of the club whores—Cruz thought her name was Billie—up the ass while several other members stood around with their gazes locked on the tableau in front of them, waiting for their president to finish so they could take their turn with the coked-out whore.

"Fuck no. Just ready for the party to start." Cruz took a swig of the beer he'd been nursing for a while and waited for Camel's response.

"Word is some of the prospects will be voted in tonight."

Cruz knew Camel was fucking with him. He simply nodded.

"What? Not curious if it's gonna be you? Don't you want it?"

Playing his part, Cruz answered, "Fuck yeah, I want it. Wouldn't fucking be here if I didn't. But me wanting it means dick. Ransom'll let me in when he wants to and not a second before."

Camel nodded in agreement and approval. "Got that shit right."

"When're the bitches getting here?" Cruz was hoping Angel's friends would be late and wouldn't get caught in the raid.

"Around an hour I think. You hear we have a special guest tonight?"

Cruz turned to him. He didn't know what the man was talking about. "Nope." Hoping his lack of questioning would make Camel open up more, Cruz held his breath.

"Yeah, the fucking Bad Boy himself will be here tonight."

Fucking hell. "Chico Malo?"

"Yup. Heard he was all pissed off at Ransom and his demands. They had some words and the prick decided to head up here himself to see what the fuss was all about. Apparently he and Ransom had a heart-to-heart and they're all buddy-buddy now. Ransom invited him to check out the new rich pussy we've got and to show him why we need more blow."

It was the most Cruz had heard Camel say at one time. He needed to get ahold of Dax and let him know the shit had just hit the fan, big time. It was quicker and easier to contact his friend, and Cruz knew Dax would pass the information on to the FBI and the rest of the team. Having Chico Malo at the compound when they were just expecting to take down Ransom and the club members was fucking huge. It upped the danger factor by a hundred and ten percent—but it would also make their job a hell of a lot easier if Chico Malo was indeed here in their territory and not hiding behind his evil minions across the border. Of course, it'd only be easier if Chico didn't bring his army of thugs with him to the party though.

"Fuckin' A. It's gonna be a hell of a party." Cruz lifted his bottle to Camel in a toast.

"Fuck yeah, it is," Camel responded, then drifted off toward the gang bang that was now happening in the corner of the warehouse.

Cruz stood leaning against the makeshift bar, trying to look as nonchalant as possible. He had a bit of time before the task force would be heading out. He couldn't bring attention to himself. He had to hang out and wait. Discreetly pulling out his undercover cell, he shot off a text to Dax. No one seemed to notice or care what he was doing, since a cheer went up in the corner of the room as Billie whipped off her bra and did an impromptu strip tease.

Cruz observed more people entering the large room. Slowly but surely it was getting more and more crowded. It looked like the entire MC had shown up for the special party. Dixie and Bambi were there, along with some of the stripper whores from the club.

The alcohol was flowing and, at least for the old ladies and the whores, the drugs were as well.

He couldn't help but watch Dixie swallow Ransom's cock as soon as she was led to him. She knew the score. To get drugs, she had to service the president, but she wasn't able to get him off before he threw her away from him and ordered Bambi to bend over the arm of the couch.

Cruz had to give the man one thing, he was always able to get hard. He had no idea how he did it, but he watched for the second time that night as Ransom fucked a whore in front of his MC as they cheered him on.

Finally, Ransom pulled out and jacked himself off all over Bambi's back. She looked at him and smirked. Cruz observed Ransom slapping her on the ass then reaching into his pocket. He pulled out a small baggie and threw it onto the cushion in front of her.

Bambi didn't bother pulling her skirt over her naked ass before she snatched up the bag of drugs. She hurried over to a small table, fell to her knees in front of it and opened the bag. She poured the white powder out on the glass tabletop and immediately leaned over to snort it. She pushed away another one of the women who had come in with her when she tried to horn in on her stash. The woman fell back on her ass as the club members laughed.

Vodka hauled the second woman up with a hand on her neck. He leaned down and said something to her, most likely promising her own stash of drugs if she took him. She nodded enthusiastically, turned away from him, bent and grabbed her ankles, readying herself to be taken.

Meanwhile, as Vodka unzipped his pants, preparing himself to take her right there, Bambi was getting screwed by Tick as she leaned over to snort another line of the cocaine Ransom had given her, not even caring who was behind her fucking her.

Apparently the party had officially started.

Another hour passed and the members got rowdier and rowdier. The old ladies weren't passed around as the whores were, but the members had no problem taking their women in the main room in front of everyone. Even though the old ladies were respected, mostly, by the members of the club, they weren't treated well by any stretch of the imagination. They were expected to fetch drinks for the men, clean up, take the club whores to task when the men decided they needed it, and to service their men whenever and however they wanted.

Eventually, Angel's friends started arriving. Each time one walked into the room, one of the club members would intercept her and take her to the other side of the warehouse, away from the gang bangs, and get her to snort a few lines of coke. It was obviously all planned out in advance. They'd then pass her a joint and a shot of tequila and settle her into a tamer part of the clubhouse, away from the orgy but still in sight of it.

The club needed the money from the women, but

they weren't willing to tone down their lifestyle in the long run. There was a better chance of the women accepting it if they were high than if they weren't. Ransom was hoping the high they got from the drugs was enough for them to overlook the harsher aspects of club life.

Cruz kept Angel's friends in his sights as they started floating from all the drugs and alcohol they'd ingested in such a short period of time. The looks in their eyes reminded him too much of Sophie and how she'd looked at him the last time he'd seen her. He'd gone down to the police station after his friend, Quint, had called him and let him know she'd been arrested for prostitution, again.

He'd wanted to try one more time to get her some help. She'd looked up at him and smirked. "Hey, Cruzie. You here to get me out? Want to party?"

He'd simply shaken his head, asked Quint not to tell him when she was arrested again, and left.

Cruz was sipping his beer when the door to the warehouse opened. He saw Angel's Asian friend—he couldn't remember her name—enter the space, along with another woman, one he hadn't seen before. She was curvy and sexy as all get out. Cruz's gaze went from her hips and chest, up to her face—and he almost choked on the beer he'd been about to swallow.

Roach and Steel sauntered over to the duo and each took hold of their arms and steered them to the other side of the room, as the other members had done with all of Angel's friends.

Cruz's feet were moving before his brain could fully comprehend what he was seeing. He recognized the sway of those hips, the short black hair that brushed against her neck, now with a pink streak along the side...the wide-eyed look of innocence in her eyes.

Fuck. It was Mickie, and she'd just walked straight into hell. They were both fucked.

CHAPTER 16

MICKIE TRIED NOT to hyperventilate as the meanest man she'd ever seen took hold of her arm in a grasp she knew she couldn't break, and steered her toward a corner of the large room. She'd only been able to catch a glimpse of the area before she'd been hauled off, but she knew what she'd seen would haunt her forever.

There were women bent over pieces of furniture all over the left side of the room. Most were completely naked, while some were still wearing some sort of top, but all were being fucked. None were struggling, but none were actually participating either. They just lay there, or stood there, as someone pumped into them. Mickie also noticed, in the quick glimpse she'd had, that there were men waiting to take their turn with the women. They had their dicks out and were cheering their buddies on as they waited.

The music was loud, and the stench in the room

was eye-watering. Body odor, alcohol, weed, smoke, and who the hell knew what else.

Mickie had regretted her stupid decision to come as soon as they'd pulled up. Li had tried to reassure her, but Mickie knew in her gut she'd made a horrible mistake. There was no way she'd be able to covertly film whatever was going on inside the warehouse. She was an idiot.

She'd tried to get Li to let her take her car home, promising to come back and get her whenever she was ready, but Li refused, saying that no one was allowed to drive her car, but her.

Li had driven them to a part of San Antonio Mickie had always avoided like the plague. It was industrial and notorious for always being on the nightly news because of the area's high crime rate. The music was loud even outside the building, and there were no lights on. The parking lot had been pitch-black, and only the light from the small flashlight on Li's keychain had illuminated the concrete as they'd walked to the side entrance of the building.

Mickie tried to wrench her arm out of the hold of the man who was propelling her forward, with no luck. She started panicking—but then heard the last voice she ever thought she'd hear in this hellhole.

"Let the fuck go, Roach, I got this one."

"Fuck off, Smoke. I got to her first. She's mine. When I'm done with her, you can take your turn."

"I said, let go."

"Fuck you. These tits and ass are all mine tonight."

Cruz didn't bother arguing, he simply hit Roach in the face with everything he had.

Roach fell with a thud, and didn't move. Cruz had knocked him out with one punch. No one put their hands on Mickie except for him.

"Wh—"

With the punch, Cruz knew he now had the attention of most of the club members so he had to play the next few minutes exactly right or they'd both be dead. Cruz cut Mickie off and grabbed her arm in the same place Roach had. "Shut the fuck up. Let's go."

Mickie kept her mouth shut. Cruz was pissed and she was scared out of her mind. She had no idea why the other man had called him Smoke, but she knew she was in deep shit. But when all was said and done, she'd rather Cruz have a hold of her than any other man in the place.

Cruz hauled Mickie over to a table covered in white powder. He had no idea how he was going to get through the next few minutes, but knew it was critical they both keep their cool. He couldn't screw this up now. Not when they were so close to shutting everything down.

Dax and the FBI knew Chico Malo was in play and they'd be at the compound within the hour, as planned.

Cruz brought them to a halt in front of one of two small tables and held his hand out to Steel. "Bag."

"Never known you to take such a liking to pussy before."

"Yeah, well, look at it." Cruz gestured to Mickie's tits crudely. "You blame me?"

Apparently it was the right thing to say, because Steel laughed. "Fuck no. I, myself, like Asian pussy." He put his hand over Li's crotch and stroked harshly, ignoring her nervous giggle. "It's smaller and tighter... but can't deny your taste is good."

"Thank you," Cruz ground out. "Bag," he demanded again.

Steel pulled a small bag filled with coke out of his back pocket and tossed it to Cruz. He caught it with one hand and kept the other tightly around Mickie's arm. He felt her squirm next to him and try to pull away from his grasp. "Stay still," he ordered gruffly, opening the bag with one hand.

Cruz could feel the sweat beading at his temple. Fuck. He kept Steel in his peripheral vision; he was bent over Angel's friend, his hand at her breast and his mouth at her ear. Cruz didn't waste any time. He stepped so that he was between the two small tables and, more importantly, blocking Steel's view of Mickie.

Mickie's heart was racing a million miles an hour. She couldn't believe Cruz was here, and had spoken about her so crudely to the other biker. She almost didn't recognize him. He had on boots with enough chains on them to set up a swing set. His chest was bare and he was wearing a leather vest that was open in the front. He was frowning and had at least a day-old beard that made him look scary as hell and Mickie was quickly putting two and two together.

All the times he'd asked about Angel, how he'd magically shown up right after Mickie had argued with her sister. He'd played her. Apparently he was a member of the same MC she'd bitched about all those times they were together. He wasn't going to talk to his coworkers about the club…he was a *part* of it.

She was the dumbest woman on the face of the earth and she was going to pay for her stupidity big time.

Cruz's voice interrupted her mental flogging. It was only slightly less harsh than a few seconds ago. "I'm going to put two lines on the table. When I push you down, breathe out slowly and blow lightly without pursing your lips. It'll spread the powder out to look like you snorted it. Whatever you do, don't inhale. "

Cruz didn't wait for her acquiescence. He poured two short, thin lines of cocaine on the table and closed the baggie and tucked it into his pocket. He put his hand on the back of Mickie's neck and forced her over the table roughly, or at least what he hoped looked rough to Steel and anyone else who might be watching.

He'd put his free hand against her hip, and when he pushed her against the table, he moved the hand just enough so the table bit into his hand instead of her skin. "Snort it, bitch. That's it. You know you came here just for that shit."

Cruz let out a relieved breath when he saw Mickie doing just as he'd demanded. She didn't struggle against him, simply breathed gently on the line of cocaine and it dissipated amongst the other powder residue on the table. She put on a good show, moving her head and cupping her hand as if she was actually snorting the drug. If Cruz hadn't been watching carefully, he would've been fooled.

He wrenched her upward when the lines were gone and hooked her around the neck and backwards, until she was clutching his biceps, much as she'd done the other night as he'd pounded into her. She was arched over his arm, completely at his mercy. Cruz didn't give her a chance to say anything, but covered her lips with his and drove his tongue into her mouth roughly. With the way he was feeling, there was no way he could be gentle.

Cruz kissed Mickie with all the pent-up frustration, worry, and stress he had within him. Even with their situation, and how pissed he was at her for putting herself in the middle of a fucked-up motorcycle club party that was about to get raided by no less than three different state and federal agencies, the kiss quickly turned carnal. Mickie didn't lie in his arms docilely, she gave as good as she got. It was as if the danger surrounding them gave their attraction an extra edge. Their tongues intertwined and they sucked and nipped at each other as they relearned the taste and texture of each other's mouths.

Hearing Steel clapping behind him, and coming to his senses, Cruz finally lifted his head and stared into Mickie's eyes, keeping her immobile in his arms, hanging backwards. There was so much he wanted to say to her, so many things he needed to say, but now wasn't the time or the place. All it would take was one wrong word and they'd both be fucked.

Cruz finally whipped Mickie upright. Keeping his arm around her neck, Cruz turned to Steel. "Fuck yeah," was all he said.

Steel laughed and looked at Mickie's chest as he roughly grabbed Li's breast and squeezed. "When you're done with those titties, I'll take a taste for myself. I might like Asian pussy, but their tits leave something to be desired."

Cruz looked down and cursed under his breath. Mickie's nipples had popped over the top of her low-cut bra and were poking through the mesh tank top she had on. The sight was erotic, and Cruz wanted to gut Steel for looking at what was his.

Mickie looked at herself and gasped. Obviously being held over Cruz's arm had been too much for the miniscule material of her bra. She was totally flashing the scary man standing with Li, and everyone else for that matter. She brought a hand up to cover herself, but Cruz grabbed it and squeezed her fingers tightly. She held back a gasp.

"I don't think I'll be done with these tits for a while, Steel. Sorry." Cruz held Mickie's hand in his own and turned her away from Steel and his fucking eyes.

"I know, Mickie. I know. Hang on, I'll cover you in a second," Cruz whispered the words as he leaned down to her chest to put on a show for the guys sitting in the corner with the other women. He licked up the side of Mickie's neck and nibbled on her earlobe.

"Throw your head back and put one of your hands on the back of my head."

When Mickie hesitated, Cruz ordered curtly, "For Christ's sake, Mickie. If you want to fucking live to see another day, do it. I'm not going to hurt you."

Cruz felt her hand timidly rest on the back of his head, and he died inside as he felt her fingers trembling against him. Deciding to cut this little tête-à-tête short, he moved his head to her chest. Pretending to nuzzle against her, he grabbed the edge of her bra through the mesh with his teeth and pulled it up and over her nipple, covering her again. He did the same to the other side, making her at least mostly decent once again.

He lifted his head and refused to look at her. Cruz couldn't bear to see the disgust in Mickie's eyes. If he could get her out of this fucked-up situation in one piece, he'd take her hatred. He should've prepared for this. He'd known Mickie was scared for her sister. She'd even flat-out suggested that she do something crazy to help Angel...this was certainly that. Fucking hell.

Mickie tried to control her breathing. From the second she'd entered the warehouse, she'd been off kilter. From the sounds and what she'd seen on the other side of the room, to the big scary man grabbing her, then seeing Cruz there and him acting so weird...it was all so overwhelming.

Just when she'd thought she'd been completely wrong about Cruz, she'd finally figured it out.

She'd thought he was going to force her to snort the

drugs on the table, but he hadn't. Then when he'd cushioned her against the table with his hand as he'd shoved her, and finally just now, when he'd covered her so she wasn't flashing everyone, she understood what was really going on. At least she thought she did.

No matter what she heard, Cruz's actions toward her were telling. Cruz was in security, he had a "thing" that night, he hated drugs... While she might not like the words he was using, or how he outwardly treated her, she got it. He *had* to be undercover—and Mickie swore not to do anything to fuck it up for him.

If he wasn't undercover, he was actually a member of this club, but thinking back to everything she'd learned about him...after seeing where he lived...she didn't think that was the case. She didn't like that he'd obviously lied to her, but at the moment, all she cared about was getting out of there in one piece. She'd talk to him later and learn just how much he'd lied about. But as of right now, he was the only thing standing between her and her worst nightmare. She'd keep her mouth shut no matter how awful things got.

For the first time since entering the building, Mickie relaxed. Cruz was here. He'd make sure nothing happened to her. He was one of the good guys, she was betting her life on it.

She glanced around quickly, inwardly wincing at the actions on the other side of the room. She didn't see Angel anywhere, which relieved her, but also freaked her out as well. What if she was in a backroom doing something worse than what was happening out here in the open? No, she refused to believe that. Angel always liked to make a grand entrance, she was most likely trying to be fashionably late or something.

Cruz led Mickie over to the tamer side of the room. He kept his arm around her neck and put one hand low on her ass. There were no open seats, so he simply leaned against the wall and pulled Mickie into his side. He kept her head pushed against his chest. He knew she'd be able to hear his heart beating way too fast, but Cruz didn't give a shit.

"Hey, Smoke," Tiny called from a nearby chair. "Didn't think you were into club pussy, man. Wanna swap when you're done? I'd love to bury myself between those fat thighs—"

"Shut the fuck up, Tiny," Cruz growled, tightening his arm around Mickie's waist. "I'm not fucking swapping. She's mine until I'm done with her, and I don't fucking share."

Tiny just smirked. "All right, but when you get sick of that, you can have some of this." Tiny pulled down the shirt of the woman who was sitting on his lap until her breast was exposed, and he squeezed so hard everyone could see his fingers turn white with the pressure. The woman yelped and squirmed against him futilely.

Cruz felt Mickie shift uneasily next to him. "Turn your head, hon. Don't look." His words were muffled and gruff…and tortured.

They all looked to the door when it opened once more. Angel strode into the room as if she were the

Queen of England and there wasn't a drug-filled orgy going on in front of her eyes. No one stepped up to greet her and she looked around for Ransom.

Mickie tried to pull out of Cruz's arms, but he tightened his hold on her. He wouldn't let her look up at him. "Stay the fuck still. If she recognizes you, we're both fucked."

Mickie held her breath and stared at the scene unfolding in front of her, her heart breaking.

Angel kept searching the room until she found Ransom. He was on the other side of the space, where his club members were screwing the strippers and whores. He was sitting on a couch with two women kneeling in front of him. His pants were around his thighs and the women were taking turns sucking him off, as they, in turn, were being hammered from behind by two other men.

Ransom smirked at Angel and lifted a hand and crooked his finger at her. As if planned, and it probably was, the music abruptly stopped. Besides the sound of sex echoing around the room, it was fairly quiet.

Angel hesitantly walked over to Ransom.

"You want this? On your knees, bitch. Suck me."

"But, Ransom...I don't understand."

"What don't you understand?"

"I thought, we...you... I'm your girlfriend."

"Girlfriend?" Ransom threw his head back and laughed. He held one of the women down over his cock as she deep-throated him. She began to gag, but he still held her. "I don't have fucking girlfriends. What do you think this is, high school?"

He let up on the woman and she pulled her head off him with a gasp, saliva and pre-come dripping from her mouth. Ransom pushed her away and reached for the other woman's neck. He forced her head down on his cock and held her there as he had the first woman.

Angel continued to stand in front of him as if in a trance. It was as though she couldn't believe what she was seeing.

"Why would I want to tie myself to one woman when I can have all of this?" Ransom flung out a hand to encompass the room. "You were a nice change of pace for me, but you were just a fuck, Angel. You'll always be just a fuck. Now be a good girl and go join your friends. Snort some coke, but don't forget to pay for it first, then see if you can find one of my brothers willing to fuck you. I'm sure they'll line up for the chance. After all, they've heard from me what a tight cunt you have."

Ransom allowed the second woman to come up and off his dick, and she coughed harshly as she too gulped in air. Ransom gestured to Angel, "Unless you want to come sit on my dick and get me off first? I'll take that pussy any day of the week."

"Are you kidding me? I'm not going to fuck you after you've probably had your dick in these whores' cunts." Angel's words were acidic.

Ransom laughed mercilessly. "Bitch, there's no 'probably' about it. If you think yours was the only pussy I was getting, you're delusional. I fuck whoever I want, whenever I want, and don't give a shit what *you* want. I like your money. I like your rich friends' money. I like your pussy, ass, and throat around my cock, but honestly, I don't give a shit whose hole my cock is in as long as I get off."

The music started up again after Ransom's harsh words and people went back to what they were doing before his little show.

Everyone laughed as Angel spun away from Ransom and headed to the other side of the room as if she didn't know where she was going. Roach had picked himself up off the floor where he'd landed when Cruz had punched him, and was quick to get to Angel's side to comfort her. Ransom merely leaned back on the couch, smiling as one of the completely naked strippers came up to him and offered to sit on his dick and finish him off.

Mickie mumbled into Cruz's chest, "I need to go to her." She really didn't want to go anywhere at the moment. Cruz's arms made her feel safe in a definitely unsafe world. Even if he agreed, Mickie wasn't sure her feet would be able to move.

"Fuck no."

Mickie squirmed against Cruz, thankful for his answer but feeling guilty nonetheless. "Please?"

"No."

"Problem, Smoke?" Steel asked from a chair nearby. He had Li on his lap and his hand was buried under her skirt. Her eyes were closed and her head was thrown back, obviously enjoying Steel's attention.

"No problem. Bitch just needs a firm hand." Cruz grabbed the back of Mickie's neck and let go of her waist enough so he could bend her over. He held her there with his hand holding her still and the other planted in the middle of her back. He pushed his foot between her legs and spread them so they were shoulder-width apart. She was completely helpless in his grasp. Her head was parallel with the ground now and Cruz leaned over to furiously whisper in her ear.

"Stop it right fucking now. In case you haven't noticed, we're in deep shit here. Keep your mouth shut. Angel can take care of herself. *You're* my concern right now, not your sister. You can help her tomorrow. Do what I tell you, *when* I fucking tell you, and don't bring any more attention to us. Got it?"

Mickie tried to nod, but couldn't. She sobbed once, but ruthlessly held it back. Even though Cruz had a tight hold on her, he wasn't hurting her. His words were mean and harsh, but he was exactly right. Mickie held no illusions about what would happen if someone, anyone, figured out what Cruz was doing there.

Cruz whipped her upright and pulled her into his embrace again, her head shoved against the top of his chest. He held her against him with a hand on the back of her neck and his fingers digging into her side.

"You need any help with that, just let me know," Steel commented dryly. "But it seems you have a good handle on her."

"Yeah. I got this. She's just got to learn to do what I fucking want her to do."

The other MC members laughed, high-fived, and agreed.

When the attention of most of the members went back to the women they were fondling or to their drinks, Cruz relaxed a fraction. Fuck, that had been close. He didn't know what time it was, but watching Ransom push the naked woman off his lap after he came, and pull up his pants, Cruz figured it was about time Chico Malo showed. There was no other reason for Ransom to make himself presentable.

Roach had steered Angel over to the tables covered in coke residue and encouraged her to snort six lines of the stuff. It was way too much, but Angel obviously wanted to forget what she'd just seen and heard, and was just stubborn enough not to leave the party altogether. After she'd snorted the drugs, and downed two shots of tequila, Roach took her to the other side of the room, away from her friends. Cruz figured she went with it because she was trying, unsuccessfully, to make Ransom jealous. The second they were seated, Roach had one hand on her crotch and the other on her breast, but Angel's eyes never left Ransom.

Just as Cruz was working through his head how he could get Mickie the hell out of there before everything went down, the door opened. A tall, slender Hispanic man entered the room, followed by at least ten other men.

Chico Malo had arrived—and all hopes of safely

getting Mickie out of the middle of a turf war between a pissed-off Mexican drug lord and a cocky motorcycle club president disappeared like a puff of smoke.

As the door shut behind Chico Malo and his thugs, Cruz could only silently pray Dax and the rest of the task force would get there sooner rather than later.

CHAPTER 17

"WELCOME TO MY CLUB!" Ransom boomed, striding to greet Chico Malo before he made it too far into the room.

Three men moved so they were standing in front of their boss, preventing Ransom from getting too close to him.

"What's all this? Can't I greet a friend in my own club?"

"Stay back," one of the bodyguards growled, putting his hand on the butt of the gun in his waistband.

"Come on, Chico! Look around. Look at how much fun is being had. You want a woman? A smoke? A drink? Name it and it's yours."

Taking Ransom at his word, the drug kingpin slowly looked around the room. The music had been turned down after his arrival, but the strippers were still undulating against the poles that had been erected for the party, their eyes glassy, and bodies moving to the music. There were a few MC members passed out around the room and more not even bothering to pause their screwing of the club whores to greet the newcomer.

Chico Malo's gaze roamed to the other side of the room where Angel's friends were huddled with various members of the club. His eyes went to each woman, and Cruz's stomach clenched when they stayed on Mickie's ass a bit too long for his taste.

"¿Qué es esto?" Chico Malo asked, gesturing toward the right side of the room, obviously noticing the difference in the caliber of women on that side.

"Glad you asked," Ransom smirked. "That's the high-class pussy side of the room. See, this here's the reason we need to up our stakes in the market. These bitches have money to spend, and they want to spend it on my cocaine. You like what you see? Help yourself. My brothers would be glad to share."

Chico Malo looked back to Ransom and raised an eyebrow.

"Yeah, take your pick. It's the least I can do for a gentleman like yourself. And you know what, if we continue to do business together, you can have all the high-class pussy you want, whenever you want it."

"You don't think I can get it on my own?" Chico Malo growled. "You don't think we have high-class Mexican pussy?" His words were ground out in obvious irritation, his accent making the words seem caustic and biting.

"No, no, I didn't mean that. I just thought that

maybe you'd like to partake in American high-class pussy, to break it up a bit. You know, for variety."

Chico Malo seemed to consider Ransom's words. He smiled and then turned and stared right at Cruz. "I want that one. The curvy one in black."

Cruz tightened his arms around Mickie as she gasped in horror. "No. Oh God."

"No. She's *my* fuck." Cruz bit the words out, his heart hammering in his chest. Dammit all to hell. A bad situation just got a hundred times worse.

"Prospect, you fucking know better than that. You don't *get* club pussy, remember? And any woman who steps foot in my clubhouse becomes club pussy unless she's an old lady." Ransom's words were hard. He waved his hand at Bubba, who strode across the room toward Cruz, determined to do his president's bidding.

"Mickie? What the *fuck*?"

Angel's words rang out across the room. She'd pulled herself away from Roach and was standing near Ransom, on the other side of the group of Mexican men. Her bra had been undone under her tank top and her short skirt was askew, though still covering the important bits. Her voice came out slurred, but still understandable. "Are you spying on me?"

Ransom turned toward Angel for a moment, then looked back at Cruz. "Well, well, well. The prodigal fucking sister has entered the lion's den. Looks like you were doing just as I asked and keeping a close eye on her after all. Bring her here, Bubba. I think we need to give her a proper Hermanos Rojos welcome."

"I said no," Cruz ground out, his teeth clenched. He'd seen what Ransom and the club did to the whores who wanted to be "regulars."

"You don't fucking *get* to say no, Smoke. Everyone in this club belongs to me. What I say goes. If I want to bend the bitch over and fuck her up the ass right here in front of everyone, I'll fucking do it. In fact, now we're *all* going to do it. Give her to Bubba and back the fuck away."

"No way! No fucking way!" Angel screeched at her sister, stomping her feet as if she were ten years old. "Ransom is mine. *Mine*! I'm the one who sucks his cock. *Me*! He sticks his dick in *me*! I'm the one he wants. Why would he want *you*? You're a fat, stuck-up, prissy little nobody! You're just here to fucking babysit me." The drugs and alcohol in Angel's system had clearly made her lose any filter she might have had.

"Angel, shut the fuck up and get out."

Angel, obviously high enough that she didn't care what her former boyfriend was saying, refused. "No!" She stomped her foot again for dramatic effect. "I found the club first. It's mine! Not hers. You can't want *her*. You like fucking *me*."

She turned to the scum of humanity who was standing amongst his henchmen smirking. "And you, fucking Hispanic jerk. You can't have her either. If you want your cock sucked, *I'll* do it. I'm better than she is! She's a fucking prude. Her own husband didn't want to fuck her, he kept his real love on the side and couldn't wait to fucking divorce her ass so he could be with her.

Hell, Mickie probably called the cops before she even got here! She hates this MC. She hates *you*," Angel said, looking at Ransom. She turned back to Chico Malo, "And she doesn't even know you, but she probably hates you too."

Cruz swore under his breath. This was quickly getting out of control. The only thing he knew was that he wasn't going to hand Mickie over to fucking Ransom or a Mexican drug lord. He'd have to kill them first. His mind whirred with every scenario he could think of to get them out of this.

"You can't control your women very well, Ransom. *This* is the example you show me of high-class pussy?" Chico Malo growled, clearly annoyed at Angel's words, and Cruz's refusal to hand over the woman of his choice.

"I'll deal with this, Chico, no worries. Give me a second." Ransom stepped close to the still-fuming Angel. She smiled nastily, obviously thinking she'd won and had gotten what she wanted.

Ransom reached into the back of his jeans and pulled out a large knife. Without a word, he pulled the sharp blade across her neck from ear to ear, with a slow, methodical swipe.

Angel made one startled gurgling noise, then fell heavily to the floor.

Cruz spun Mickie around so that she was facing the wall as she gasped in shock. He stood next to her, holding her tightly with his left hand and partially blocking her with his body. He quickly growled,

"Whatever the fuck happens, do *not* turn around. You got me, Mickie? I'll protect you, but you stay right here and don't watch."

"Angel—"

"You can't do anything for her right now. We'll be lucky if *we* get out of here in one piece."

Cruz didn't wait for her agreement, but turned his attention back to the clusterfuck happening right in front of him.

Angel twitched a couple of times on the ground as the pool of blood around her grew larger and larger. The men standing around were laughing as her body convulsed on the floor at their feet.

"Very nice, Ransom. Didn't think you had it in you." Chico Malo grinned. "Maybe this partnership will work out after all."

"Feel free to fuck her if you want...her pussy'll be warm for at least another thirty minutes."

It was as if Ransom's words broke through whatever spell was on Angel's friends. They suddenly completely freaked out, jumping away from the hands of the MC members who had been holding them and shrieking at the vision of their friend dying on the floor and bleeding out.

Ransom was yelling at his club members to control them while Chico Malo's goons looked on with humor, enjoying the chaos that had erupted around them.

Through the shrieking and crying of Angel's friends, Cruz heard Ransom call out, "Bring the fucking sister over here, Bubba. Now."

Cruz could feel Mickie trembling as she huddled against the wall. No way in fuck was Bubba, or anyone, getting their hands on his woman.

Just as the thought went through his head and Cruz readied to fight Bubba for Mickie, all hell broke loose in the room.

Flashbang grenades went off all around them, and even though Cruz had training on how to lessen the effects of them, his ears rang and his vision went dark from the unexpected explosions. He leaned against Mickie, covering her ears with his hands and crowding her, trying to cover her as much as he could.

The cavalry had finally arrived.

Cruz didn't relax. Even though Dax and the FBI task force had finally made their entrance, he and Mickie still weren't safe. Ransom and Bubba were gunning for Mickie, and probably him too, now that he'd refused to give her up. The MC members had knives and most likely a stash of illegal weapons. The Mexican drug lords obviously didn't want to get caught either, and they were certainly armed to the teeth.

"Crouch down, sweetness. Come on, that's it." Cruz urged Mickie to get as low to the ground as possible. He knew she probably couldn't hear him because of the loud percussion of the flashbang grenades, and was most likely in shock with what she'd seen and what was going on around them now.

He knelt with her and engulfed her in his arms, protecting her as best he could. It killed him not to be out in the fray, helping his friends and brothers in arms ferret out the bad guys and keep them contained, but at the moment all he could think about was Mickie, and keeping her safe. Now that Ransom knew she was Angel's sister, who knew what he'd do to get to her.

There were gunshots and shouts all around them. Cruz knew if they didn't get struck by a stray bullet, it'd be a miracle. He kept his arms around Mickie even as he put his hand on her head to push it farther down, to make her as small a target as possible. He literally put himself between her and the bullets that were flying around the room in the chaos.

When the commotion died down a bit, Cruz took stock, trying to get his bearings. There were several MC members on the ground with their hands on their heads being guarded by officers in riot gear. The women in the room, in various stages of undress, were being herded to a corner. The old ladies right along with the naked strippers and whores.

Most of Chico Malo's men were lying on the ground bleeding. Chico Malo himself was lying motionless on the floor with a bullet hole in the middle of his forehead.

Fuck. The FBI had wanted to take him alive. Cruz had no idea how he'd been killed, but his death would set off a power struggle in the drug world, most likely on both sides of the border, the likes of which hadn't been seen in quite a while.

Cruz could see three officers lying on the ground bleeding as well. Dammit. Although casualties were usually in the back of every police officer's mind, it was always a dark day when it actually happened. Cruz was relieved none of the injured men were Dax or Quint or anyone else he knew.

He looked around the room again—but didn't see Ransom anywhere.

It seemed quiet enough over where Angel's friends were all huddled together, sobbing. There were no MC members around them, but there weren't any officers with them either. It was a crap shoot on whether Mickie would be safe with them, but he didn't have many options at the moment. Cruz put his hand on her head and leaned close. "Go over to the other women. I'll be back." Before letting go, he took her chin in his hand and brought her lips to his. He kissed her once more, regretting everything that had happened.

Finally, without another word and ignoring the pleading look in her eyes, Cruz helped Mickie stand and gave her a slight push in the right direction. She took a stumbling step, then another, before she gathered her strength and headed straight for the relative safety of the group of Angel's friends, crying in each other's arms.

Cruz headed purposefully for the backrooms of the clubhouse, ignoring the shout for him to stop from one of the officers. The officer was either playing his part well in keeping Cruz's undercover status intact, or he honestly had no idea who Cruz was in the chaos of the raid. He didn't have time to stop and figure it out now.

Ransom knew the warehouse like the back of his hand. There was no way, after everything that had happened and everything he'd done, Cruz was going to let him get away. Not now, no fucking way. He knew right where Ransom would be holed up.

It was time to show the president who was really in charge.

CHAPTER 18

CRUZ PROWLED down the hall behind the big open room of the warehouse, intent on finding and killing Ransom. The hell with his oath to protect and serve. The man had murdered Angel with no second thought and had threatened Mickie. Mickie would never be safe if Ransom got away. He knew who she was and he'd come after her. Cruz had no plan in mind other than making sure the man paid for what he'd done and could never hurt what Cruz now thought of as *his*.

He came to Ransom's office. Cruz could hear the officers on the task force continuing to search the building farther down the hall from where he was. Realizing they'd already looked in the office and had found it empty, Cruz eased in and shut the door behind him.

This showdown would be between Ransom and him.

"You can come out, Ransom, it's just you and me."

Cruz waited, knowing the man wouldn't be able to stay in hiding. He was pissed off and had something to prove.

Within moments, Ransom pushed the heavy panel in the floor back and climbed out of the panic room he'd built into the office floor. Not expecting it, but not entirely surprised, Cruz watched as Bubba also appeared out of the hidden room. Bubba being there would make the fight a bit lopsided, but Cruz wasn't backing down now. He was ready and willing to take them both on.

"Hiding like a girl, huh? Figures," Cruz taunted.

"You're a pig, aren't you?" Ransom correctly guessed. "I should've known; you're too fucking pretty to be a real man. Mall cop my ass."

"Took you long enough to figure it out, asshole, but whoops, guess not quick enough I'd say, wouldn't you?"

Bubba growled. "Let me fucking stick him, Ransom."

Ransom held up his hand. "I don't think so. He wants a fight? He'll get one."

Cruz nodded. "You think you're so fucking smart, but your downfall was Chico Malo. Axel knew you were in over your head, he sung like a canary the second he was faced with jail time." Seeing Ransom look at him in surprise, Cruz smirked. "Yeah, we got Axel. He knew Chico Malo would never let him live after he'd been arrested. He wasn't scared of *you* at all, a small-time, wannabe MC president."

Cruz could see the vein in the side of Ransom's

neck throbbing, but he continued, knowing he was getting to the man. "You just couldn't be satisfied with owning the drug market on this side of the city, could you? Your strip club, whores, old ladies…none of it was enough. You were too greedy, Ransom. Once you crossed the line to Angel and her friends, you were done for, you just didn't realize it."

"Angel was a fucking whore, just like all the rest. She took what I gave her and was glad for it. A whore's a whore, even if she's wearing nice clothes. Just like her sister. But Mickie cleans up well, doesn't she? All tits and ass. Guess I was wrong about her being a muffer, wasn't I?"

Cruz refused to rise to Ransom's bait. "You're done, Ransom. You think anyone's gonna do business with you ever again? Your name's been reduced to shit. The second you step foot outside this clubhouse you'll be a giant target for every Mexican drug lord, not to mention your local rivals as well. You're finished."

"I had it all and you fucked it up!" Ransom yelled, finally losing his cool. "Loyalty to One. That *One* is fucking *me*! I was gonna rule this town and you fucked it up. You're gonna pay, Smoke! You're gonna fucking pay!"

"Come on then." Cruz egged Ransom on. It might not be professional, but he'd had enough of this asshole. Cruz felt as if he'd somehow allowed Mickie's sister to be killed. He didn't protect her and he couldn't bring her back now. He hadn't saved her, just as he

241

hadn't saved Sophie. Oh, his ex wasn't dead, but she might as well be.

On top of that, Cruz knew Mickie would never forgive him. After what she'd seen and what Cruz had said to her, about her, that night. He might have lost the best thing that ever happened to him. If he could take down one more drug dealer in the process, all the better.

Ransom leaped forward, a knife materializing in his hand as he attacked. Cruz grabbed the wrist that held the knife and wrestled Ransom to the ground. They flipped each other over, and as Ransom frantically tried to make contact with Cruz's face, or neck, or anywhere, Cruz used his fist to pummel the asshole's face, and wherever else he could get in some licks. He was gaining the upper hand, until Bubba grabbed him from behind and wrenched his arms behind his back.

Smirking, Ransom pulled himself off the ground and wiped his bleeding nose on his sleeve. He spit on the ground before turning to Cruz. "Now what're you gonna do, asshole?" Ransom ground out, throwing his knife from one hand to the other, taunting Cruz.

When Cruz didn't answer, but continued to fight Bubba's hold, Ransom went on, "I'm gonna cut you, pig. Won't kill you though. Just hurt you enough so you can't fight back. Then I'll disappear, but when she least expects it, I'm gonna find the fat sister and I'm gonna steal her ass away. I'm gonna tie her down and fuck her. I'll leave her tied up and I'll fuck her in every hole she's got until she's bleeding and begging me to stop.

Then I'll let Bubba fuck her. Then I'll invite every asshole motherfucker I can find to come in and take her. Then I'll leave her there, tied up and bleeding. But I'll film the entire thing and send it to you, so you can watch it over and over."

Ransom leaned in close to Cruz, who was struggling harder to get out of Bubba's grasp. "And you'll take your last breath knowing it was *you* who did it to her. Do you know why I'm called Ransom? Usually I ransom the girls off. Send videos back to their families, ask for money. And they give it. Every fucking time. It's what I do. Bet you and your pig friends didn't know that about me, did you?"

Ransom laughed. "Drugs aren't how I make my money. Fuck no. The *real* dough is in kidnapping and collecting ransom money. But I'm not ransoming the bitch sister. I'll send you the video, but I won't tell you where she is. I'll tell her you refused to give me the money I asked for to let her go. She'll lie there, bleeding out of every orifice, dying, knowing it was *you* that put her there, and that you didn't want her enough to pay to get her back."

Ransom drew his hand back when he stopped speaking and swung the knife forward as hard as he could.

Expecting it, knowing Ransom was careless in his arrogant belief that he had him right where he wanted him, Cruz lurched to the side—just enough so the blade cleared him, sinking into Bubba's fleshy belly instead.

Cruz easily wrenched out of Bubba's now-lax grip and punched Ransom as hard as he could. The first punch dazed the man; the second knocked him out altogether.

He then turned to Bubba, who was on his knees holding the knife that had been in his belly. He pulled it out and made a halfhearted lunge at Cruz, but fell unconscious next to the MC president when Cruz's boot made contact with his face.

Cruz leaned over, putting his hands on his knees and taking a deep breath. Then another. Then one more. His adrenaline was through the roof. Ransom's words echoed through his brain and he curled his lip in disgust. How many lives had the man ruined? Cruz had always wondered why he was called Ransom, but none of the men in the club had known. His evilness was bone-deep.

He'd been able to visualize what Ransom had taunted him with. He could all too easily picture the look on Mickie's face as she lay hurt and dying at the asshole's hands. It'd been close. Too close. If Cruz hadn't moved quickly enough, or if he hadn't been able to dodge out of the way of Ransom's knife, Mickie would've been right where Ransom had insinuated she'd be.

Ransom had to die, and Cruz was just the man to do it.

He'd taken a step toward the knife lying on the ground when the door behind him slammed open and Cruz spun around, ready and willing to do battle.

Realizing it was the cops, Cruz reluctantly put his hands on top of his head in surrender. The adrenaline coursing through his veins made him want to continue to fight, but these were his brothers in blue. He wouldn't fight another police officer.

"Yeah, turn around, asshole," the officer sneered, slamming Cruz up against the wall. As he wrenched his arms behind his back, he leaned in and whispered, "Hang tight, we'll get you out of these as soon as we can." Cruz was glad the large officer knew he was one of the good guys; he hadn't been particularly gentle as he'd sent him crashing into the wall.

Cruz kept an eye on Ransom as the other agents called for medical attention for the two men. He knew it was probably too late for Bubba; Ransom had obviously hit something vital, because the blood pooling under the man was way too large for a simple stab wound. He hoped he died a slow, painful death.

Cruz was shoved back into the main room of the warehouse and he'd been docile enough, following the directions of the officers to the letter. He had no doubt Dax and the FBI would get to him eventually.

As he was led toward the door, he looked around frantically for Mickie. Where was she? Was she safe? He flexed his hands in the cuffs. Fuck, why'd he let them put the cuffs on him before he'd made sure Mickie was safe? He couldn't help her with his hands behind his back.

Cruz's eyes roamed from the weeping women in the corner of the room to Angel's body...and found

Mickie. She was sitting on the ground next to her sister with one hand on her arm and the other clenched tightly at her side. She looked up as they went by and Cruz could see the tracks her tears had left on her cheeks. Her mascara had run down her face, but it was the look Mickie gave him as he passed that nearly made his knees buckle under him.

Devastation. Emptiness. Despair. Her emotions battered him as if she'd physically assaulted him.

"Keep moving, asshole," the officer griped, playing his part to the hilt, not understanding the gut-check Cruz had just been dealt.

Cruz looked away from Mickie, devastated. He'd done that to her. He'd failed her, just as he'd failed Sophie. Just as he'd failed Angel. He couldn't help any of them now. As much as he wanted to take Mickie into his arms and comfort her, he not only didn't have the right, but he was physically unable.

Cruz stumbled once and managed to right himself as the finality hit him. He'd never have another chance to sit next to Mickie and watch her eat. He'd never smell her again, never feel her hand clasp his as they walked. Never see her laugh as she sat next to him when they watched movies. Never read a text from her again. Never look down at her beautiful face as her warm, wet folds engulfed him.

The officer opened the back door of a cop car and roughly pushed him in. As the door slammed, locking him inside, Cruz turned his head and looked out the window of the cruiser.

It was a beautiful night. There wasn't a cloud in the sky; the stars were shining brightly over his head. As the police car pulled away from the warehouse, Cruz wondered how it wasn't raining. With the way his heart hurt, it should've been foggy and raining.

He closed his eyes and swallowed hard as a tear, the first he'd shed over a woman, ever, fell from each eye and dripped onto his leather vest and slid down the fabric. It wasn't manly, and it wasn't macho. But he couldn't stop those tears if his life depended on it.

CHAPTER 19

Mickie sat on a bench under a large tree, watching as cemetery workers nearby lowered Angel's coffin into the ground and began filling the hole with dirt.

The last week had passed in a blur. After watching in shock as Cruz was led out of the warehouse in handcuffs, Mickie had been pried away from her sister's body by the EMTs who had been on the scene. They'd treated her for shock and had even given her a shirt to wear since she'd been shivering and was obviously not dressed appropriately.

She'd been extensively questioned by the police and the FBI for hours. Mickie had to call their parents and let them know about Angel. They hadn't shown a lot of emotion, but they'd at least had the decency to show up for the service and the funeral.

Angel's friends had been questioned as well, and Mickie hadn't heard from many of them. Li had texted her to let her know she'd started seeing a counselor and was in therapy. Most of the women weren't so hooked on the drugs that they'd needed in-patient treatment, but Mickie hoped like hell they were all getting some sort of help. It wasn't as easy as it might seem to wean yourself off of a drug like cocaine, even though they hadn't been using for a long time.

Mickie allowed herself to think about Cruz for the first time in a week. She'd been busy, too busy to really think about all that had happened. But now, sitting in the fresh air, on a beautiful day that wasn't too hot for Texas, watching her sister being put to rest, Mickie could think.

A part of her had expected Cruz to show up at either the memorial or the graveside service, but she hadn't seen him. Mickie lowered her head and stared at her hands. Cruz. She'd asked about him when she'd been questioned by the FBI and no one seemed to know of him, or at least they weren't admitting it to her. Even with evidence that might suggest otherwise, she refused to believe he was an actual part of the motorcycle club. He'd been too protective that night. Too concerned about making sure she was safe.

Mickie chuckled under her breath. Now she was acting like Angel. Refusing to see what was right in front of her eyes.

She pulled out her new phone and fiddled with it. She'd had to get a new one because the FBI had confiscated her old one due to the video she'd taken.

She'd turned on the video feature right before she'd entered the warehouse that night. It had recorded until her phone had run out of memory. It had caught most of Cruz's words as the night had progressed. The video was shaky and made her nauseous to watch, but if Mickie closed her eyes, she could still hear Cruz's words. Some had been harsh and crude, but it was the others that she clung to in her head.

"Hang on, I'll cover you in a second.

I'm not going to hurt you.

She's mine until I'm done with her, and I don't fucking share.

Turn your head, hon. Don't look.

We'll be lucky if we get out of here in one piece."

He'd tried to reassure her. He'd kept her safe.

Mickie was cried out. She felt like she'd been crying for a week straight, but her eyes welled up once again. Damn.

"Hey, Mickie, right? Can I sit?"

Mickie looked up in surprise to see a petite, shorter-than-she-was, brunette, gesturing to the concrete bench she was sitting on. "Uh…" Mickie didn't want her to sit, didn't want to share a bench when there were several others in the cemetery this woman could sit on. She wanted to be alone.

"My name is Mackenzie Morgan. We talked on the phone…"

Mickie struggled to remember, then suddenly it came to her. "Mack?"

"Yeah. So…can I sit?"

Mickie moved over without thinking and nodded.

"Thanks."

They sat there in silence for a moment before Mack started to speak. "He asked me to check on you, you know."

Mickie knew exactly who "he" was. "Was anything he told me the truth?" Her voice was soft and hitched once, but she controlled it. She got right to the point, needing to know.

"I don't know what Cruz told you, but I'm guessing as much as possible was."

Mickie turned to look at the pretty woman sitting next to her. "I'm having a hard time with all of this. I mean, I like him. I do. But this has all been so…unreal. I'm just so confused."

Mack put her hand on Mickie's leg, showing her silent support. "I'm sorry all this happened to you. I'm not trying to be a pain in your ass. But I know Cruz, and if you could see him now… Okay, will you let me tell you what I know about him? Then you can decide if what you've learned over the last few weeks is a lie or not."

Mickie nodded and waited for Mack to begin.

"Cruz is FBI. He was undercover in the Hermanos Rojos MC. His ex-wife is a drugged-out prostitute, who he didn't know was a drugged-out prostitute until he caught her servicing three men in their bedroom. He feels like it was his fault he didn't realize it or recognize the signs in her. He volunteered for this assignment so he could try to get some of the drugs in San Antonio off the street. He was supposed to find out information from your sister, but instead he met you.

He wanted to call the whole thing off. He told Dax, my boyfriend, that he wanted out, but didn't know how."

Mack took a breath and then continued. "He loves you, Mickie. I'm not sure he's told you, or if he even realizes it, but he does. I've never seen a man so broken in my life. I've only seen him once since that day, and he looked like shit. That was today. He knew you were burying your sister and wanted me to come and make sure you were all right. I don't know what happened last week. Dax won't tell me, and it's not in the papers, but whatever it was…it broke him. He's put in paperwork to be transferred out of Texas. He won't talk about it. Not to me, not to Dax, not to any of his friends. We've bugged him, begged him, annoyed him, and flat-out ordered him to tell us what's going on in his head, and he refuses."

"I don't know what you want me to say," Mickie said, confused. Cruz had been honest with her. Almost everything he'd told her had apparently been true. The security job thing was a bit of a stretch, but technically Mickie supposed being in the FBI *was* security.

"I don't know either. I guess I'm just letting you know how much this has torn him up. If you care, at all, maybe you'll try to do something about it." Mack changed the subject abruptly. "I'm sorry about your sister."

"Me too. I should've done more."

Mack laughed, a humorous sound that had Mickie turning to look at her in shock.

"I'm not laughing at you. I'm laughing because that's

the exact same thing Cruz told Dax when he talked to him last. I picked up the other line in the house and listened in on their conversation."

At Mickie's incredulous look, she said, "I know, terrible, but I was worried about Cruz. He's my friend. I'd do anything for him. Did you know Cruz was the one who found me when I was kidnapped?"

Mickie's head spun with the change of subjects, but she shook it anyway.

"Yeah, he wouldn't tell you about that...typical. I'd died. Taken my last breath. Dead. As a doornail. Dax saw me take my last breath on video and there wasn't a damn thing he could do about it. They didn't know where I was. While Dax was watching me die, Cruz searched the house the bad guy was in, and found a coffin in the basement. The bastard had pretended to bury me alive, but really had me in the basement of his house so he could hook up cameras and watch me die a slow, horrible death. Cruz didn't just stand there while Dax was watching me die; he searched the house until he found me. They got me out and I'm here today as a result. What I'm telling you is that Cruz doesn't give up. Ever. But whatever happened last week has made him *want* to give up. He's leaving San Antonio and has asked to be transferred to Victim Assistance.

"Now, I'm not saying he wouldn't make a great advocate for people who have been assaulted, raped, or any victim of any other kind of crime, but it's not where his heart is. He's good at what he does, Mickie. And for him to think he was responsible for whatever happened to your sister, or you, is just wrong. That's why I was laughing. You think *you're* responsible, and he thinks *he* is."

"I miss him."

"He misses you too."

"I don't know what to say to him."

"Well then, I think you're perfectly matched because I don't think he has the first clue what to say to you either. But one of you is going to have to make the first move, and I don't think it's going to be him. Look, next week is the annual law enforcement versus firefighter softball tournament. I'd love it if you came with me."

"I don't know."

"Cruz is going to be playing, along with my boyfriend and the rest of their group. Won't you please come and keep me company while the boys and girls duke it out on the field? I love all the guys, and it's hysterical seeing the firefighters do their best to trip and otherwise cheat their way to a win. And while I will always support Daxton, I'll tell you right now those boys in blue aren't afraid to do some cheating of their own. But no pressure. Promise. But it might be a good place to start if you're serious about missing him."

Mickie bit her lip, she knew it was going to take some time to work through not only what had happened with her sister, but also to herself and what had happened with Cruz. But the bottom line was that she did miss him. She'd found herself checking her phone several times a day, just in case there was a text waiting for her. It was stupid, but she'd gotten so used to talking to him that way every day, it'd become a habit.

Realizing Mack was waiting for her answer, she quickly nodded. "Okay. I'll come."

"Great! I'll pick you up if you want. Daxton is going early—he says to warm up, but it's really to talk smack to all the firefighters. The whole thing is really actually hilarious. It's gonna be really fun."

"I'd like it if you picked me up. Are you sure you don't mind?"

"Not at all." Mack stood and her tone turned serious once again. "He has a personal phone—his real phone, not the one you were communicating with him on. He had to turn in the one he was using as Smoke to the FBI. They had a tracker on it so they could keep tabs on where he was."

Mickie looked up at that. "So all the texts I sent…"

"I hope you didn't send him any naughty pictures, 'cos if you did, the FBI has them now." Mack smiled.

"No, I didn't, but…"

Mack handed her a piece of paper. "Here's my phone number and Cruz's real number. Reach out. If nothing else, maybe you can convince him to stick around here. Cruz is important to me and my boyfriend. We don't want to lose him."

Mickie took the paper without a word and looked down at it.

"I'm really sorry about your sister, Mickie. I don't know what I'd do if I lost either of my brothers. They drive me crazy sometimes, but they're still my family.

I'll text you soon to figure out the details about the game." Mack put her hand on Mickie's shoulder, then turned and walked out of the cemetery.

Mickie continued to sit beside her sister until the cemetery workers had tamped down the last of the dirt and put up the temporary marker. The one Mickie had ordered wouldn't be ready for another few weeks.

Finally, as the sun got low enough in the sky that Mickie couldn't clearly read the words on any of the gravestones around her anymore, she got up and left.

She never saw the man watching, and guarding, her from the other side of the cemetery. Never saw him put his fingers to his mouth and sadly blow her a kiss as she drove out of the fenced-in cemetery grounds toward home.

CHAPTER 20

Mickie sat nervously in the stands at the charity softball game between Mack and an officer she'd been introduced to, Hayden Yates. She worked for the sheriff's office and had told Mickie that she'd recently hurt her shoulder in an altercation with a drunk driver, so she wasn't playing that day.

She'd also been introduced to all of Cruz's friends. Mickie recognized their names from one of the many conversations she and Cruz had late one night. Daxton was the first to come up to her and Mack when they'd arrived. He'd given Mack the kind of kiss Mickie had only seen in the movies...full of passion, as if they hadn't seen each other in years, instead of merely hours.

Dax was a Texas Ranger, and Mickie recalled Mack's story of how she'd been buried alive and ultimately saved by Cruz and his other friends. Quint introduced himself next. He was a lieutenant for the

SUSAN STOKER

San Antonio Police Department. He'd taken her shoulders in his hands and gazed into her eyes for a long time before finally speaking.

"It's very nice to meet you, Mickie Kaiser. Whatever you do, don't give up on him."

"I'm not sure—"

"He's spoken of nothing else but you since that night. How brave you were. How sorry he was that you had to see what you did. How he hoped he'd be able to patch things up with you. I get that what you went through was horrible. I wouldn't blame you for wanting to forget everything about that night…for wanting to forget *him*…but if you care anything about him, please give him another chance. You'll never find another man more willing to move heaven and earth to keep you safe."

Mickie was surprised at the sentiment. She wasn't used to such deep speeches from men she'd just met. All she could do was nod, and hang on to him when he gave her another long hug.

They were interrupted by another man, who Mack introduced as TJ. Apparently he was a highway patrolman and the joker of the group. The introductions came in quick succession after that, luckily with no more deep speeches. She met Calder, a medical examiner, and Conor, a game warden, and of course, Hayden.

Cruz was also there, but didn't talk to her for long.

"Hello, Mickie. You look good."

"Thanks. You too."

He'd given her a quick hug and a brief kiss on the cheek, before joining his friends back on the field.

Mickie's head was spinning, but she couldn't deny the bubbly feeling deep inside at seeing him again.

"So, you gonna put that man out of his misery or what?" Hayden asked, not unkindly.

Mickie looked over at the small woman next to her. Hayden was built and obviously strong. She had the most beautiful auburn hair and her skin was pale, with freckles spattered across her nose. She looked fragile, but she spoke with the confidence that comes with many years of being in law enforcement.

"Look at him," Hayden said, gesturing toward the field with her head. "He can't keep his eyes off of you."

Mickie didn't need Hayden to point it out. She hadn't been able to keep her eyes off of him either. "A lot happened."

"I know. But you have to decide if what happened was too much to come back from."

"What do you mean?"

"I've seen it time and time again. Couples who go through extreme situations, as you and Cruz did, sometimes can't work through it to stay together. I'm not saying you guys can't get past this, but it takes a lot of effort. I wouldn't be a good friend to Cruz if I didn't make sure you were willing to put in that work."

Mickie looked away from the woman and back to the field. Her eyes blurred with tears as she thought about everything that had happened. Hayden was right. If she wanted to make whatever it was she and Cruz had successful, they'd both have to wrestle their own demons. She had no doubt that Cruz had them, just as she did.

Her voice came out just above a whisper. "I don't want everything that happened that night to have been too much."

"Good. Then you have my support."

"Mine too," Mack chimed in. She put her hand on Mickie's leg. "Welcome to the family."

Mickie glanced over at Mack. "What family?"

"This family," Mack replied instantly, throwing an arm out, encompassing the field. "This big, crazy law enforcement family. They're outrageous, they work too hard, they'll make you insane, but you've not only got me and Hayden as sisters, you've got all of them as brothers."

"But I just met them today," Mickie protested.

"I'm not talking about just Dax, Calder, and the others," Mack told her, laughing. "All of them. See all those firefighters out there?" At Mickie's nod, Mack continued. "They might treat this game as if it's the last battle of Waterloo, but everyone's actually on the same team. Moose, Sledge, Crash, Squirrel, Chief, Taco, and Driftwood are from Station 7, and if asked, they'll drop everything and come to your aid. To any of the guys' aid. Sometimes it can be annoying to have to share Daxton with them, but honestly? It's wonderful. I love seeing how well they all get along.

"But I have one word of advice...when you want an uninterrupted night, and Cruz isn't on call...turn off the phone. The guys have the uncanny ability to know when we're about to have sexy times. They've interrupted us more than once."

Mickie laughed, as she supposed Mack meant her to. It was nice to lighten the mood a bit. The rest of the afternoon went by quickly and Mickie only had the chance to briefly speak with Cruz once more before she left.

She'd been waiting for Mack to say goodbye to Dax —the guys were going out with the group of firefighters Mack had pointed out earlier—when Cruz came up beside her.

"How are you doing?"

"I'm good."

"I'm glad. For what it's worth…I'm sorry about your sister."

"Thanks."

"I'll talk to you later?"

Mickie had nodded and watched sadly as Cruz walked back toward the other men. She wasn't brave enough to say anything right then, there was too much going on around them anyway, but she'd made the decision to reach out to Cruz to see if they could salvage their relationship. She just had to figure out how to do it.

CHAPTER 21

Mickie stared down at her new phone. The FBI had allowed her to write down any contact information she'd wanted from her old phone before they'd confiscated it. She was one of the holdouts and had never set up her stupid Cloud, but as soon as she had time, she was going to make sure she did it. It was a pain to have to re-enter all the settings and contacts.

They'd said she would get her old phone back eventually, not that she cared too much. There were some pictures on there that she wanted to keep, but it wasn't as if she could complain about them taking it. If the video she took would put some of the MC members away, she wouldn't put up a fuss.

She'd saved Cruz's new number Mack had given her into her contacts two weeks ago at her sister's funeral, and was now debating whether or not she should hit send on the text she'd written. She hadn't lied to Mack; she missed Cruz. She missed texting him, she missed talking to him, and she certainly missed the feel of him holding her.

Spending time at the softball game with Mack and Hayden, and seeing how well all the men had gotten along and how close they were, had solidified Mickie's desire to try to work through all that had happened with Cruz. He'd been giving her space, which she appreciated, but she'd finally decided it was time to reach out to him.

She'd thought about what Mack had told her at the funeral; in fact, hadn't slept that great as a result of not being able to *stop* thinking about it. Cruz believed he was to blame, but when Mickie really examined everything that happened, the person responsible for Angel's death was Angel. And Ransom, and all the other assholes in the motorcycle club. Cruz was there to do good, and he'd done what he could to protect Mickie.

She had been stupid enough to put herself in danger. Mickie never should've gone to the party that night, and in turn had put Cruz in danger. It was obvious he knew the club was going to be busted, but he did what he could to shield her from the worst of it. He'd protected her and risked having his cover blown as a result. She'd been terrified out of her mind when the crazy drug lord had decided he wanted *her*, but not once did she think Cruz would hand her over. Even with everything going on around them, she knew he would protect her and somehow get them out of there.

It was that bone-deep realization—that when the

shit hit the fan, Cruz would protect her—that had made her type out the text in the first place.

The whole situation was fucked up and it killed Mickie to know Cruz blamed himself. It wasn't his fault; *none* of it was his fault.

She pushed the send button on the phone before she could analyze what she'd written anymore. Heck, Cruz probably wouldn't even know what the hell she was talking about. Probably wouldn't even know it was her.

She sat on her couch clutching her phone and trying not to hyperventilate.

CRUZ LAY on his bed with one hand under his head and the other resting on his stomach. This was where he came when he needed to feel…something. He'd been numb for the last few weeks. Nothing seemed to be able to penetrate. But here, in his bed, where he could still smell Mickie, *here* he could feel. It hurt, but it was something. He shifted onto his side and turned his head into his pillow. Yup, he could still smell her, barely. He hadn't washed his pillowcase, which he knew was probably disgusting, but if he had, he wouldn't be able to smell Mickie. He'd be empty again.

He thought about the raid. Cruz had been taken to the police station and the officer removed his cuffs when Quint met him at the door. Cruz had turned and shaken the officer's hand and thanked him.

He'd been debriefed by the SAPD and his boss at the FBI. They'd informed him Mickie had taken an audio recording, and a very crappy video, of most of what had happened at the warehouse. They now had that video and audio in their possession and were going to use it against as many people as they could.

Cruz had had to sit down upon hearing that. Apparently she'd gone to the party in the hopes she'd be able to gather proof that Ransom wasn't a good guy that she could bring to the cops, to get him away from her sister. Well, she'd certainly gotten more than she'd bargained for.

Bubba *hadn't* survived the knife wound Ransom had given him by accident and Ransom had been arrested. He'd only been in the county jail for three days before he'd been found dead in his cell. It was ruled a suicide, but Cruz had his doubts. Ransom was too conceited, too in love with himself, to do something so final as to take his own life.

Chico Malo might be dead, but whoever his successor was had found a way to take down his competition with a vengeance. At least Cruz didn't have to worry about his or Mickie's safety anymore. The other MC members were either dead or sitting in jail. And since no one but Ransom and Bubba had known Cruz was undercover, his identity was safe.

Cruz should feel glad. He'd gotten the Red Brothers MC shut down and had a part in dismantling a major international drug supplier. But he couldn't stop thinking about Mickie. He'd give it all back if he could have her in his life again.

Realizing that was impossible, Cruz knew he couldn't live in the same city as Mickie and not completely lose his mind. He didn't think she hated him, not after the softball game where he'd noticed she'd kept her eyes on him, but her not hating him and them being able to have a relationship were two completely different things. Not sure he could handle seeing her and not having her for himself, Cruz had put in for a transfer. He didn't care where, as long as it wasn't in Texas. He'd volunteered to work in Victim Assistance. He could still honor Avery, and now Angel, and their memories by helping victims of crime get their lives back.

Cruz's phone buzzed. He was tempted to ignore it. Mack and Dax had been on his ass to get back into the land of the living. Not to mention the other guys. TJ and Quint typically called him once a day, and even Calder and Conor tried to convince him to go out to dinner one night with them. Hayden, the lone woman in their circle of friends, had attempted to sweet talk him into taking her to see the latest action movie in the theaters. He'd turned them all down.

Quint had sat him down and had a long talk with him after the softball game the other day. Cruz had been surprised to see Mickie there, but should've known Mack wouldn't let a chance to throw him together with Mickie go. She was his biggest fan, other than Dax, and he knew she wanted him to be happy.

He and Quint had had a long talk about what it was they wanted out of their lives, and Cruz was surprised to learn that Quint felt much as he did, especially after seeing how happy Dax and Mack were. Quint had flat-out said he didn't care if the woman meant to be his wasn't perfect...as long as she loved him as much as Mack loved Dax, it wouldn't matter.

Thinking about that conversation, as well as the look of longing in Mickie's eyes at the game, made him want to grab ahold of her and never let go.

He made the decision to reach out to her. If he didn't try, he knew he'd always regret it. And she'd shown up at the game...that had to mean something.

Cruz reached for the vibrating phone, knowing if he didn't respond, whichever of his friends it was, wouldn't leave him alone.

He read the text in confusion. It made no sense.

I remember you used to drive that crappy blue Chevy Nova. What do you drive now?

Cruz didn't drive a Chevy. He had a Harley and a black Toyota. It wasn't in the best shape, but it wasn't crappy by any stretch. Cruz was about to ignore the text, assuming it was a wrong number, when something niggled at his brain.

He sat up and stared at the number. It was local, but not a number he recognized. Cruz struggled to remember what he needed to in order to respond. Finally, it came to him. He hoped like hell he wasn't wrong about who'd sent the text. He could feel his heart literally leap in his chest. Cruz painstakingly typed out a response.

The same crappy blue Chevy Nova.

He held his breath.

You want to accidently be at the same place at the same time tomorrow to feed ourselves?

Cruz closed his eyes and choked back the emotion crawling up his throat. Mickie. Thank God.

She'd reached out with a line from *Beverly Hills Cop*, then asked him the same thing he'd asked her all those weeks ago when he'd asked her out for the first time. He suddenly felt stronger and more with it than he'd felt in a few weeks.

Yeah. I'd like that.

I know a good Mexican place on the River Walk :)

Cruz tried to smile, but couldn't quite make it.

How about my place? I make a mean BLT.

It was several minutes before Mickie texted back, and Cruz could swear his heart stopped beating until she did.

What time?

One?

Okay. See you then.

I've missed you. Cruz wasn't going to go there, but couldn't help himself.

I've missed you too. See you tomorrow.

Bye.

Cruz clicked off his phone and lay back on the bed, holding the phone to his chest. He had one more chance with Mickie. He didn't want to fuck it up. The depression that had settled on his shoulders seemed to disappear as if by magic.

He got up off the bed. He had a ton of shit to do. Mickie wasn't just going to accept him back without him working for it, so he was going to do whatever he could to convince her to give him another chance. She apparently had more gumption than he'd expected. He hoped like hell her reaching out meant she was considering giving him another shot. Her text was just what Cruz needed to get his head out of his ass.

He wanted Mickie. He wanted his life in Texas... with Mickie. He was going to do everything in his power to make her realize how good they were together. Even if it took months, he was up to the challenge. She was worth it.

CHAPTER 22

MICKIE NERVOUSLY WIPED her hands on her thighs as she waited for Cruz to open his door. She wasn't sure why she was so nervous, except she really wanted this to work out. She knocked softly.

Cruz opened the door almost immediately. "Hey, Mickie."

"Hey, Cruz."

"Come in. Please."

Mickie brushed past Cruz into his apartment. She heard him close and lock the door behind her and she continued walking into his living room.

"Want to sit at the table to eat? Or the couch?"

"Either."

"Couch okay then?"

"Yeah." Mickie hated the stifled conversation between them, but didn't know how to fix it. "Need any help?"

"Sure, if you want to grab the drinks, I'll get the plates."

Mickie grabbed the two soft drinks and brought them over to the coffee table as Cruz followed with their sandwiches. They both sat down, and Cruz turned sideways with one leg hiked up on the couch, facing her.

Mickie sat straight forward, feeling awkward. She grabbed her sandwich and took a bite. She put it back on the plate and rested her head against the cushions. She turned her head to see Cruz watching her intently. She swallowed hard. "Cruz—"

"Thank you for coming over today, Mickie. I've said it before, and I'll say it again. I'm very sorry about Angel."

Mickie nodded. "Yeah...thanks."

"I was going to sit next to you and make small talk while we ate. Then I was going to suggest a movie, maybe *Beverly Hills Cop 2*. Then I was going to ask if you wanted to go out again...soon."

"You *were* going to do all of those things?" Mickie asked, clearing her throat nervously.

"Yeah, but now I'm not."

"You're not?" Mickie felt like a parrot, repeating back everything Cruz said to her.

"No. I can't." Cruz held up a hand between them. "Look, I'm shaking. I'm so afraid you only came over today to tell me what an asshole I am. And I *know* I'm an asshole, I know what I did was wrong, but I—"

He stopped speaking abruptly when Mickie reached

up and took his shaking hand between both of hers. She lowered their hands to his knee and rested them there. "You aren't an asshole, Cruz."

"Mickie—"

"Seriously. Listen to me for a sec. I was hurt after that phone call. I'd just had the most amazing experience with you and thought you felt the same. When I heard what those guys were saying, I couldn't understand how you could go and cheapen what we had by telling them about us."

"I didn't tell anyone anything."

"I know that *now*, Cruz, but I didn't at the time. And it hurt. And then I saw you at that party. I was scared and confused and when you talked about me like you did to that first guy, I was completely freaked out. But then you protected me. You didn't make me do the drugs, you covered me back up when I inadvertently exposed myself, and when push came to shove, when the cops came and the bullets flew, you shoved me against that wall and made sure not one inch of my body was vulnerable. You literally put yourself between me and stray bullets."

"Mickie—"

"I'm not done."

"Sorry, go ahead." Cruz couldn't help but smile. She was so cute.

"I have a question for you. If you answer it right, I… I want to see where this can go between us."

"And if I don't?"

Mickie shrugged. "Then you'll get transferred and we'll both go on with our lives."

Cruz turned his hand within hers and brought it up to his face. He rested his forehead against the back of Mickie's hand and nodded once. He took a deep breath and looked into her eyes. "Ask."

"Was it all a lie? Were you using me to try to get information about Angel, and thus about the MC?"

Cruz didn't even think. "No. It wasn't all a lie. I had thoughts about trying to get in with Angel, to find out what she knew, to see if she knew anything about how the drugs got into the club in the first place, but I found out pretty quickly she was an innocent bystander. Ransom was using her. I had no intention of getting involved with you, but when Ransom got pissed at you for trying to butt in with Angel, I wanted to protect you.

"You were right about the tires. Ransom ordered one of the club members to do that. I didn't know about it until you called me though. But the thing is... once I started protecting you, it stopped being about the club and the job, and started being about you. I should've gotten the hell away from you, but I couldn't. I knew from the first time I saw you that you were an open book. Not only that, I knew what else you were."

When he didn't continue, Mickie tentatively asked, "And what was I?"

"Mine."

"What?"

"Mine. I know that sounds terribly chauvinistic, but it's what I thought. Sitting across from you, talking to you, touching your hand. A part of me knew you were what I'd waited my entire life for. You were the reason why I'd been married to Sophie. If I hadn't been married to her and experienced what I did with her, I wouldn't have been driven to take this undercover assignment. And if I hadn't taken the assignment, I never would've met you. I never would've smelled you, tasted you, felt what you feel like when I was deep inside you. I might not have been there when you went to try to save your sister. Who the hell knows what would've happened to you. I'm pretty sure I'm in love with you, Mickie."

"Cruz…"

"You'll never know how scared I was when I realized you'd walked into that warehouse. There were men having full-out gang bangs, people snorting cocaine, and me—me being an asshole. You were in danger and there wasn't a damn thing I could do about it and keep my cover. But you should know, I'd already made the decision that I didn't give a shit about my job, or my cover. I was going to do whatever it took to make sure you got out of there in one piece. You will always be more important to me than my job. Always."

"I'm sorry, Cruz. I never should've done it. You told me not to do anything crazy and you were right. I was an idiot and I can swear to you that it'll never happen again."

"Damn right."

Mickie smiled for the first time that night. Cruz sounded so disgruntled.

"The thing is, Mickie, for the first time in my career, the job wasn't important. I'd been undercover for almost three months and the only thing I cared about was your safety. I wasn't going to let Roach, or Vodka, Chico Malo, or even Bubba touch you. I didn't care if I blew my cover, but they weren't going to fucking touch you. I would've died getting you out of there untouched, Mickie. You're mine." Cruz's voice broke, but he continued on.

"I'll do whatever it takes to have you trust me again. I'll quit and see if I can get hired on at the SAPD. I'll tell you anything you want to know. I have no secrets from you, never again. We'll honor Angel's memory somehow, however you want…"

"Will you have to go undercover again?"

"No."

"You sound sure."

"I'm sure. Most of the time, we don't get sent undercover, sweetness. Agents volunteer for that shit. If I have you, I don't ever want to go undercover again. I wouldn't want to be separated from you and I certainly wouldn't want to put myself in danger like that again."

"I don't want you to quit the FBI. You're good at what you do. I think I love you back."

"Me going undercover could put you in danger as well, and I won't do it. I'll even—wait…what?"

"I love you."

Cruz could only stare at Mickie in bewilderment.

His badassness was gone. This woman was his world and she had him completely under her thumb. "But, Mickie... I killed your sister."

Mickie sighed and scooted closer to Cruz, until he had to drop his leg and turn so he was sitting correctly on the cushion. She pulled her feet up and lay her head on his shoulder. Her left arm went around his chest and she pushed until her right arm was between his back and the couch. She smiled when Cruz tentatively put his arm around her shoulder and pulled her close.

"You didn't kill Angel. Ransom killed Angel."

"But if I—"

"*No*. Ransom killed her. There's enough blame to go around to everyone. Ransom, Angel herself, me, you, her friends, my parents...I could go on and on, but the bottom line is, the only person responsible for taking her life is Ransom."

They were both quiet for a heartbeat. "The service was beautiful, hon."

Mickie lifted her head. "You were there?"

"Yeah, I was there."

"Mack said you sent her to make sure I was all right."

"I did. But I was there too. I hung out at the back of the church and I was there at the cemetery until you left that evening."

"I didn't see you."

"I know. I want us to work. I want to get back to where we were, but this time, I want you to hang out with me and my friends. I want to be able to talk to you about my job, at least what I can. I know it's going to take some work, on both our parts, to get completely past what happened. But I'm willing to try. I'm hoping you are too."

"I am," she replied immediately. "I was thinking the same thing. I'm sorry for what happened, I'm sorry you had to worry about me and Angel in the middle of having to worry about keeping your cover and staying safe while everything was happening. I'm happier than I can say to be here with you." Mickie put her head back down and buried it in Cruz's neck. She inhaled deeply. "I've missed you, Cruz. So much."

"I've missed you too. Are we good?"

"Yeah, I think so, why?"

"Because I've spent the last few weeks missing you more than I thought I'd ever miss anyone in my entire life. I've thought of nothing but you. My friends are ready to disown me and I'm completely useless at work."

Cruz disengaged himself from Mickie and stood up. He held his hand out to her. "Let me show you how much I've missed you. I'm in love with you, Mickie. I want to take you to my bed and not get up for days. I need you. Will you come with me?"

Mickie didn't hesitate. She put her hand in his and squealed when he pulled her upright forcefully and bent so she was sailing over his shoulder. He caught her and wrapped his arm around the back of her legs. He turned and headed down the hall to his bedroom.

He dumped her on the mattress and she laughed as she bounced.

"I think we've done this before," Mickie exclaimed, referring to the last time he'd dropped her on his bed.

"No, this is gonna be something completely different. I know we went slow before, but I can't this time. I came too close to losing you and it's been too long since I've held you in my arms. Tonight will be fast, at least the first time, but I promise to make it good for you."

"Cruz...God."

"I love you, Mickie. It has to be love. I've spent my whole life waiting for you. I might not be able to take it slow this time, but you'll love everything I do, I promise."

Mickie sat up, propping herself up with one hand and reaching for Cruz's face with the other. "I will, because it's you doing it to me." She fell back and arched, anticipating his touch. "Do your worst."

"One question before we get started and I can't think about anything but your scent and your body..."

"Yes?"

"Will you wear that outfit for me sometime? Just for me?"

Mickie smiled up at the man she loved, knowing exactly what outfit he was talking about. "I *did* enjoy the way you got creative with your teeth when you covered me back up..."

"I'll take it that's a yes?"

"It's a yes."

Cruz looked into her eyes. "I promise to show you every day how much you mean to me. I won't lie to you again. We'll work through any issues that come up."

"I'll do the same, Cruz. The thought of losing you was eating me alive."

"I'm here now. Let me show you how much you mean to me. Take off your shirt. I've got to see you."

Mickie eased her shirt over her head and gazed at Cruz. She loved the look of adoration in his eyes. "Yours too?"

"Of course. I've got to feel you against me."

Mickie quickly stripped off her pants and shed her bra and panties and scooted up on the bed as Cruz took off his clothes. Before even a minute had passed, she felt Cruz's heart thumping against her chest. She figured he could feel hers too, as it felt like it was beating out of her chest.

"You're beautiful, and I swear I feel like the luckiest guy in all the world that you're here with me."

"I think I'm the luckiest girl for being here with *you*," Mickie countered, smiling.

Cruz didn't bother to argue with her, he simply dropped his head and covered her lips with his. His hands moved over her body as he devoured her mouth, relearning her taste. He flipped them over and held onto Mickie's hips as she got her balance on top of him.

"Take me, Mickie. I'm yours. As fast or as slow as you want."

Mickie looked down and saw that he'd put on a

condom before coming to her on the bed. She'd been worrying about her own clothes so much she'd missed it. "Are you ready?"

He laughed as if she'd said the funniest thing he'd ever heard. "Sweetheart, I took one look at those nipples of yours and I was ready."

Mickie smiled shyly down at him and rose up on her knees. Her smile grew as he groaned at the first touch of her hand on his cock. She stroked him once before fitting him to her, then sank down on him inch by inch, groaning along with him as her hot, wet body engulfed his hard length.

She stayed motionless when he was inside her as deep as he could go. She felt his thumbs caressing her hips, but otherwise neither of them moved.

"Are you okay?" he asked in a quiet voice.

"Never better." Mickie lifted up an inch, then dropped back onto Cruz. His hands tightened on her hips, letting her set the pace.

"That's it. Move on me. Do what feels good."

"Everything feels good."

They looked into each other's eyes as she continued riding him. Mickie braced her hands on his chest as she increased her thrusts against him. She knew when Cruz lost his battle to let her have control when he held her in place above him and rocked his hips up and into her.

Sensing he was close, Mickie quickly moved one hand from his chest down to her clit and frantically rubbed herself as Cruz fucked her. She threw her head back and shuddered over him, in the midst of a monster orgasm when Cruz pumped into her one more time and held her on top of him as he exploded.

Several moments later, when Mickie's muscles felt like Jell-O and she lay on top of Cruz, just as they had after the first time they'd made love, connected in the most intimate way two people could be connected, Cruz cleared his throat and Mickie expected to hear something romantic or sexy come out of his mouth.

"By the time the average American is fifty years old, he has five pounds of undigested red meat in his bowels."

Mickie had watched *Beverly Hills Cop* five times in the last couple of weeks, simply trying to be closer to Cruz. She giggled as she responded appropriately, "And why are you telling me that, Cruz? What makes you think I have any interest in it at all?"

Cruz nuzzled the top of Mickie's hair and whispered, "Well, you eat a lot of red meat."

"I love you, Cruz Livingston."

"And I love you, Michelle Kaiser."

EPILOGUE

MICKIE GRINNED at the group around the table. They were having lunch on a Saturday, almost three months after Cruz's undercover mission had come to a screeching halt. All of his friends were there, and Mack was trying to convince the guys and Hayden that they needed to do a sexy calendar photo shoot to raise money for her nonprofit group.

Not surprisingly, no one was very keen on the idea.

"Come on, you guys. It'll be awesome. It's not like you have to get naked or anything. And we can even invite your firefighter friends. Think you can get Squirrel or Chief…hell, *any* of them to say yes? It'll be epic if you can get everyone to agree!" Mack tried pouting, hoping it'd get her what she wanted, but everyone just laughed at her.

Mickie put her hand on Cruz's knee and smiled when he immediately covered it with his own.

The last three months had been wonderful. She and

Cruz had moved into a new condo together last month. They both knew they were moving their relationship along very quickly, but it felt right. Marriage wasn't in the plans yet, but it was definitely a possibility in the future.

Mickie thought back to this morning. She'd been dreaming the most wonderful dream, that Cruz was making slow, sweet love to her, and had woken up to the reality of Cruz running his fingers up and down her chest and nuzzling against her neck.

"I love you."

"I love you too."

"I want you."

Mickie had smiled and her nipples tightened in his grasp. "Then take me." She'd thought he'd pounce on her, but instead he took his time. He worked his way from her chest, down her belly, until he'd made himself comfortable between her legs. He'd grabbed a pillow and shoved it under her butt until she was just where he wanted her. He'd feasted on her folds until she was begging for mercy. Then, and only then, had he crawled up her body and entered her slowly. As much as Mickie had begged, he'd taken her at his own pace, whispering words of love and adoration the entire time.

Finally, when Mickie had exploded again, he put both hands on the mattress at her shoulders and lost control. He'd pounded into her, not taking his eyes away from hers. He'd pushed in one last time and held himself as far inside her as he could go and filled her with his come.

They'd lain in bed for another long while, simply enjoying being alive and connected. While they'd made love countless times since everything had happened, that morning was one of the most memorable…besides their first time.

Mickie was brought out of her semi-dazed state when Cruz leaned over and nuzzled behind her ear as the good-natured ribbing continued around them. "I'll pose for Mack's calendar if you pose with me in your biker-babe outfit."

She turned her head and kissed Cruz quickly before pulling back. "As if you'd allow me out of the house with that on."

"Who said anything about 'out of the house'?"

Mickie smacked Cruz lightly on the arm. "You're so bad." They grinned at each other and Mickie soothed Cruz's arm where she'd smacked him. She looked down and grinned at the addition Cruz had made to his tattoo. Alongside Avery's initials was now a large AK, in tribute to Angel. She hadn't been very nice to Mickie, especially at the end, but she was Mickie's family, and a victim. She deserved to be remembered and honored.

"I love you, Cruz. Not only that, I'm very proud of you."

"I love you too, Mickie. And while there are times I know I'll probably do things that will piss you off, I'm going to try to live every day to make you proud to be by my side."

Mickie leaned her head against his arm and closed her eyes. She had no idea how she'd gotten so lucky, but she wasn't going to give Cruz up. No way, no how.

A large crash rang out through the restaurant and made Mickie jump away from Cruz in surprise and a little bit of fright.

"Easy, sweetness. You're okay."

Mickie nodded and she looked over to where the sound had come from.

A woman was standing in the middle of the restaurant apologizing profusely to the man she'd just run into. It was a busboy and he'd dropped an entire tub of dirty dishes.

"Jesus Christ, are you blind? Watch where you're walking, why don't you?" The man was standing with his hands on his hips, glaring at the tall, slender woman in front of him. "How would you like it if I came to your workplace and made you look like a schmuck in front of everyone?"

Quint scooted his chair back and stalked quickly over to the duo, intent on preventing the situation from escalating. Most of the time, just the sight of his SAPD uniform could chill out the angriest individual.

"As a matter of fact, I *am* blind," the woman said, sounding a bit peeved. "I already apologized for running into you, but if you'd been paying attention as well, you would've seen me and you could've gone around me."

"Everyone all right here?" Quint asked, making his presence known to the two angry people.

"Hunky-dory," the busboy groused, dropping his attitude after seeing Quint's uniform, and squatting down to start cleaning up the mess.

"Miss? Why don't you just step over here out of the way." Quint put his hand on the woman's elbow and led her away from the shattered plates and water spilled from the cups. "Are you okay? You didn't get hit by any flying glass or anything?"

"No, I think I'm all right. Thank you."

"Can I help you—"

"I'm not an invalid, no matter what you might think of blind people."

"I didn't—"

"Yes, you did, most people do." Her voice was partly resigned, as if she was used to being thought less of because of her disability, but there was also a bit of irritation not quite hidden beneath her words.

Quint couldn't remember the last time someone had spoken to him with such disdain.

"I really just wanted to make sure you wouldn't slip on the water on the floor."

"Why? Because I can't see it? Because I'm an idiot and I'd go tromping through the middle of the spilled stuff to prove a point?"

"Well, no, because I'm trying to be a gentleman."

The woman snorted. "A gentleman. Yeah, like there are any of those left in the world today."

Smiling, not offended in the least, Quint looked

down at the stressed-out, prickly woman in front of him. She was tall, only a few inches shorter than his six foot two. She had long blonde hair that was pulled back into a messy ponytail and eyes so blue they didn't look natural. They were almost more turquoise than blue. As he looked closer, if he had to guess, he'd say they were most likely contacts or prosthetics.

She had wisps of hair that were escaping the tight confines of the band that held it and she wore no makeup. She was wearing a T-shirt that fit her like a glove and a pair of jean shorts that were neither too short nor too long. On her feet were tennis shoes and a cute pair of pink socks. She had a long white cane with a red tip hooked around her arm.

Quint reached out and touched her hand briefly, not knowing the protocol for wanting to shake someone's hand when they were blind and couldn't see the gesture. "My name is Quint Axton, I'm happy to meet you."

She didn't hesitate, but reached her hand out to him. "Corrie Madison."

"Are you meeting someone here, Corrie?"

"Yeah, he should be here any moment. So you can just leave the poor blind woman here against the wall and he'll be along to take care of me soon." Her voice was still laced with a bit of irritation.

"Maybe I should start us off again." Quint brought Corrie's hand up so it rested over the badge sitting on his chest. "My name is Officer Quint Axton with the

San Antonio Police Department, and I'm pleased to meet you."

"Oh my God," Corrie whispered, her tone of voice immediately changing to one of chagrin and snatching her hand back after moving it over his badge and realizing what she was feeling. "Uh, yeah, sorry. I didn't mean any disrespect, I mean…"

Quint laughed and put her out of her misery. "I just wanted to make sure you knew before you said something you might really regret."

"I really am sorry. I'm not usually like this. I've had a really really *really* bad week."

Quint chuckled, remembering the story of how Mackenzie had said the same thing after TJ had pulled her over all those months ago. "It's okay. Now, are you *sure* you're all right here? The person you're waiting for will be here soon?"

"Yeah, he's my lawyer."

"Your lawyer?" Quint scrunched his eyes together in concern.

"Yeah." Corrie continued in a low voice, "I heard a murder. I think someone's trying to shut me up, and I have to figure out what's going to happen next."

Look for the next book in the Badge of Honor Series: *Justice for Corrie* . Get it NOW!

Would you like Susan's Book Protecting Caroline for FREE?
Click HERE

JOIN my Newsletter and find out about sales, free books, contests and new releases before anyone else!!
Click HERE

Want to know when my books go on sale? Follow me on Bookbub HERE!

Continue scrolling to read the first chapter of Justice for Corrie….

BLIND SINCE BIRTH, Corrie Madison relies on her other sharpened senses in her job as a chiropractor. Never did she imagine she'd have to depend on them to identify a killer. But when a man enters her practice, murdering everyone in his path, Corrie is the only witness—putting her directly in the killer's crosshairs.

Officer Quint Axton wasn't looking for love, or even a relationship, until he meets Corrie. Beautiful and brave, resilient and intelligent, she's everything Quint wants—if he can keep her alive long enough to explore their mutual attraction. The threats on Corrie's life are escalating. Surely a blind person is helpless against a ruthless killer?

Hardly. Corrie is about to prove that disabled does not equal defenseless.

**JUSTICE FOR CORRIE* is the 3rd book in the Badge of Honor: Texas Heroes Series. Each book is a stand-alone, with no cliffhanger endings.

ABOUT THE AUTHOR

New York Times, USA Today and *Wall Street Journal* Best-selling Author Susan Stoker has a heart as big as the state of Texas where she lives, but this all American girl has also spent the last fourteen years living in Missouri, California, Colorado, and Indiana. She's married to a retired Army man who now gets to follow *her* around the country.

She debuted her first series in 2014 and quickly followed that up with the SEAL of Protection Series, which solidified her love of writing and creating stories readers can get lost in.

If you enjoyed this book, or any book, please consider leaving a review. It's appreciated by authors more than you'll know.

www.stokeraces.com
susan@stokeraces.com

Also by Susan Stoker

Badge of Honor: Texas Heroes Series
Justice for Mackenzie
Justice for Mickie
Justice for Corrie
Justice for Laine (novella)
Shelter for Elizabeth
Justice for Boone
Shelter for Adeline
Shelter for Sophie
Justice for Erin
Justice for Milena
Shelter for Blythe
Justice for Hope
Shelter for Quinn
Shelter for Koren
Shelter for Penelope

Delta Team Two Series
Shielding Gillian
Shielding Kinley (Aug 2020)
Shielding Aspen (Oct 2020)
Shielding Riley (Jan 2021)
Shielding Devyn (May 2021)
Shielding Ember (Sept 2021)
Shielding Sierra (TBA)

Delta Force Heroes Series

Rescuing Rayne
Rescuing Aimee (novella)
Rescuing Emily
Rescuing Harley
Marrying Emily (novella)
Rescuing Kassie
Rescuing Bryn
Rescuing Casey
Rescuing Sadie (novella)
Rescuing Wendy
Rescuing Mary
Rescuing Macie (novella)

SEAL of Protection: Legacy Series

Securing Caite
Securing Brenae (novella)
Securing Sidney
Securing Piper
Securing Zoey
Securing Avery (May 2020)
Securing Kalee (Sept 2020)
Securing Jane (novella) (Feb 2021)

SEAL Team Hawaii Series

Finding Elodie (Apr 2021)
Finding Lexie (Aug 2021)
Finding Kenna (Oct 2021)
Finding Monica (TBA)
Finding Carly (TBA)
Finding Ashlyn (TBA)

Ace Security Series

Claiming Grace

Claiming Alexis

Claiming Bailey

Claiming Felicity

Claiming Sarah

Mountain Mercenaries Series

Defending Allye

Defending Chloe

Defending Morgan

Defending Harlow

Defending Everly

Defending Zara

Defending Raven (June 2020)

Silverstone Series

Trusting Skylar (Dec 2020)

Trusting Taylor (Mar 2021)

Trusting Molly (July 2021)

Trusting Cassidy (Dec 2021

SEAL of Protection Series

Protecting Caroline

Protecting Alabama

Protecting Fiona

Marrying Caroline (novella)

Protecting Summer

Protecting Cheyenne

Protecting Jessyka

Protecting Julie (novella)
Protecting Melody
Protecting the Future
Protecting Kiera (novella)
Protecting Alabama's Kids (novella)
Protecting Dakota

Stand Alone
The Guardian Mist
Nature's Rift
A Princess for Cale
A Moment in Time- A Collection of Short Stories
Lambert's Lady

Special Operations Fan Fiction
http://www.AcesPress.com

Beyond Reality Series
Outback Hearts
Flaming Hearts
Frozen Hearts

Writing as Annie George:
Stepbrother Virgin (erotic novella)

Made in United States
Orlando, FL
02 May 2022

17391339R00165